Praise for Leslie O'Kane
and her Molly Masters mystery,
The Cold Hard Fax

"Endearing characters, touching family and friend relationships, and a feisty heroine."
—DIANE MOTT DAVIDSON

"O'Kane delivers a satisfying whodunit."
—*San Francisco Chronicle*

"Molly Masters is a sleuth with an irrepressible sense of humor and a deft artist's pen."
—CAROLYN G. HART

"O'Kane is certainly on her way to making her Molly Masters series the *I Love Lucy* of amateur sleuths."
—*Ft. Lauderdale Sun-Sentinel*

Please turn to the back of the book for an interview with Leslie O'Kane.

By Leslie O'Kane:

DEATH AND FAXES
JUST THE FAX, MA'AM
THE COLD HARD FAX*
PLAY DEAD*

*Published by Fawcett Books

PLAY
DEAD

Leslie O'Kane

FAWCETT GOLD MEDAL • NEW YORK

A Fawcett Gold Medal Book
Published by The Ballantine Publishing Group
Copyright © 1998 by Leslie O'Kane

www.randomhouse.com/BB/

Library of Congress Catalog Card Number: 98-96043

ISBN 0-449-00159-8

Manufactured in the United States of America

First Edition: December 1998

10 9 8 7 6 5 4 3 2 1

To Tam, the noble collie of my childhood, and to Taffy, my equally noble cocker spaniel.

Chapter 1

Talk about "dead air," I thought as I scanned the shabby lobby of the radio station. KBXD was completely deserted. At two P.M. Friday on a gorgeous spring day in Boulder, Colorado, I'd expected that my upcoming radio interview would not glean many listeners, let alone new clients. I had, however, expected to see some personnel.

I opened a heavy wooden door and entered an unadorned L-shaped hallway. Puzzled, I listened to a woman's halting, sniffling speech, and followed the sound to the nearest corner of the shiny faux-mahogany–paneled wall. A built-in speaker blared what I realized, with a sinking feeling, was not a TV soap opera, but the actual KBXD radio broadcast.

"—just can't believe they would shut us down with no notice like this," the woman's voice, strained with barely checked emotion, was saying. "So we want all our listeners to call in throughout the rest of our programming today. Complain. Share the memories. Share the sorrow. You're listening, for the last time, to the *Tracy Truett Show*."

"Oh, great," I muttered to myself. My first radio spot ever and the station is shutting down? I cautiously rounded the corner, considering my options. I shuddered at the idea of trying to talk enthusiastically about my newly chosen profession, all the while with "listeners" calling in to share their grief about the radio station closing.

1

Through an interior window, I spotted radio host Tracy Truett. She was a large, square-jawed woman with short blond hair in wet spikes surrounding the headband of her black earphones. Her heavy makeup was smeared. She was wearing what was probably a nice-looking outfit when she'd first come to work that day—sky-blue pants suit, paisley blouse—but the jacket was off and hanging haphazardly on a chair back, and the bow on the neckline of her blouse was untied and unbuttoned, revealing a sturdy bra strap. One thick, black shoe was on top of the table between Tracy's microphone and a liquor flask.

She continued into her microphone, "—Or, should I say, after a word from our soon-to-be-*former* sponsor, is our regularly scheduled program, 'Boulder Business Women.' Today, we'll be talking with Allida Babcock, who's just opened her new business here in town as a dog psychologist."

"Did you say a dog *psychologist*, Tracy?" a male voice broke in. He was not in my vision, but I quickly surmised that this must be the voice of the show's producer, speaking from the control room overlooking Tracy's booth.

"That's right, Greg. So now both our depressed listeners *and* their depressed pooches can call in and cry with us. Or howl, as the case may be."

I cringed, then made a swift executive decision. I turned on my heel and headed for the exit. Just then, from the corner of my eye, I saw Tracy Truett rise and gesture for me to come in.

Before I could make a clean getaway, Tracy leaned out the door and called, "Are you Dr. Allida Babcock?"

I turned back and forced a smile. "No, I just came in here to use your bathroom."

"You are too," Tracy stated crossly. "You sent us this photo of you in your press release, remember?"

I glanced at the eight-by-ten glossy in Tracy's hand, which was unmistakably my likeness—short, sandy brown hair, dark brown eyes, button nose. As if the facial features alone weren't enough, I realized to my chagrin that I was now wearing the very same bright yellow cable-knit sweater I'd worn for the photo.

"True, but I meant I'm not a doctor. Technically, I'm a behaviorist. I just call myself a dog psychologist in my advertisements because I thought it would catch people's attention faster."

"Yeah?" Tracy said, arms akimbo and eyeing me as if I were a disobedient child. "Looked to me like you were trying to leave us in the lurch. It's people like you, not showing up for their interviews, that caused our owners to shaft us in the first place."

I held the woman's gaze. "It's just that, with the station suddenly closing and everything, I assumed you wouldn't want guests on your show. Wouldn't you prefer to reminisce amongst yourselves?"

"Sure. But that's not what it says on today's program schedule, now is it? *I* fully intend to act like a professional, even if nobody—"

"Tracy? Get back in here!" the same male voice boomed over an intercom. "You've got dead air!"

Tracy grabbed my wrist and pulled me into the sound booth, then rushed over to the nearest mike. "Yes, dear listeners, we're still here, for today, at any rate." She rounded the table and reclaimed her chair, using one hand to give herself a swig from her flask, and gesturing frantically at me with the other hand to sit down at the second mike. "Today, our guest is Allida Babcock, who's here to tell us all about her new business as a dog psychologist." She shot dagger looks over the table, but her voice was pure honey. "Welcome, Allida. Glad you could join us." She slipped her earphones back on as she spoke.

"Thank you, Tracy," I said as smoothly as I could while sitting down. The chair was way too low for me. The air in the small room smelled of whiskey. Sheets of gray foam rubber were haphazardly stuck on the walls as though a child had gone wild with packing material. The low-hanging ceiling tiles gave me the impression that the roof was about to cave in on us. Somehow, I'd always pictured radio studios as fancier than this. I craned my neck and said into my microphone, "It's a pleasure to be here."

"However short-lived," Tracy added under her breath. "So, Allida. Speaking of which, you're extremely short, aren't you?"

"Yes, I am, Tracy. Thank you."

"What are you? Four-ten? Four-eight?"

"I'm five feet even," I answered, which was only accurate when I poofed my hair a little and raised up on my toes. Determined to make the most of this mess and keep the conversation focused on my profession, I continued smoothly, "Yet my height has never adversely affected me when training dogs. You see, even though a dog might greatly outweigh his or her owner, dogs are pack animals. What's important for training purposes is that you quickly establish that you, not your dog, are the top dog, the alpha dog, the leader of the pack."

"Maybe so," Tracy said with a chuckle, "but from where I'm sitting, you can barely see over the table, not to mention the microphone. How old are you, anyway? Twelve?"

"Thirty-two, actually, and I've spent twenty-five years now training dogs. During that time, I—"

"Greg," Tracy interrupted. Though she'd turned in her seat to face the pimply faced man in the control room, she still spoke directly into her microphone. "We've got to get this poor girl a dictionary or a pillow to sit on.

She's going to sprain her neck at this rate. Got a dog bed back there anywhere we can fold up and stick on her chair?"

"As I was saying, Tracy," I continued, hoping my rising agitation was not reflected in my voice, "I've trained dogs for many years—" I rose to surrender my chair to the dutiful Greg, who had yanked off his own earphones, left his post, and entered the broadcast booth "—and am now working specifically with the so-called behavior-problem dogs."

Tracy let out a loud burst of laughter, then asked, "Got any tips for badly behaved employers—such as station owners?"

"Not unless they're canines," I said calmly, though my face was growing warmer by the moment. Beside me, Greg chuckled quietly as he cranked the chair into a higher position. He was older looking than his pimples and wardrobe—jeans and Boyz II Men T-shirt—would normally indicate. I guessed him to be in his late thirties. Unshaven and potbellied, he reminded me of the janitor who worked at my school in Berthoud, Colorado, more than a decade ago.

Tracy Truett scoffed and took another drink. "You could call 'em dogs, all right. Or heartless swine."

Watching her, all I could think was: Are you nuts, lady? Don't you *ever* want to work in radio again? Heart pounding, I forced a smile and leaned over the mike to say as sweetly as I could, "I can't imagine why they've canceled your show, Tracy. That's such a shame."

"Yeah, me neither. We got a call on line one." She flipped a switch on the phone opposite her shoe and liquor bottle and said, "Hello, Russell, you're on the air."

"Hi, Tracy. I'm calling with a question for Ms. Babcock."

Thank you! I thought. Any interruption in the show

was a welcome relief, although I recognized the voice of Russell Greene, an electrical engineer who'd rented half of his two-room office to me. Russell Greene had been in love with me—or thought he was—from the minute we met three weeks ago. I'd answered his ad for office space to rent. Handsome-featured with thick, shiny dark hair and mustache, Russell had risen when I came to see him about the ad, and, as our eyes met on an even plane, his face lit up. He seemed to interpret our mutual vertical challenge as a sign that we were fated for each other—two of the same miniature purebreds.

Problem was, there was no chance, as far as I was concerned. He didn't like dogs.

"Go ahead, Russell," Tracy said.

"Ms. Babcock, I was wondering if you're as beautiful as your voice makes you sound."

I clenched my teeth and sank into the seat that Greg had adjusted and was now holding for me. In truth, I'm "cute," not beautiful, and I hate the sound of my own voice. Now able to speak into the mike without neck strain, I said evenly, "My physical appearance has nothing to do with the psychology of dogs. In fact, that is one of the many appealing aspects of dog ownership—our dogs love us regardless of how we look."

"Let me just ask one follow-up question, Ms. Babcock. Are you busy Saturday night? I was thinking a candlelit dinner for two at the Flagstaff House, for starters."

I put my hand over the microphone and whispered, "Oh, good Lord. Just kill me, now." Cheeks burning, I mentally ticked through the list of friends and associates I'd told about this show. The worst embarrassment of all was knowing my mother was probably listening to this fiasco.

Tracy took a swig from her flask. "Oh, hey, Rusty, hate

to tell you this, but I'd have to say Allida here is turning you down flat. However, I'm free Saturday. What time you want to pick me up?"

There was a click on the line. Without missing a beat, Tracy said, "We've got another caller," and flicked a switch. "This is Tracy Truett, and our segment's called Boulder's Business . . . Broads." She guffawed as Greg shook a fist at her while reentering his control room. "Ah, lighten up, Greggy. What are you gonna do? Fire me? And considering our guest here works with female dogs, I coulda said something a lot worse." She laughed at her own liquor-influenced wit. "Let's hear from our caller. You're on the air."

A deep, all-business woman's voice said, "I have a question for Miss Babcock."

Mom! Though relieved to hear the familiar voice, I automatically straightened my shoulders and stared at the phone.

"Allida, I mean Miss Babcock, my friends and I are here in my kitchen with our *many* dogs, and we just want to say what an intelligent, competent person you seem to be."

"Thank you." I smiled at my mother's fib. My mother was far too much of a loner to have more than one friend in her house listening to the broadcast.

"We all want to bring our dogs to see you, and we just want to know where your office is located and how we can go about getting an appointment with you."

I felt such a rush of love and gratitude that my eyes misted. I gave my exact address in downtown Boulder, then my phone number, and said, "It is important that you call me first, because many times I can tell over the phone if my services are going to be helpful to you and your dog. For example, I would almost always first want to ensure you've consulted a veterinarian. Also, I can determine over the phone whether my initial encounter with your dog should be in my office or at your home."

I heard a familiar woof in the background, and my heart lurched a little as I instantly recognized the deep tones of Pavlov, my German shepherd. I wished I could be with both of my dogs right now. I was currently renting a room in a house—all I could afford till my business got established. Sadly, the owner forbade dogs. Though my cocker spaniel, Doppler, had won the woman over—influenced, no doubt, by my insistence that I would not move in without at least one of my dogs—she drew the line at the German shepherd.

"Did you have any other questions for our guest?" Tracy asked my mother.

"No, though I must say that you are the worst interviewer I've—"

Tracy flicked a switch and said, "Oops. Line went dead. These darned phones. But we got us another caller. You're talking to Tracy True-It-Is. How ya doin'?"

"Hi, um, my name's Beth Gleason," said a quiet, youthful, female voice. "Actually, I have a problem with my dog?"

"Yes, Beth. What's the problem?" I asked.

"He won't eat. It's like, he's starving himself to death."

"First off, when a dog won't eat, it's usually a medical problem. Have you taken him to a vet?"

"Yeah, and they say there's nothing wrong with him. He's a collie. I got him from the shelter after his owner died."

"I see. And do you know much about his former owner—especially, what your dog's feeding routine and brand of dog food were?"

"Oh, yeah. Absolutely. I know a lot about the former owner. Just about everybody in Boulder knew her. You probably read about her death in the papers. It was all over the news about six weeks ago."

I had moved back to Colorado less than a month ago, but didn't want to distract Beth from her story, so I merely said, "Go on."

"It was that rich lady, Hannah Jones, who was found shot to death in her house, and they finally ruled it a suicide."

Across the table, Tracy grinned wild-eyed at me, then at Greg in his control booth, and let out a low breath, mouthing the words, "Hot damn!"

"Beth, my first reaction is that we probably shouldn't go into all of this on the air."

Tracy immediately gestured at me and tried to shout within a whisper, "Yes, we should!"

Doing my best to ignore Tracy, I continued, "I would very much like to help, though. You might want to call my office. Just tell me one more thing. Do you know if you're giving your dog the same brand of dog food Ms. Jones had been giving him?"

"Yeah, like I said. I'm giving Sage, that's my dog's name, the same food he always had. I got the original food itself. The people watching him after Hannah died brought Sage's forty-pound bag of dog food to the animal shelter with him. But—" She paused. "I know this sounds crazy, but . . . It's just, like, the way Sage barks like mad at men—especially, well, really *only* if it's a man wearing a coat."

That was interesting and gave me some immediate theories, but again I thought it best not to interrupt.

Beth continued, "And Sage, you know, flinches from loud noises? I just—I really think he's trying to tell me that Hannah Jones didn't commit suicide. This is so embarrassing, so you can tell me straight out if you think I'm nuts here."

She paused, and I could hear her take a deep breath. Beth said, "I really think Sage witnessed Hannah's death. I think a man in a raincoat shot her."

Chapter 2

I was still stunned at the murder suggestion when, across from me, Tracy Truett let out a squeal of delight and, with her sturdy arms and fists in the air, said into the mike, "Remember, you heard it first on the *Tracy Truett Show*! Hannah Jones was murdered, and her collie dog, Sage, can identify the killer!"

Incredulous, I stared at the show host. The last thing this poor, starving dog needed was to be turned into a local celebrity! Tracy folded her arms and leaned on the table, then gestured with a sweep of her hand that it was my turn to speak.

My heart pounding with pent-up frustration, I wrapped my hands around the base of my microphone and said, "Beth, there are many possible causes for Sage's reaction to men in raincoats. The very least likely cause is that Sage witnessed a murder by one."

"Yeah, but—" Beth began.

"So you're saying it *is* possible," Tracy Truett broke in.

I glared at Tracy, angered that the show host's eagerness for a flashy story was interfering with my attempts to help a seriously distressed dog. "What I'm saying is that it's extremely unlikely." I focused on the phone, my only connection to Beth Gleason and her collie. "My immediate concern is for Sage. Beth, from what you've

11

said, it sounds as though your collie is having extreme troubles adjusting to his new situation. Even so, a grieving or depressed dog will usually eat at least enough to sustain himself."

"Sage isn't eating anything at all. He won't even go near his bowl, and if I try to hand-feed him something, he backs away."

"We have to—"

"Hey, Allida," Tracy interrupted. "Here's an idea."

I automatically looked up. Tracy was already nodding wide-eyed at me to gain my consent. "Have Beth bring the dog here to KBXD. We'll put his entire therapy procedure on the air. We'll attach wireless mikes to the three of you. Then we'll—hey, Greg, you wouldn't mind putting on a raincoat for the sake of science, would ya? We'll get 'im a plastic gun and test Beth's theory. What do you think, Doc?"

What I thought was that Tracy needed to switch from whiskey to coffee. I ignored my host and asked calmly, "Beth, are you still there?"

"Yes. What should I do?"

I rose, but leaned toward the mike. "Can you and Sage possibly meet me at my office, 1197 Mapleton, at three P.M.?"

"Wait! Inquiring minds want to hear this therapy session!" Tracy gestured at the phone, where all five buttons were flashing. As I pushed my chair under the table, Tracy's voice switched into genteel tones as she cooed into the mike, "Time for a brief commercial break." She flipped a switch, got to her feet while ripping off her earphones, and pointed a finger at me. "Listen, honey, you don't seem to understand that a series on Hannah Jones's canine witness could save KBXD from extinction. You've got to stay on my show!"

"I can't *do* that! You're talking about bringing a traumatized dog who, from all indications, hasn't eaten in days, and turning attempts to help him into a circus act!"

Tracy smiled and took a swig of whiskey. She said in a throaty voice, "No, Missy Babcock. I'm talking about giving your doggie's shrink practice such a boost, you'll be turning collies into shelties on a regular basis."

"Thank you for having me on your show, Miss Truett. I only wish I'd been on yesterday, instead of today." I'd listened to that broadcast. She'd been sober then and had done a good job. But no use crying over guzzled whiskey. I walked out of the studio.

"Hey, Greg," I heard Tracy exclaim from the speakers in the hallway. "Don't just sit there! Stop her!"

I hesitated in the lobby for just a moment, thinking I wouldn't mind giving Greg an earful, now that I was off the air. He didn't come after me. I crossed the parking lot, got into my cherry-red Subaru wagon, started the engine, and heard the voice of Tracy saying over the air, "—listeners' poll on how many of us think Sage did indeed witness the murder of—"

I clicked off my radio and drove west toward my downtown office and the Flatirons, craggy mountain faces that towered over the town of Boulder. The least I could do to vent, I decided, was throttle that ignoramus Russell Greene for asking me for a date during a live broadcast.

Despite trying to focus on my officemate and not to draw conclusions before meeting Sage and his owner, I found myself mulling Sage's possible status. Depression in dogs over the loss of a beloved owner has been well documented. I'd recently heard of a dog in London who, every day for seven years, returned of his own volition to wait on the steps of the hospital in which his owner had died.

On the other hand, I wondered if Beth's conclusions about "a man in a raincoat" were an example of what I liked to call "The Lassie Syndrome." It was all too easy to read a human response and thought process into each little dog-like action of a beloved pet.

I pulled into my reserved space next to Russell's avocado-colored Volvo on the formidable hill by my building. I got out, descended the concrete steps where my office entrance was cut into the hill, and marched straight through my office and into Russell's. Empty. Probably ran for cover, I thought. The coward.

The light on my answering machine was flashing. Four calls in my brief absence. That was a personal record, but then, they might all be sympathy calls from friends and relatives who'd heard the broadcast. I pressed the play-back button. I had a pair of quick hang ups, but also messages from two prospective clients: a fox terrier too rough with the children, and a golden retriever destroy-ing the house whenever the family was away. I grinned. Ironic that bad news for others meant good news for me. If I was *really* lucky, half of the dog population in Boul-der would run amok and make their owners' lives truly miserable.

Before I could return my first call, the door creaked, and I whirled around, hoping to see Beth and her col-lie. Instead, it was a very humble-looking Russell Greene. His dark hair and mustache were as neat as ever. Today he wore newly pressed jeans and a white shirt with a striped tie.

My high heels negated the six inches he had on me. I strode toward him, doing my best to sound like a growl-ing pit bull as I said, "Russell—"

He took a step back, but held up a colorful bouquet of spring flowers as if it were a shield. "Before you say anything, Allie, I just—"

The flowers only caused a momentary distraction to my instantly accessible anger. "It's Allida," I snapped. "In fact, it's Miss Babcock for you, from now on."

"Sorry, uh, Miss Babcock."

Now that I heard him call me that, I felt a little silly and had to resist a smile.

Russell cleared his throat. "What I'm trying to say is that I'm *really* sorry. Believe it or not, I just wanted to impress you by demonstrating how . . . er . . . spontaneous and fun I could be. Rumor has it that we electrical engineers are not known for our spontaneous wit. I thought you'd . . . be charmed."

"You thought it was *charming* to call into the live radio show I was only doing to advertise my *profession* and ask me for a date?"

He gave me a sheepish grin, which, framed by the bouquet in his arms, was rather charming—though I was not about to admit that to him. "Yes, but then I listened to some more of the show, and I realized you weren't enjoying yourself and I probably embarrassed you." His cheeks growing redder by the second, he offered me the bouquet, already in a jar full of water. I recognized from the wrinkled mayonnaise label that this was the jar that had been catching drips underneath the sink in our bathroom.

I decided not to make a wisecrack about the makeshift vase. He handed me the flowers. His eyes were sparkling, and he truly was an attractive man.

"Thank you. They're lovely." I took a deep breath of the sweet fragrance, then set the jar and contents on the corner of my desk—a "slightly used" oak set I'd gotten from a bankruptcy sale, along with the other sparse furnishings—two gray two-door file cabinets, a pair of hard-backed chairs, a folding table, and a personal computer.

"Could I . . . take you out to dinner to make this up to you?"

"No, Russell." Sheesh! I silently added. I've worked with wolf hybrids who had an easier time taking no for an answer.

There was a light tapping on the glass door just behind Russell, who stepped back to reveal a disheveled-looking young woman with a sable collie. This could only be Beth Gleason and Sage. Russell surveyed the two of them and, demonstrating his usual dog phobia, held up a palm, murmured, "I'd better get back to work," and strode into his office, shutting the door.

The dog and his owner entered. I gave a quick glance at Beth, mentally registering that she was in her twenties or so, attractive, very tall, and wore loose-fitting dark clothing, then I turned my gaze on the collie.

By show standards, Sage could not be called beautiful. Though his coat was full and in the classic sable pattern—snow-white ruff, tan body and muzzle, white paws and tail-tip—he had a face only a dog person could love. His nose was not only Roman, but oversized and bumpy. One of his black ears was up, the other down. He walked as if carrying the weight of the world on his back—head hanging. The midsection of the leash dragged on the ground like a jump rope.

"You're Allida Babcock?" Beth asked nervously.

"Yes," I answered, "and you must be Beth Gleason." I flashed a quick smile at her. She bore the same dispirited countenance as her dog, as well as the nearly identical shade of reddish brown, long, shaggy hair. I noted that her entire outfit, including her socks and sandals, was black.

Returning my gaze to Sage, who flopped down in front of the door, I said, "Hi, Sage." I moved toward him slowly. He looked up at me with his beautiful brown eyes, his chin still resting on his paws. I stroked his head, then gently moved my hand down his body. Sage's ribs were protruding, though this was hidden by the thick coat, which was shedding between my fingers.

"We walked here," Beth said. "I live about a mile east on Pine Street."

A residence on that part of Pine meant lots of traffic and a small yard, I thought. Problematic for a large dog. I reached into the bottom drawer of my desk and grabbed a premium-quality dog biscuit, which I brought over to Sage. Strangely, Sage sniffed at it but jerked away as if afraid he'd get an electrical shock. "He's been drinking plenty of water?" I asked.

"Yeah," Beth answered, her voice rife with concern, "but he won't go near his food."

"What about table scraps. Will he eat those?"

"Isn't it bad to feed a dog table scraps? I've always been told that."

The ever-present list of "thou musts" and "thou must nots," I thought. If I were Sage's adopted owner, I'd feed him filet mignon straight off the plate, if that were my only means to keep him from starvation. I suspected that if more owners trusted their own instincts instead of seeking expert advice, their dogs would do just fine. However, since I was one of those "experts," this was an opinion I kept to myself.

"Mixing table scraps into a dog's dry food is not necessarily wrong. I sometimes do that with my own dogs. At this point, we need to know whether or not Sage will eat *anything*. We need to ensure he doesn't starve while we're still trying to identify the cause of his problem."

Beth shrugged, her hands buried in her pants pockets, and chewed on her lower lip. "I'm a vegetarian, so it never occurred to me to try to give him some of my food."

I tried what was perhaps the oldest and most obvious trick in the book. I broke the biscuit in half and pretended to eat my half, palming it, then offering it again to Sage. To my mild surprise, he chomped both halves of the biscuit down with a ravenous hunger.

"Wow!" Beth exclaimed. "How did you get him to do that?"

I grabbed the box of biscuits and selected a second biscuit, letting Sage watch my every motion. I held it out for him. He rose and sniffed the dog bone carefully, keeping an eye on me, trembling in his widespread stance as if set to bolt if I made a move. He gobbled it down. I offered him a third, and this he ate without hesitation.

"I've tried the dog biscuits he's used to, but he wouldn't take them from me at all." Beth sighed. "Maybe Sage just doesn't like me. Or doesn't trust me to feed him."

"I doubt that's the problem. You offer him one." I gave Beth the box of dog biscuits. Beth coaxed in a babyish voice, holding out a biscuit. Sage panted, watching her, and then glanced at me. He wouldn't take the biscuit. "Act as though you're eating it." She did, and Sage immediately gobbled the treat in her palm.

Sage's eating problem seemed to be related to his actual dog food, so I explained that I needed to make a house call. First, we discussed fees and the possible length of treatment. Then I got Beth's address and said I'd meet them there once I returned some phone calls.

My heart lurched as the collie hesitated before following Beth, instead looking up at me and lifting a paw. "Good dog, Sage," I said.

The collie turned to follow his owner out the door with all the resignation of an animal that knows he is about to be beaten.

With renewed determination to help Sage as quickly and completely as possible, I replayed my first message and dialed the number. The woman's voice that answered was the same as the one on my recorder. I identified myself and said, "I understand you have a fox terrier who's snapping at your children?"

"Oh, yes. Let me get my husband. He asked me to call, but it's really his dog."

That struck me as a bit odd; in my experience, most women claimed ownership of all matters regarding their children. The woman dropped the phone with a thud and called, "John!" at the top of her lungs. In the background, I could hear what sounded like young children laughing and a high-pitched yap of a dog.

"Allida Babcock?" a deep voice finally asked on the other end of the phone.

"Yes." I looked at my notes where I'd jotted the name Sarah Adams and said, "Is this John Adams?"

"O'Farrell, actually. John O'Farrell. Adams is my wife's maiden name. I listened to your show, so I can tell you right off the bat that, yes, I've taken Mugsy to a vet, and he told me my dog badly needed some obedience training."

"Has he actually bitten one of your children?"

"She. Yes, she's nipped at both my five- and my seven-year-olds' ankles, but never hard enough to really hurt them. The bites didn't even break the skin, or—" He paused, and I could hear angry murmurs of his wife's voice. "Just the top layer of skin got a little scratched. It healed in no time." Again, there were angry murmurs in the background. He said into the phone, "We're on our way out.

Can we set something up now? Maybe have you come to my house to do an observation?"

"Sure, that would be—"

"How 'bout tomorrow? I know it's a Saturday and everything, but weekends would really be best for me. That way we can all be here. I could pay double your going rates for a house call, since you'd have to give up part of your weekend."

"I suppose tomorrow would be all right," I said, trying to sound slightly downhearted at the concept of "having" to work the next day. At this stage of my career, I would drive to Wyoming on the Fourth of July if that meant establishing a client base. "I don't charge extra for weekend visits." I took down the address and set an appointment for ten A.M.

The next call—whose golden retriever was chewing up house and home—also had a schedule that he thought was best observed during the weekend. I set up my visit to his house for late Saturday afternoon, then made the short drive to Beth's and pulled into a space by the curb.

Beth was watching out the front window and opened the door for me before I could knock. "Sage is in the kitchen," she murmured. Her eyes were red-rimmed and her nose pink, as if she'd recently been crying. "I tried that trick you taught me . . . pretending to eat the dog food and offering it to him. He all but ran away from me."

I placed a reassuring hand on Beth's forearm. "Let me see what I can do."

Beth took a halting breath and said, "You've got to do something to help me. I just don't know how much longer he can last."

I tried to project confidence as I nodded at Beth's words, but I had no idea why Sage would starve himself here, yet eat dog biscuits in my office. If there was one thing I knew for certain from my three decades of being in the company of dogs, it was that neither I nor anyone else could ever truly know what was going on in a dog's mind.

Sage was lying on his side in front of the refrigerator. Despite his lethargy, which was no doubt a result of his starvation and the walk to and from my office, Sage's tail thumped on the grimy maroon linoleum when I entered the small, dark, and messy kitchen. I petted him, feeling heartsick at his skeletal body.

"Can I see his feeding supplies, please?"

Beth pulled out a nearly full forty-pound bag from beside the refrigerator. It was the same top-of-the-line brand that I fed my German shepherd. I grabbed a handful of the dry dog food, then dropped it back into the bag. My palm felt strangely sticky afterwards.

"This is the food you got from the animal shelter?" I asked.

"Uh-huh. Hannah's neighbor, Dennis, was taking care of Sage for a couple of weeks after Hannah died. He donated his food and dog treats to the shelter."

Underneath the window by the heater was a large red dog bowl, with the name SAGE in white letters. I grabbed a kibble from the bowl and squeezed it between my fingertip and thumb. I sniffed it. It smelled perfectly normal. The kibble had such a tacky surface it stuck to my index finger, and I had to shake it off to drop it back into its bowl.

I touched my fingertip to my tongue. An acrid taste filled my mouth. "Can I see the dog biscuits, too, please?"

"Sure." Beth held out the box. "Why? Is there something wrong with the food?"

I grabbed a bone-shaped biscuit and scraped its surface with a fingernail. I touched that fingertip to my tongue. Again the taste was so bitter my lips nearly puckered.

"The dog food's been tainted."

Beth's face paled. "You mean, someone poisoned it?"

"Not exactly. It's been treated with something, probably an odorless dog repellent, such as Bitter Apple. It's not poisonous, but it makes the food taste repulsive to dogs."

Chapter 3

Beth Gleason's jaw dropped. "What do you mean? How could that be? I don't—"

"Could anyone have doctored Sage's dog food after you got it?"

Beth began to pace in tight circles, combing her fingers through her hair. At length, she shook her head. "No, that isn't possible. Somebody had to have done this to the food before I got it. Oh, God. This makes me so sick! Here I've been trying to get Sage to trust me, and I've been offering him only inedible food!" She punched her thigh. "Why didn't I think of that? But, how could I have known? I mean, it's so . . . weird."

Beth sat down on the floor beside Sage and lifted his head onto her lap. She said under her breath, "I could kill whoever did this!"

Why would anyone want to hurt Sage? Was it possible somebody wanted him dead because of what he'd witnessed? Surely not. Even assuming, despite the suicide ruling, that Hannah Jones was murdered, Sage could do nothing more threatening than to bark at the killer.

The dog might have been used as a guinea pig in some food-aversion experiment or training exercise by his former owner. Could Hannah Jones have been that cruel?

"The good news," I said, "is with some new food, we can restore Sage's strength and spirit very soon. Though

23

he'll have to be retrained to know that he can eat kibble and dog biscuits again. I need to try to find out why and when this happened. That will help me determine my course of treatment."

"That's what I'd like to know, too," Beth said, gently scooting out from under Sage's head. She hopped to her feet and started rifling through a layer of papers spread across the off-white and gray speckled Formica top of her kitchen table.

"What are you looking for?"

"I can't believe Hannah would have done this to her dog. It had to be . . . the people who were taking care of him in between her and me. I've got Dennis's number here someplace. That's his name. Dennis Corning."

"Why don't you think Hannah Jones was responsible?"

Beth paused from her search to meet my eyes. "She loved Sage like he was her kid or something. She used to bring him to class and everything."

"Class?"

Beth nodded, returning to her search. "I took vegetarian cooking lessons from her. That's where I first met Sage and decided I wanted to get a dog just like him." She grabbed a small strip of paper that looked as if it had been torn off the bottom of a sheet of yellow notepaper. "Here." She handed me the slip of paper, which contained only the name Dennis Corning followed by a phone number, then she whirled on a heel and headed toward the refrigerator.

"I just realized. I got a new thing of tofu in the 'fridge." She began rifling through her refrigerator and said over her shoulder, "Can I see if Sage'll eat that?"

"Uh, sure," I answered, wondering what feeding a half-starved dog tofu would do to his digestive system. "Just give him a small portion, though. His stomach has to be extremely sensitive at this point. It isn't used to having any food in it." Let alone tofu.

Beth slid the white, rectangular block of tofu out of its plastic container. It landed with a wet-sounding *shwock* on the gray Formica countertop. She sliced off an inch, which she offered to Sage on her palm. He gobbled it up. Watching him, I could only think how ironic this scene was in a town sometimes referred to as the tofu-eating capital of the world. Boulder, Colorado, where even the dogs eat bean curd.

"Don't give him any more," I said. This angelic dog had already been conditioned to think dog food was bad. This was going to further program him to think only tofu was good. I glanced at my watch. I had plenty of time left on Beth's hour, and I needed to make sure Sage got a decent meal as soon as possible. "Let's go to PetsMart and get him some dog food. The key is going to be to give him small, frequent feedings and to gradually nurse him back to his full weight."

Beth returned the tofu to the refrigerator, then dried her palms on her black pant legs. Not exactly Martha Stewart, I thought, averting my gaze.

"Should we just take your car?" she asked.

"Sure. I want you to purchase a small bag of both Sage's brand and a second brand. We'll mix the two together, so that you won't cause too much upset to his digestive system by switching brands, yet the food will smell different so he won't associate it with the Bitter Apple. But before we go, I think you should call your vet and explain Sage's situation. I've never worked with a dog this undernourished before. Your vet undoubtedly has."

Beth nodded, chewing on her lower lip as she watched Sage. "This just kills me," she murmured, then grabbed a once-white phone off its wall mount. She dialed and was soon speaking to who I gathered to be the receptionist. Beth hung up and said, "My vet's gonna call me back. He's always slow with that. Let's go now."

She led the way out her door, letting the screen door bang behind her before I, followed by Sage, could reach it. I stepped out onto the porch, quietly closing the door on Sage. "Don't you want to lock this?" I asked.

"Nah. I never lock anything. I always figure, if someone wants to get in, they're gonna get in, so you may as well save yourself the broken glass."

A philosophy which, in this case, left her dog and his food vulnerable to trespassers. So far, Beth had struck me as a nice, caring person. Yet she also seemed to be a kibble or two shy of a full serving in the firm-grasp-on-reality department.

"Beth, I think you should consider changing your habits, now that you've got Sage." Ironic, I realized even as I spoke, that I was suggesting she be more careful to lock her house, now that she owned a watchdog. "What if you've got some neighbor who hates dogs? He or she could have waltzed into your house while you were out and ruined his food."

Beth, standing on the sidewalk, stared up at me on her porch. "Jeez. I hadn't thought of that." She glanced at the houses on either side of hers. "I've never even met my neighbors."

I looked back at the house, where Sage was watching us, his long nose pressed against the narrow window alongside the door. Though my rational side assured me I was just being paranoid, I had visions of his being nabbed in our absence. "Let's take Sage with us."

Beth stared at me blankly for a moment, then shrugged. While I unlocked the car and opened the door to the backseat, Beth jogged back to her house and got Sage, but did not lock the door afterwards. Good thing much of my work with Sage's eating problems would be with her collie and not with Beth Gleason. The dog seemed more trainable.

Beth jogged down the steps, and Sage came bounding alongside her with surprising energy. This, after all, was a large dog operating solely on a slice of tofu and a few dog biscuits. He hopped in and immediately settled down on the pink blanket spread across my backseat. The blanket was so embedded with dog fur it looked like angora.

Beth clicked her tongue as she looked at him. "Riding in the car is the only time Sage shows any liveliness. I really think he always expects me to take him to Hannah's house."

That was probably exactly what Sage was hoping, I thought. Beth crammed her long legs underneath the dashboard though her seat was all the way back, while I slipped easily into my seat, all the way forward. Must be awful to have to bend down as far as she had to whenever she picked something up off the floor.

I gave myself a quick check in the rearview mirror, glad to see that my short, wispy, light-brown hair and slight touches of makeup maintained a reasonably professional appearance. I started the engine and pulled away from the curb, comforted by the familiar soft sounds of a large dog panting in the backseat.

It seemed quite possible that some disgruntled, oddball neighbor of Beth's was behind the food tainting. Yet, if that were true, Sage's reaction should have been to mistrust Beth; she would be the variable that had changed from the last time Sage had good food. Therefore, Sage should have shown much more reluctance to eat her tofu or the biscuit she'd fed him at my office. Sage's actions had been more in keeping with a dog that knew his dog food tasted bad, not that all food *Beth* offered him tasted bad.

"Did Sage ever eat any of his food? On the first day you got him, at least?"

"Not even once," Beth answered firmly. "The very first

thing I did when we came into my house was to pour him a bowl of food, but he wouldn't eat it."

That effectively put the neighbor theory to rest, I thought. "You met Sage at this cooking class taught by Sage's former owner. What happened next?"

"I read about Hannah's death in the *Daily Camera*. I called Hannah's house and left a message on her machine that if nobody else wanted Sage, I sure did."

"And somebody from her estate called you to let you have him?"

She shook her head. "No, no one ever called me, but the shelter did when he was brought in. See, I'd also left my name at the animal shelter as wanting to adopt a collie."

"And the people at the shelter also gave you the name and number of the person who'd been watching Sage?"

"No, I . . . found that on the piece of paper I gave you. It was in the bag of dog food."

This was more than a little bizarre. Fortunately, we were at a stoplight, because I hit the brakes to face Beth. "You found a man's name and number inside the bag of dog food? The food that had been tainted with a repellent?"

"Uh, yeah. Right on top. So I, um, called the number out of curiosity, and a lady answered and told me they'd been taking care of Sage." Her cheeks had colored and she picked at a nonexistent piece of lint on her black T-shirt as if she didn't know what to do with her hands. She reached back to stroke Sage's fur and avoided my gaze. Why was she acting so uncomfortable on the subject of Hannah's neighbors?

"Did they say why their number was in with the dog food?"

"She said they cared a lot about Sage and wanted to keep track of him. But I wouldn't give them my address. It just . . . felt wrong to me. Kind of like telling your kid's birth parents where you are and everything, once you've already adopted him. I mean, what if they change their minds about giving Sage up?"

"Hmm." I was starting to feel more and more suspicious about all of this. Traffic eventually allowed me to make a left at the intersection, and we passed the round, windowless, white stucco structure that was appropriately named the "Toadstool" playhouse. "I have to say that it seems a bit strange that this Ms. Jones, who was so devoted to her dog as to take him to class with her, would commit suicide and not make any arrangements for Sage."

"I know," Beth said, nodding vigorously. "That's why I don't think she committed suicide in the first place. Especially shooting herself in the head like that, while Sage was in the house with her." She leaned over and whispered to me, "And wait'll you see how he acts around men in raincoats. He turns ferocious."

Beth's not wanting Sage to overhear made her theory about her collie having witnessed a murder all the more difficult to take seriously. Why, then, was I battling this mental picture of Sage barking helplessly as a man in a trench coat shot his owner to death and doused his dog food in Bitter Apple?

"Once we restore Sage's diet and health, I'll look into his behavior around men. Is it any particular type of raincoat, or just any man in any type of coat?"

"Oh." Beth narrowed her eyes and stared out the windshield thoughtfully. "I guess I'd have to say it's any type of long coat on any man. Just not, like, suit jackets or ski jackets. Good thing the weather's so nice today, or we couldn't even trust Sage not to go ballistic at some guy while we're at PetsMart."

I turned on the blinker and drove through the parking lot to the opposite end of the Albertson's shopping center where PetsMart was located. PetsMart encourages customers to bring their pets into the store, but Beth announced that she hadn't brought Sage's leash, then headed with long strides into the store, oblivious as to whether I was following. The collie looked completely settled in anyway, his body taking up every inch of the backseat, the same way Pavlov's did. I cracked the windows but locked the car, then joined Beth in the store.

By the time I caught up to her, Beth's cart was half filled with dog bones, chew toys, and two big bags of food despite my suggestion that she start small in case Sage didn't care for these brands. While we waited in line at the cash register, Beth pulled out a thick wad of twenties, and I asked, "What do you do for a living, Beth?"

"Huh?" Beth did a double take at me, then said, "I'm a student at CU. I already have a couple of degrees, in fact, but I haven't found any careers that speak to me."

I couldn't help but chuckle a little at that. Beth gave me a puzzled look. I held up a hand in apology and said, "I don't mean to laugh. It's just that I got this image of a voice from the clouds calling down to you, 'Beth. Become a dental hygienist.' "

She grinned. "Actually, I gotta admit, a career would probably speak to me a lot sooner if I didn't have such a big trust fund. My father's getting a little tired of all my changes in majors." She led the way outside, pushing the cart at what I'd begun to realize was her typical, impressive clip.

"Maybe *he'll* speak to you about that," I commented as the automatic doors opened.

"I'm half expecting him to . . . to . . ."

Her voice faded as we heard a dog's frenzied barks. I immediately scanned the parking lot for my car. Sage was going wild, clawing at the window on the far side of the car.

"Oh, my God," Beth cried. "He must have seen a man in a raincoat or something."

She tore across the lot, her cart making a tremendous clatter as she shoved it ahead of her over the bumpy asphalt. I followed as fast as I could in my tight skirt and stupid high heels.

"Stop it! Stop it! Sage, it's me," Beth called as she ran around to the window on the far side of the car where Sage was still clamoring.

I grabbed the box of dog biscuits from the cart Beth had deserted near my car. I ripped the box open and unlocked the door opposite to Sage. "Sage, come," I called. After a few more seconds of barking, he looked at me, and I repeated the command. He came over to my side and I gave him the biscuit.

A frumpy middle-aged woman parked directly across from me got out of her car. She wagged a finger at me and said, "You need to get that dog of yours under control, young lady! He scared me half to death!"

"He started barking at you?" I asked, noting that she was wearing a miniskirt and blouse, which was not at all flattering, but more significantly, could in no way be misinterpreted as a raincoat.

"No, not at me, at some man. But *I* had to sit here and listen to that racket for the last five minutes!"

"Was the man wearing a coat?" Beth asked, rounding the car toward us.

"Why would I have noticed what the man was wearing? I was just sitting here, minding my own business, waiting for my sister to finish her grocery shopping."

Beth got into my backseat and cuddled Sage. He seemed to have completely reverted to the calm behavior he'd displayed at my office and at Beth's home. "Where is this man now?" I asked the woman.

"He drove off." She waved her hand in the air as she spoke, her brow still knitted.

"Did he just happen to be walking past my car?"

"How should I know?" She whirled on her stiletto heel. "All these stupid questions! No wonder nobody wants to get involved these days." She stomped back to her car, got in, and slammed the door shut.

Beth, in the meantime, emerged and pushed the cart to the back of my car. "Sage seems fine now. Let's throw this stuff in your trunk and get going."

"Sure wish I could ask our Good Samaritan over there to answer a few more questions," I muttered as I unlocked the hatchback. Technically, I didn't have a "trunk."

Beth shrugged. "Bet you anything some guy in a coat walked by. That's the only thing that could get Sage so upset." She hurled a bag of dog food into the back of my car. I was impressed. I can lift a sack that heavy, too, but not without whimpering and looking truly awkward. "Believe me," Beth went on, "I've seen Sage do this four or five times now." I loaded the lighter dog paraphernalia, while she moved the second bag of food in beside the first.

She struggled with one bag that was, for Sage, a new brand of kibble. "Know how to get these open?"

"It's one of those string things that seem to start working the moment you give up on them. I just save myself the time and slice it open with a knife."

"Okay. In that case, allow me." Beth pulled something out of her fanny pack. With an effortless flick of her wrist, a gleaming, five-inch-or-so blade emerged.

Incredulous, I asked, "You carry a switchblade around with you?"

"Gift from my boyfriend," she replied with a shrug.

A switchblade as a lover's present. And they say romance is dead, I mused.

Beth promptly cut a hole in the bag, but also let out a cry of pain as she sliced her thumb.

"Let me see that."

"It's nothing," Beth said, shutting the knife and dropping it back into her pack as she grabbed a tissue, which she wrapped around her thumb. The tissue didn't seem to be soaking through, so I took her at her word. "Let's see if Sage'll eat a little."

She grabbed a handful of dog food with her good hand and offered it to Sage as we got in. Sage eagerly gobbled it down. "Thank goodness," Beth said under her breath.

We drove back to Beth's house. Though deeply concerned about whatever had caused his reaction in the parking lot, I was tremendously relieved to know that Sage wouldn't starve. I helped Beth carry her food and supplies inside, then supervised Sage's initial feeding. He wolfed down a cup of kibble, then stood at the ready for more. I reminded Beth to check her messages for instructions from the veterinarian, but also said that my recommendation would be to wait an hour for a second feeding.

We set an appointment for Monday morning at my office, and I broke my own newly established procedures and gave my home phone number, telling her to call any time if Sage was having any serious troubles over the weekend.

What if Hannah Jones *had* been murdered? I asked myself as I got into my car. Sage might have been barking because he recognized the killer in the parking lot. My stomach knotted at the thought. That was crazy, I decided. Even if it were true, there was no reason to think that person could have staked out my office and followed us to Beth's and then PetsMart. And yet, something was tugging at me—a memory that wouldn't quite return in full color.

It was after five, and I was beginning to feel anxious to be with my own dogs—especially Pavlov. It was terribly hard to own such a wonderful, intelligent animal as my shepherd and only have weekend visitations. Yet I had the slip of paper from Sage's dog food bag burning a hole in my pocket. I decided to stop into my office and call the number.

Russell's Volvo was already gone. That was unusual. He tended to work long hours. The door to our joint entrance—the only access to Russell's office was through mine—was locked. Curiously, the overhead lights in both offices were off, but the small reading light on my desk was now on, though I hadn't used that lamp all day. I made my way over to the lamp. It was angled so as to shine on a ticket to a CU Buffs basketball game, along with the note:

Dear Miss Babcock,
I happened to have an extra ticket to tomorrow's 11:45 A.M. game. (It's the early game on national TV and supposed to be a great match.) Use it, don't use it, give it away to an attractive female friend. What-ever. No pressure. I'm including my business card with my home address and phone number, just in case you're concerned about pollution and want to ride over there with me.

Yours always,
(and I mean that in a friendly, casual sense)
Russ

I smiled and shook my head, thinking: No thank you, Russ. And I mean that in a friendly, casual sense.

I dialed the number on the piece of paper Beth had given me and held it up to the light as I waited for some-one to pick up. There were some telltale translucent ar-eas, as if the paper had been soaking up the additive for some time. A woman answered. I identified myself, then explained that I got this phone number from Sage's new owner.

"Oh, yes! You're the dog psychiatrist lady," the woman cried, her voice filled with awe as if she were talking to a celebrity.

Psychologist, I silently corrected, wondering just how many listeners today's show could have had, considering it had been axed. "You were listening to the broadcast?"

"Yes, once my neighbor called and told me you were talking about Hannah and her dog. I should introduce myself. My name is Susan Corning. Dennis, my husband, and I were taking care of Sage after Hannah's death. Hannah lived next door to us, so we're especially interested in any stories about her." She paused, then said, "How's Sage doing? I understand he won't eat anything."

"I think he's going to be fine. Was he eating when he was with you?"

"Well, yes and no. He would eat Shakespeare's food, but he wouldn't touch his own. And Shakespeare—that's our shih tzu—was getting so upset by that, of course, that we just figured Sage preferred Shakespeare's brand, so we started putting that in Sage's bowl, too, by the second day he was here. That worked out fine. We wanted to keep Sage for ourselves, by the way, but Shakespeare was just too jealous. Plus, we have a two-year-old who kept trying to treat Sage like a pony, and we weren't sure how long Sage'd put up with that."

So at least Sage was eating well until Beth adopted him, I thought. I considered telling Susan about the Bitter Apple, but, not knowing the motive behind the food dousing, I decided I'd rather err on the side of reticence, at least for the time being. "Can you tell me anything about Hannah's relationship with her dog?"

"She treated Sage like he was a person. Better, actually." In the background, I heard what was either a shrill-pitched bird or a squeeze toy. "She was always cooking sirloin for him, which she wouldn't even eat herself. She was the original Boulder vegetarian, and an eccentric one at—Brian! Don't put that in your mouth! That belongs to Shakespeare!"

"I swear," Susan grumbled, this time to me. "This happens every time I'm on the phone."

"Ms. Jones didn't have any ethical objections to feeding her dog meat?" This "sirloin" shot down the only reasonable theory I had formulated—that Hannah Jones had been making some ill-conceived attempt to convert Sage to vegetarianism.

"Well, yes and no," Susan replied for the second time. "As a matter of fact, she had been trying to invent a meat-less recipe that Sage liked. But the woman was eccentric, not stupid. She did realize that Sage was—Brian! No!—that Sage was a dog and needed meat."

"Were you surprised that she committed suicide?"

"Surprised?" There was a long pause. She lowered her voice and said, "She told us she owned a handgun, which made us nervous, of course. She used to baby-sit for Brian every now and then. The gun belonged to her late husband, and the rumor was that *he'd* used it to commit suicide. In five years of living next door to her, we never saw it, and she certainly never used it. I guess she must have . . . gotten tired of living with the cancer and decided to join her husband."

"She had cancer?"

"Leukemia. It had been in remission, but maybe her condition had recently taken a swing for the worst."

"I'm a little surprised she didn't make arrangements for someone she knew to take care of Sage after her death."

"Yes, that did seem odd, for Hannah."

"I'll let you go. Thank you for speaking with me." I hung up, gathered my belongings, and locked the door. I managed to hit the traffic just right to make a quick left turn onto Broadway. If I hurried home, I could pick up Doppler before Kaitlyn, my chronically depressed house owner and roommate, arrived.

Minutes later, I pulled up to the curb by my house in the northwest section of town. It was a little two-bedroom that looked to be the type of temporary house Laura Ingalls's father might have erected during one of their stopovers—Little House by the Rockies. Though the house was dwarfed—and often shaded—by a brick apartment building next door, I chose the place because of its low rent and proximity to my office. Also because it had a wonderful, large backyard with a small, Doppler-sized dog door that the previous owners had installed. I might have even considered the place cozy, had I been living with a less neurotic roommate.

I left my engine running for a fast getaway and started to trot up the concrete walkway. To my complete surprise, Doppler was sitting on the front porch. Doppler gave me his usual unadulterated loving greeting, wagging his stubby tail so hard his rear end was wagging as well. He was buff colored with patches of white on his nose and chest.

"How did you get out?" I asked, wishing he could just answer so I wouldn't have to search for holes in the wire-mesh fence.

I tried to unlock the front door, then realized it was already unlocked. The hinge creaked as the door slowly swung open.

"Kaitlyn?" I called nervously. There was no answer, and her car was not out front. Kaitlyn was the most security-conscious person I'd ever met. She would never deliberately leave the house unlocked.

Something was very wrong.

Chapter 4

My heart pounding, I shoved the door wide open and peered inside. Nothing looked out of place. Doppler waited for me to enter first, as he'd been trained to do. This was the first time my dog's training had backfired on me. Teaching a dog to wait for his owner to cross a doorway is very important in establishing the owner's rank as master—but not especially desirable when said "master" is possibly about to confront a prowler.

"Anybody home?" I called, hoping to give a would-be burglar enough warning to get out through the back door. I stepped inside. The house was silent. Reassuringly, Doppler was quiet and stayed by my feet. He has such an excellent nose that, had there been a prowler still in the house, Doppler would have darted off, barking as he followed the scent.

Nevertheless, somebody had unlocked the door and let Doppler out. "Is anybody here?" I asked again.

Silence.

The living room furnishings seemed intact. I wandered toward the kitchen. Doppler sat and tilted his head as he watched me, puzzled by my actions. Still fearing the possibility of stumbling onto a burglar—who would be sorely disappointed by our offerings—I wanted to make some noise. I sang the only song that popped into my head, "I'm an Old Cowhand," which was a very odd choice, as I only know the one lyric—that the guy was from the Rio Grande. Repeating that one lyric, I checked the bedrooms, hall-way, and bathroom, finding nothing amiss.

Doppler trotted along beside me as I circled the interior and returned to the living room. "Sure wish you could tell me how this happened, sweet dog," I said to him. He, of course, didn't answer. I knelt and nuzzled against his soft fur.

There was a clatter and a bang from the still-open door-way behind me. "Allida?"

I recognized my roommate's voice. I winced and slowly turned. It was even worse than usual. Kaitlyn Wayne had to have been crying for hours to get her face that blotchy. How could she have managed to drive in this condition? Maybe that explained the unlocked door. Perhaps Kaitlyn had come home early and then left, so emotionally over-whelmed, she forgot to lock the door.

Under unemotional circumstances, she was an attrac-tive woman—five foot five, nicely built despite her own continual assessment that she was "so overweight I'm dis-gusting," and auburn hair. Yet I wasn't even sure what color her eyes were, the irises were so overwhelmed by her eyes being frequently bloodshot and red-rimmed.

"Oh, Allida," Kaitlyn whimpered. "Thank goodness. There you are."

"No, there I'm not. I'm just passing through." I rose for emphasis. "I have to go to—"

"He called."

"Your husband?" I asked, unable to keep the amaze-ment from my voice.

Kaitlyn nodded, sniffling.

Uh-oh. Maybe he was back in town. "He doesn't still have a key to the front door, does he?"

"Of course he does. The house belongs to *both* of us."

I grimaced. So much for my impression of her being

security-conscious. The man had left her three years ago, but Kaitlyn clung to the hope that he would see the error of his ways and return to her. For a spacious bedroom and access to the whole house, she had charged me well below market value, on the condition that I "be prepared to move out the minute my husband returns."

"What did he say?" I asked.

"I don't know. Bill didn't call *me*. He called a real-estate agent we both know here in town. He told *her* to call me and see if I was interested in selling our house and giving him half the proceeds. Do you believe that?"

Yes, actually. "What are you going to do?"

"Nothing. I'm not going to sell. Not until he comes back for me. I told the agent to tell him that. She claims she doesn't even know where he is or what his number is. That she has to wait till he calls her again. I asked her when that would be, but she *claims* she doesn't know." Kaitlyn started to weep openly, a tiny whimper that would gradually increase to a wail.

Doppler began to let out whiny little pants, not able to understand why Kaitlyn was crying. I stroked his sleek fur. The first few times Kaitlyn had done this, I had been sympathetic. However, after only three and a half weeks of living with her, I'd lost track of the crying jags I'd witnessed and was now only looking out for myself and my dog. "Kaitlyn, when I got home, the house was unlocked and Doppler was sitting on the porch."

She instantly stopped crying and looked at me. "Then he was here! He must have been!" Kaitlyn's expression turned to joy, which should have been a refreshing change—if she hadn't been quite so manic. She grabbed my arms and did a couple of cheerleader hops, squealing, "Bill's back!"

"Are you sure you don't want to wait until you talk

to . . . Bill before you get all excited? Just to make sure he's feeling—"

"Did he leave me a note?" Kaitlyn raced through the house, frantically searching.

Thinking this was a game, Doppler began to bark, then trotted alongside her, hopping up at her, which he knew very well he wasn't supposed to do.

She looked devastated by the time she returned. "There's no note. Nothing. Why would he just come in here and not leave me a note, or something?"

Because he's just casing the place, wanting half the proceeds from its sale, and he wants nothing to do with you. I left my comment unspoken.

Kaitlyn whined, "What should I do?"

"I'm sorry. I try not to give advice to people. My psychology's only good for dogs."

"Fine." Kaitlyn sank into the nearest chair and flicked a soggy tissue in my direction. "You just go. I'll be all right here by myself. Like always." She turned her face to the window.

I gritted my teeth and stared at the back of my house-mate's head, wondering what would happen if I told Kaitlyn how I really felt; that she needed to get a grip on herself and start living for herself instead of pining after some man like a lovesick puppy dog. At that last thought, I gave my own loyal dog a pat, then said gently to Kaitlyn, "Maybe it's time you tried to meet somebody else."

"Somebody else?" She scooted around in her seat to face me. She looked stricken. "You mean, start dating again? How can you even suggest that? I'm a married woman!"

I turned on my heel and grabbed the leather leash that hung on a hook by the door. "Yes, well, this is why I work with dogs. They don't ask for my advice and then argue with me. I need to get going." I patted my thigh and said, "Doppler, heel," not bothering to hook the leash on my very obedient cocker spaniel. Doppler followed me out the door and down the walk, then sat and waited for me to open the door to the backseat. I pretended not to notice the curtains parting on the front windows, as a chronically depressed Kaitlyn Wayne watched us drive away.

"Boy, Doppler. I wish I knew what to do about that housemate of ours." I knew full well that Doppler couldn't understand me, but I was appreciative of the fact that dog ownership is a nice excuse to talk to oneself. "I know I should try to be more patient with her and try to cheer her up, but she doesn't want to be cheered. She just wants company in her misery."

At the light, I glanced back. Doppler, whose front paws were pressed against the ledge of the closed passenger-side window of the backseat, seemed to smile and nod at me. It was a long drive to my mother's place, nearly an hour at this time of the evening. My thoughts kept turning toward the shadowy images of a man in a trench coat shooting a white-haired woman in the head, then drenching Sage's dog food and treats in Bitter Apple, while Sage barked helplessly.

My mother had gone back to work shortly after my father's death and still worked part-time as a flight instructor. She lived in a blond brick ranch-style house in Berthoud, Colorado, a small town northeast of Boulder. She had a fully fenced two-acre backyard, which had been dog paradise to the half-dozen golden retrievers we'd owned over a thirty-year period. Mom's most beloved dog, Star, had passed away two years ago, and she'd yet to feel up to another.

Pavlov, my two-year-old female German shepherd, anticipated my Friday visits and was watching through the window. Pavlov's loud woofs greeted me through the doorway, causing Doppler to bark back in excitement. Though redundant, I rang my mother's doorbell.

"Doppler, sit," I commanded. The little dog was over-stepping his bounds by standing in front of me, wagging his stubby tail and whimpering in excitement. Doppler gave a sad whine, but took his rightful place slightly behind me.

My mother opened the door. "Hi, dear," she said. I stepped in and Doppler scooted past our ankles. "How was your week?" These were the exact same phrases she'd used to greet me for each of the last three Fridays since I'd moved in with Kaitlyn. My mother is a great listener, but her questions tend to be predictable. That was good, because right now, I had to be cautious with my answers. If I started talking about Kaitlyn's problems, Mom would suggest I move back home, which wasn't a good idea for either of us.

"Things have been a bit trying, of late. How was yours?" I patted Pavlov's large head and rubbed her ears, which she really loves. "Hi, Pavlov. How's my big girl?"

"Judging by the Trudy Truttle show, I'd say your week was worse than merely 'trying.' "

"Tracy Truett," I corrected, my arms wrapped around Pavlov's massive chest. My mother, on the other hand, was not the hugging sort. "Wasn't she a kick?"

"Yes," she answered with a snort. "If you like drunks." She paused and studied me. She rarely saw me in a skirt and heels, which were highly impractical for dog training. "You look nice. Why did you get all dressed up for a radio show?"

"Thought my outfit would make me feel and sound more professional." Pavlov gave my face a lick—which was something I'd trained her not to do but which had recently reappeared under my mother's care. Then the two dogs launched into their own circling, sniffing dance of greeting. The two canines could pick up more information from smelling the various scents on each other's fur than

I was likely to extract verbally from my mom this entire visit.

Though I look like a younger version of my mother in many ways, she was, at five-six, considerably taller. Her long braid of once light-brown hair was streaked with gray, which she referred to as "natural highlighting." She led the way toward the kitchen. Judging by the aroma, she'd made her fabulous lasagna. These free, Friday evening meals were a great enticement for my visits, in addition to seeing Pavlov. And my mother.

"Did you recognize my voice on that call-in show?" she asked.

"Yes, right away."

"Darn. I was trying to disguise it. I guess my sultry intonations didn't work."

"That's 'cause you always sound sultry, Mom."

She laughed heartily. The table was set for two; the lasagna was already on a trivet on the table and two glasses of burgundy were already poured. My mother always drank a glass of red wine with her meals and could either never remember—or deliberately ignored—the fact that I never drank more than a sip or two of wine. It gives me headaches.

"You don't have to make dinner for me every time, you know. How about if I bring you dinner next week?"

"No, thanks. I'd rather cook than eat McDonald's take-out."

"Actually, I was thinking KFC."

I washed my hands in the kitchen sink, then stepped out of my shoes, which were killing my feet. Much as it was nice to be taller for a change, I'd sooner strap two-by-fours to my feet.

As I dried my hands on the dish towel, my mother, watching from her seat at the table, said, "I can't help but

feel that this whole business of starting up a dog psychologist practice is just . . . such a lot of work. Maybe
you should think of a contingency plan if the whole thing
doesn't fly. Speaking of which, have you given any more
thought to getting your pilot's license? Just as a fall-back
position. After all, your brother's done well by it."

Drat! Not the dreaded be-a-pilot-like-Kevin conversation. A decade or so ago, Mother had given me flying
lessons, which I'd greatly enjoyed till an unanticipated
downdraft during our lesson had left me permanently
shaken.

Mom really *is* wonderful, and if we weren't mother
and daughter, we'd be the best of friends. But, in addition
to her predictable questions, she has a couple of pet top-
ics of conversation that she periodically drags out, dusts
off, and thrusts at me like an old scrapbook. My choice
of career had been embossed on those figurative pages
ever since I not only refused to fly, but deserted a relatively lucrative technical writing job back in Chicago in
favor of my one-time "moonlighting" job as a dog trainer.

I gave a glance at the photo of my handsome younger
brother in his United Airlines pilot's uniform. My photo-
graph was there, too, hung on the same wall, but it was a
smaller picture, the same size as all of the photographs
that she had of her late dogs.

"Kevin and I are very different people," I began, taking my seat, annoyed at myself for so easily falling into
this all-too-familiar verbal exchange.

"I realize that. I had enough time alone with the two of
you to know your personalities."

Oh, great. Now she was spicing up her Be-All-That-You-
Can-Be-So-Long-As-You're-a-Pilot speech with a pinch
of guilt. Though a pilot himself, my father had died in a
car accident more than twenty years ago.

I took my energy out on the lasagna as I stabbed the

spatula into it and shoveled a large portion, silently daring my mother to say, "Are you sure you're going to be able to eat all that?" My mother's lips were pursed and she was staring at my plate, no doubt biting her tongue.

"The point is, Mother, as you seem to keep forgetting, *I'm afraid of heights*! Airplane passengers tend not to feel confident putting their lives into the hands of a pilot who's afraid to look out the window."

"Oh, I wish you would just get over all of that fear-of-heights nonsense. It's all in your head."

"So are brain tumors, but I wouldn't want to fly with a pilot with that problem, either. Mom, when I'm up high and look down, I get vertigo. Everything starts spinning. How exactly do you expect me to be able to steer when my vision's going in circles?"

"Oh, gosh, dear, I don't know. By looking at a compass, perhaps? By going up with me a couple of times till the vertigo goes away?" She dished up a portion half the size of mine. She sighed and tapped her plate with her fork a couple of times while staring at my plate. Our eyes met as I took a bite. "Are you sure you're going to be able to eat all that?"

I chuckled, smiled affectionately at my mother and lifted my wineglass. "Here's to you, Mom. Cheers."

"Cheers," my mother said while we clinked glasses. "Doesn't wine give you a headache? I only poured you a glass because I didn't want to be rude."

I laughed merrily, having to dab at my eyes. Pavlov and Doppler now stood by the back door, Doppler scratching at the glass. I smiled as I got up to let the dogs out into the yard. I wondered if this wasn't a major function of the family, in general—to allow its members to be crazy within the sanctity of its walls, so that we can present ourselves as normal to the world outside.

"I heard the rest of your broadcast this afternoon," Mom

said. "Are you really working with Hannah Jones's former dog?"

"Did you know her?" I asked hopefully, quickly reclaiming my chair.

She nodded, taking a sip of burgundy. "She took flying lessons from me."

Yes! Though a loner, my mother is an exceptional confidante, and thereby had an uncanny ability to know a surprising amount about people within a hundred-mile radius. During the course of flying lessons, my mother managed to extract the entire personal histories of her students, without fail. "Tell me everything you know about her."

"She owned and operated a vegetarian cooking school and a vegetarian restaurant. She amassed a huge fortune when she sold her business, but she had no heirs. She'd been determined to spend the bulk of her fortune before she died, and was doing a good job at that, which is where my flying lessons came in. What a great tipper. Financially, that is. She kept the wings fairly level." Mom laughed, then noticed that I was not joining her and added under her breath, "Pilot humor."

"I heard she was kind of eccentric," I prompted.

She shrugged. "That's what all elderly women with spunk get called. Unless they're poor, that is. Then they're termed 'bag ladies.'"

"Do you think Hannah Jones might have been the sort to train her dog to dislike meat products?"

"What makes you ask?"

"Just a theory," I said, not wanting to allow Mom to turn this conversation around to make me the subject.

Mom looked thoughtful for a moment. "I suppose that's possible. She was a strict enough vegetarian that feeding her dog meat might have been repulsive to her."

Outside, both Pavlov and Doppler were barking. I rose

and looked out in time to see a white sedan drive away from the street along the side of Mom's property.

That's when it hit me—the memory that had been nagging at me for hours now.

I'd noticed a white car pull out from the curb just as we left Beth's house. I'd lost sight of it in the traffic on 28th Street, and Pine was a busy road, so there had been no reason to think twice about someone leaving at the same time we were.

Now that I thought about it, I was sure I'd seen a very similar car enter the parking lot at PetsMart.

Chapter 5

Kaitlyn had been asleep last night when Doppler and I returned from my mother's house. This morning Kaitlyn had—watch me do my happy dance—given me the silent treatment.

I put Doppler in the backseat to ride with me to the O'Farrell-Adams residence where I expected to observe a fox terrier named Mugsy who considered herself top dog. Last night, I had kept an eye out for suspicious white sedans and spotted none. By now, I had almost succeeded in convincing myself that I had not been followed yesterday afternoon. The operative word was "almost." If I *had* convinced myself, I wouldn't have been looking for white sedans in my rearview mirror, as I now was.

It had snowed a little during the night, just enough to make the roads sloppy. The temperature now was well above freezing—mid-forties, perhaps. I balanced my thoughts between how to jockey for position among the cars on Folsom and how to squeeze house-hunting into my busy schedule.

The O'Farrell clan lived on a street perpendicular to the South Boulder Rec Center, in a two-story colonial. I rang the doorbell, and a thin-faced, thirtyish woman with a remarkably pointy nose introduced herself as "Sarah Adams, John's wife," and ushered me inside. From somewhere in the back of the house came the sounds of TV cartoons.

"John had to run to the store, but he'll be here in a moment," Sarah said, unsmiling. "Let me introduce you to the rest of the family."

"Kids?" Sarah hollered over her shoulder, "Shut that thing off and come say hello! The dog doctor's here!"

I smiled at the thought that, from their mother's description, her children might well expect me to be a dog wearing a white lab coat and stethoscope. She arched an eyebrow and studied me. Wearing my tan cotton twill slacks and favorite striped shirt, I may not have looked as professional as I had yesterday, but I was infinitely more comfortable.

"Let's go sit in the living room," Sarah said, leading the way into a small room where an enormous sectional sofa left almost no space to walk. "Where the kids go, Mugsy goes, so I'm sure she'll be here momentarily."

To my surprise, not a fox terrier but rather a *Scottish* terrier bounded into what little floor space was left. The terrier was the classic solid black with pointy upright ears, a muzzle that I think of as sprouting a goatee, and those stubby legs that, truth be told, always struck me as disproportionately short. Not that I was anyone to talk. A split second later, a chubby, redheaded boy appeared around the corner, swinging into the room while gripping the door trim. He had a wooden gun in his hand that fired rubber bands. He pointed it at me and said, "Pow!"

"Pow yourself," I replied, eyeing his gun. The dogs of my youth had been lucky. We didn't have rubber-band guns back then, just air-propelled popguns that could spit corks all of five feet.

"Benjamin!" his mother scolded. The Scottie, in the meantime, began to bark, planting herself firmly in the center of the room between Benjamin and me, next to Benjamin's mother.

"Hi," the boy said confidently, meeting my gaze. He

walked over to stand directly beside his dog. "My name is Benjamin. I'm six-and-a-half. My little sister's shy." He turned and shouted with excess volume, "It's okay, Emmy! She's kinda pretty and she doesn't look mean!"

A little girl peered into the room. I caught a quick glimpse of carrot-colored curls. She immediately ducked from view. Maybe she disagreed with her brother's assessment of my looks.

"Hi, I'm Allida Babcock," I said to the children—or at least to the boy and to the doorway Emmy was hiding behind. "I thought you said you had a fox terrier," I said to their mother. "Mugsy's a Scottish terrier."

"Did I?" She clicked her tongue and shook her head. "John's always correcting me. Yes, Mugsy's a Scottish terrier. Terriers all look the same to me."

That was a bit hard for me to understand; not unlike claiming that all mountains look the same. Besides, Scottish terriers were quite popular. Their owners tended to name them "Scottie," just in case anyone missed the point.

"Yep," Benjamin said, grabbing the poor dog's head in a hammerlock which instantly forced me to bite my tongue, this being too early for me to offer advice. "Mugsy's a Scottie dog!"

It was not, however, too early for one of my patented, paint-peeling glares. Benjamin took one look at my face and released his grip on the dog. I love children, but my utter intolerance of pet abuse takes priority. Mugsy whined a little and backed away from Benjamin, but bravely maintained her post in the center of the room, looking in all directions as if she were a sheepdog whose flock was so scattered she didn't know which one to rein in first. Judging from her bearing and the graying fur around her mouth, I guessed her age at seven or eight—just past middle-age for a dog this size.

"I take it Mugsy was your husband's dog before you two met?"

Though I phrased the question to his mother, Benjamin immediately answered, "Our real dad lives in Oregon. Mugsy is my step-dad's dog."

"Oh, I see."

"Benjamin," Sarah said through an embarrassed smile. "You needn't bore Ms. Babcock with our family business."

"Actually, that's very much part of Mugsy's personal history, which I need to learn in order to get at the cause of her behavioral problems." I had to say this to Sarah's back while she left the room, but she soon returned with a diminutive little girl clinging to her leg.

"This is Emmy," Sarah said in baby tones. "We're a little shy, as you can probably see."

"Hi, Emmy."

The girl's eyes widened, then she buried her face in Sarah's dress.

"To tell you the truth, I h-a-t-e d-o-g-s," Sarah spelled out.

No surprise there. I looked at Benjamin, who was mouthing the letters to himself, probably deciphering the words as fast as I was.

"If it were up to me, we'd put M-u-g-s-y to s-l-e-e-p."

This remark caused the hairs on the back of my neck to rise. Put a dog to sleep just for nipping at heels a couple of times? I knelt and stroked Mugsy, thinking there was more than one bitch in the room.

Just then, the door opened, and a large, muscular man entered. He had a broad, appealing smile, and a receding hairline. "Hey, there. You must be Miss Babcock. I see you've already met my monsters," he said, ruffling Benjamin's hair. Mugsy leapt a good two inches or so, and he scooped her into his arms, let her lick his face, then gently set her down. He pumped my hand. "So, how bad are we doing here, Allida? Any fur flying?" He released my hand, then rubbed his step-daughter's back with a beefy hand and gave Sarah a kiss on the cheek.

"Mister John?" Benjamin asked. "What does 'put Mugsy to sleep' mean?"

John immediately shot a furious glare at his wife and then at me. Before I could respond, Sarah cringed and said, "Nobody's saying a thing about that, Benjamin."

"But you spelled that and—"

"That's why you should never listen when Mommy spells!" Sarah retorted. "It means she's having an adult conversation that you won't be able to understand!"

Benjamin stomped his foot. Personally, I was on his side in this particular argument and wanted to stomp my own foot. He said, "But Mommy, you spelled 'put Mugsy—' "

"Hush!" She grinned sheepishly at her husband and wrapped her hands around his arm. Over her son's protestations, she said to her husband, "I was merely trying to voice a concern to Allida about Mugsy without upsetting the children."

Emmy was now saying, "Mom?" and tugging on her mother's dress so hard only one tippy-toe was left on the ground, and Benjamin's objections were continuing in a grating, high-pitched whine.

"Doesn't look like you succeeded," John said sternly.

"Could we all sit down for a few minutes?" I asked, wishing I could join in with Mugsy and bite these people's ankles till order was restored. "I need to ask some questions about Mugsy's background and your daily routine with her."

"What routine?" Sarah quipped. "It's always a zoo around here." As she spoke, she took a seat on the sectional and hoisted Emmy onto her lap. John sat down beside her and Mugsy took an uneasy seat between the big man's feet, but Benjamin immediately climbed over the sectional, firing his rubber band at the wall in the process. "Benjamin! Sit down!" Sarah ordered. Mugsy instantly hopped up and punctuated Sarah's words with shrill barks.

"Quiet, Mugsy!" John cried.

For the first time since I arrived, a silence fell over the room. My ears were ringing. I sighed, forced a smile, and said to John, "I'm just going to take a wild guess here and say that Mugsy hadn't been around children much until you and Sarah got married."

"That's true."

I turned my gaze to Sarah. "You and the children had no pets at all until you married John?"

"That's right." Sarah asked meekly, "Are we doing something wrong?"

I very much wanted to laugh at the obviousness of that answer, but didn't. "Benjamin?" The boy was squirming around behind the couch section nearest the wall.

He raised up and said, "Yessy?"

"Can you tell me about the last time that Mugsy bit you?"

"Mugsy bit me." He averted his eyes and started fidgeting with the wooden gun in his hands, reloading a rubber band.

"Where were you at the time?"

"Don't remember."

"Were you in your room?"

He shook his head. "This room."

"And what were you doing?"

"Nothing."

"Did you have anything in your hands at the time?"

Benjamin dropped the gun on the couch as if it were red hot and said, "No."

"Benjamin!" John said. "Were you shooting rubber

bands at Mugsy? Like we told you over and over again not to do?"

"No, I wasn't!" Benjamin got to his feet and stuck his lip out. "I was shooting past her! We were playing cowboy and Indian."

John rolled his eyes and let out a chagrined puff of air. "I told you so, Sarah. Mugsy was just defending herself."

"This doesn't explain why she bit Emmy, though," Sarah said to me, stiffening. "I saw the whole thing, and Emmy didn't do a thing to the dog. Emmy is always completely gentle with everything. Aren't you, Emmy?"

Emmy nodded. She chanced a smile at me, then again buried her face against her mother. She was very cute with those big eyes and that glorious Irish-setter red hair.

"Were you scolding Emmy at the time?" I asked the mother.

"Why, yes. She'd made a mess, and I was sending her to her room for a time-out. But how could that have anything to do with the dog's behavior? The incident had nothing whatsoever to do with Mugsy."

"Was Mugsy nipping at Emmy's heels as she went to her room?"

"Yes, and like I said, Emmy wasn't doing a thing to her."

"Mugsy was trying to help you discipline your daughter by helping to hurry her into her room."

Sarah scoffed. "Oh, come on, now! Aren't you anthropomorphizing here? How can a dog want to help discipline a child? Emmy's still bigger than she is, after all, so she can't possibly know the difference in authority between us and a child."

"Sarah," John said, "you're underestimating Mugsy. She's a smart dog. Right, Mugsy?"

Mugsy barked.

Sarah looked away in disgust.

"Could we let the children go back to their television show for a minute?" I asked.

Benjamin needed no other excuse and shot out of the room calling, "Bye," behind him. Emmy waited a moment, then ran after her brother. Mugsy, who'd briefly settled down once again at her master's feet, got up and trotted to the hallway after the children, then stopped when she saw John wasn't following. She watched him for a moment, then settled down in the hallway, within eyesight of John.

I waited until the children were out of earshot. John put his arm around his wife and stared at me as if bracing himself for some serious bad news.

"There are some things I can do to help you to get Mugsy to behave better. I have no doubt that we can make some adjustments and train her not to nip at the children, with the caveat that all dogs have sharp teeth and are capable of biting. Most importantly, you both have to start by training your son to be gentler with the dog."

I leaned forward and lowered my voice. "However, Sarah, none of this might change the fact that you're not happy living with this dog."

Sarah squirmed in her seat a little, but said nothing.

I continued, "Before we can start, I need to know that you're all truly committed to keeping Mugsy. Otherwise, I'll be working with my hands tied. Dog ownership is a big responsibility. You don't need to feel guilty if it doesn't fit in with your lifestyle." I turned my gaze to John. "You need to ask yourself whether or not Mugsy and your family would be happier if Mugsy were re-homed."

"You think I need to give up my dog?" John asked.

"No, I think the first step is going to be for you and your wife to *decide* if you need to give up your dog."

"Of course we don't want to give her up. Do we, honey?"

Sarah shook her head and said, "No," but her body language and facial expression showed ambivalence at best.

I rose. "Please call me at my office after you've had some time to think about this and to discuss it. Let me know what you decide. Either way, I can help."

Sarah sprang to her feet and shook my hand, saying, "Thank you so much."

"You're welcome." I gave her a smile as close to reassuring as I could muster. Some of my best friends are dog haters. I consider this their loss, but not a personality flaw. On the other hand, none of my friends had threatened to put a dog they didn't happen to like to sleep. "I'll send you a bill for this visit, as we discussed on the phone."

"Why are you leaving? There's nothing to discuss," John insisted. "We're keeping Mugsy."

"I hope you do, but I honestly believe this is a matter for you and your wife to decide in private. It was nice meeting you all. I'll talk to you soon." I let myself out.

I hurried to the car, where Doppler was waiting. His buff-and-white colored face was pressed against the glass of the front passenger seat. "Well, that was fun," I said as I got in and petted my dog. He got into the back as I started the engine. I wondered if Kaitlyn was still home, sobbing. "Maybe she'd like a nice, loyal Scottish terrier," I said, smiling at the notion.

Actually, I considered as I drove, Kaitlyn had been paying more and more attention to Doppler over the last several days. I glanced back at my classically handsome-featured cocker spaniel. Sometimes all it took was living with a sweet, affectionate, and well-behaved dog like Doppler to convert a non-dog person. Cuddling a dog was therapeutic—good for the soul and infinitely better than waiting for some jerk ex-husband.

Not ready to go home and face my despondent housemate, I brought Doppler to my office. Doppler headed straight through my office, through Russell's, and into the bathroom. There were the unmistakable sounds of Doppler's lapping up something, which, when your dog is in a bathroom, is generally not good news. I followed him and discovered that the drip underneath the sink was leaking onto the floor.

I stepped back into my office for a container, glanced at my mayonnaise-jar vase, then looked around for something else to use. I grabbed my coffee mug, which had a badly drawn cocker spaniel on it—clients were always giving me dog-themed coffee mugs as parting gifts—and stuck it under the dripping pipe attached to the cold water tap.

Out of curiosity, I felt the pipe, and my fingertips measured an inch-long crack just above the joint. It would probably cost all of a buck fifty to replace this little section of pipe, but Russell had instead been allowing the water to drip into a jar, which he would then dump down the drain every morning. I decided I'd spur him—or the landlord—into action by doing a feeble, temporary repair job on it myself.

I grabbed a roll of Scotch tape out of Russell's office and awkwardly jammed myself under the sink to put a temporary tape-wad over the crack. I knew, of course, that this wouldn't work, but Russell would see it and be macho-ed into fixing it, and I'd get my coffee mug back. Doppler took immediate interest in my actions and joined me under the sink.

After only four orbits of tape around the pipe, a familiar female voice called, "Anybody here?" Beth Gleason, I thought.

"I'm back here." I let the tape dangle from the pipe and angled my torso out from the sink cabinet. In the meantime, Doppler tore out of the room to investigate.

"Hi, there, little fellow," Beth said.

I emerged and found Doppler bravely trying to present himself to the much taller Sage. Having been raised with a German shepherd, Doppler was not all that size-sensitive. Nonetheless, the two male dogs were doing their circling and shoulder-shoving thing while picking up each other's scents, and Doppler was assuming the submissive role and allowing himself to be sniffed. Fortunately, Doppler had rarely been in my office, or he might have acted territorial and tried to fight.

"Hi, Beth. Is anything wrong?"

"Oh. No," Beth answered, smiling sheepishly. She was wearing the same black T-shirt and jeans on her tall, lank frame as yesterday. Then again, she might have a closet full of black clothing at home that simply looked the same to me. "I was just passing by, and I saw your car out front. Sage is doing much better. I gave him three cups of dog chow, and he ate it without even hesitating. I tossed his dish and used the new one I just bought, so I think that helps, too."

"Good. I'm glad to hear that." Sage came up to me and nuzzled my hand for petting, which caused Doppler to raise his hackles and bark.

"Oh, dear. Looks like your cocker's getting jealous." Beth pulled Sage's leash taut.

"That's why I don't bring him to work with me." I sat down at my desk chair and signaled for Doppler to hop onto my lap, which he promptly did. "Actually, I'm glad you stopped by, Beth. I wanted to ask you something. Do any of your neighbors own a white sedan?"

She shrugged. "Not that I've noticed. Why?"

"I'm not sure, but I got the feeling someone in a white sedan might have been following me yesterday."

Beth made a face. "Jeez, I sure hope not. You think it might have been a neighbor of mine?"

"Actually, I'm hoping a neighbor just happened to be

pulling out at the same time we were—that I'm not being followed at all. Could you start being on the lookout for white sedans? And start locking your house, just in case. This . . . thing about Sage's former owner's death and his food being tainted has me a bit spooked."

"Oh. Sure. I'll be more careful with him." Beth gave him a loving smile, then met my eyes. "My boyfriend just stood me up for breakfast. Have you eaten?"

"No, my stomach requires at least two hours more than the rest of me does to wake up."

"Maybe we could go grab a bite someplace, after I have a chance to walk Sage back home, that is."

I glanced at my watch and considered the suggestion, somewhat surprised. She hadn't struck me as likely to want to become friends with me. Just then, Russell appeared at the entrance. He was wearing a brown, wide-brimmed hat that matched the elbow pads on his tweed jacket. He had barely managed to push the door halfway open, when Sage flew to the attack.

Chapter 6

Russell let out a brief, "Yiaa!" and backed up. Sage plastered himself snarling and snapping against the inside of the glass door. This then touched off Doppler's barking, so the two of them went at it—Doppler adding the tenor to Sage's bass tones.

Beth had been unable to keep hold of the leash and was now screaming, "No, Sage, no!" at the top of her lungs. I shushed Beth—explaining that this was just like joining Sage in barking, from a dog's perspective—and gestured at Russell to get back out of sight. Beth then wrapped her arms around Sage and said, "It's all right. He won't harm you."

"Don't fuss over him like that, Beth. He thinks you're rewarding him for his behavior." I grabbed a dog biscuit and called, "Doppler, come." Doppler gave a last little bark, then came over and sat in front of me. I gave him the biscuit.

"What am I supposed to do, then?" Beth asked, thrusting the fingers of both her hands through her shaggy, red-brown hair in frustration.

"Sage, come," I called. Sage immediately stopped his barking and came toward me. "Sit." He did so, and I gave him a biscuit.

"Isn't your giving him a dog biscuit rewarding his behavior?" Beth asked, a tinge of resentment in her voice.

"No, because I'm rewarding the dog for obeying my 'come' and 'sit' commands. Dogs don't have the cause-and-effect rationale we humans do. They only understand reward or punishment for their *current* behavior, not for what they were doing even as recently as two seconds ago." She glanced at the doorway, where Russell still had not reappeared. "Wait here, please. I've got to go see what my poor officemate wants."

I rushed outside and found a very flustered Russell Greene sitting in his car in the parking space next to mine. He looked so forlorn, sunk down in his seat, that I felt a pang of tenderness toward him. I bent to eye level and said through his open window, "Hi, kimosabi. Sorry about that."

"Dogs hate me," he muttered.

"Dogs just don't universally hate a particular person. Unless maybe he's wearing Odor de Cat cologne." I thought for a moment. Sage hadn't barked at him at all when Beth had first brought the dog over. That could be because Sage was the one entering last time, or that Russell had startled him this time. It could also have been something else entirely. "Aren't you about to head out to the Buffs' basketball game?"

He nodded. "That's why I came by. I called your house, and your roommate said you were working. I wanted to find out if you'd seen my note and the spare ticket. I thought I'd ask you in person to come with me."

He got out of his car and stood next to me. His grin was motivated, I was sure, by the fact that I was now wearing sneakers, so he could show off his full six inches of height advantage.

A cool breeze was starting to blow. "As it turns out, I'm with a collie client," I said, having to hold my wispy light-brown hair out of my eyes.

"A vicious one, if you ask me."

"Only some of the time."

"I heard about Sage's personality quirk on your radio gig. It's not like I'm wearing a raincoat, or anything, unless he considers this sports jacket a threat. Maybe it's my tie he doesn't like. Maybe it reminds him of a choke collar."

I grinned a little as I looked at Russell's red silk tie. Who would put on a tie to go to a basketball game? He was going to be the only fan in the arena wearing one. He'd probably be mistaken for an usher. "Maybe it's your hat. Would you be willing to help me for a moment?"

"Depends. Does this have anything to do with going back inside your office and facing that rabid dog?"

"Yes, but you can stay right next to the open door and duck out if he goes into attack mode again."

He paused, considering the matter, his dark eyes searching mine. "You know, Allida, that's asking a lot. The most adversity I thought I'd face today was you turning me down for yet another date." He paused and smoothed his mustache. "How long will this take?"

"Not even two minutes."

"And can I bolt out the door without you thinking I'm a dog-hating wimp?"

"Sure." I already knew he was a dog disliker, if not hater, but that didn't make him a *wimp* in my book—just not *romantic* material.

"And will you go to the game with me afterwards?" He wiggled his eyebrows at me so mischievously that I had to laugh.

"You drive a hard bargain, Russell, but yes."

"That's worth a pound of flesh. Let's go." He started to lead the way, but I grabbed his arm.

"I want you to take off your hat first. If Beth is right, it's either your hat or your jacket that's making Sage bark at you."

"I'd rather lose the jacket. The hat makes me look taller."

"The jacket makes your shoulders look broad," I said, feeling a little guilty for being so manipulative, but I really wanted to test my theory while I had the chance.

Russell grinned, his teeth white and even below his dark mustache.

"I'm going to go in first. Give me a few seconds or so, then come in, paying no attention to the dog. And, just as generic advice for the future, if a dog starts growling at you, try to stand sideways to him. By a dog's way of thinking, that's the least confrontational stance you can take."

"I would think running away as fast as my two feet can take me would be as nonconfrontational as it gets."

I laughed. "That's true, but once you turn your back on a dog, it instinctively gives chase."

"Ah. Wouldn't want that," Russell said, rocking on his heels.

I smiled and studied Russell's face, which was pale and slightly damp with perspiration. "You sure you want to go through with this?"

He nodded. "Are *you* sure you'll come with me to the game if I do?"

"Absolutely. I get a kick out of basketball, though I prefer playing to watching. I was the starting point guard for my college team."

"You were?"

His tone was so incredulous that I added, "Back then I was six one." I headed inside, where Beth was pacing.

"I was starting to wonder if you were coming back. Is that guy all right?"

"He's fine. He's going to try entering the room again. I want to see how Sage reacts."

Moments later, Russell Greene, looking very tense, appeared. He had taken very seriously my advice about a

sideways stance being less confrontational for dogs and
climbed sideways down the cement steps to the entrance.
He opened the door, still completely sideways to us, and
sashayed into the room.

Sage tensed a little and let out a couple of short, mod-
erate barks, but stayed seated.

"Should I face you now?" Russell asked timidly.

"Yes."

Doppler, who was always friendly to just about everybody, rushed up to greet Russell, who took a step back
in fear.

"N-nice doggie," he said with all of the confidence of
someone at rock bottom of the food chain. Doppler continued to wag his stubby tail.

"Wow. That's kind of weird," Beth said. "I don't understand why Sage was barking before, but not now."

"I had Russell take his hat off. That may not be what's
behind Sage's reaction, but I wanted to test the theory." I
cleared my throat, grinned, and said, "Russell?"

He met my eyes, a panicked expression on his face. He
held up his palms. "Oh, no. I knew it! You're going to
ask me to go out, put my hat on, and then come back in,
aren't you?"

Trust an engineer to figure out the best test procedure. I
mustered my sweetest voice and asked, "Would you mind
terribly?"

"All right. I'll do it. But after I escape from that big,
vicious dog trying to eat me alive, I'll meet you in my
car. All right?"

"Thank you, Russ," I said, embarrassed but still determined to go through with the plan.

"Is that your boyfriend?" Beth asked the moment the
door closed behind him.

"No, he just shares this office space."

"Boy, does he ever have a crush on you," Beth said, shaking her head as she leaned back against my desk.

"You think?"

We waited in silence for what was an inordinate amount of time for Russell simply to retrieve his hat and come back down the steps. Sage and Doppler, in the meantime, lay down on the floor back-to-back, nearest their respective owners.

Finally, Russell reappeared, doing his best to tiptoe sideways down the steps, his hat perched so lightly on the top of his head that the least little breeze would whisk it away. He barely got the door open a crack before Sage started barking wildly. Russell slammed the door and raced up the stairs.

"Weird," Beth said, over the sounds of Sage's barking. Once again, Doppler started up too, his hackles raised in excitement.

I held up the box of dog treats to Beth. "Time to try learning how to distract Sage from his barking."

She grabbed a dog bone and cried, "Come here, Sage. Come on."

I resisted a sigh and said, "Dog's name first, then the word 'come.' "

"Sage, come."

Sage immediately stopped barking and obeyed. "Good dog," Beth said, giving him the biscuit and stroking his back.

Well-trained dog, I thought. As soon as his owner could get the hang of the basics, they'd be in good shape.

Beth began to unzip a purple fanny-pack on her hip. "While I'm here, I want to pay you in advance for six weeks of treatment for Sage."

"There's no reason for you to do that. We don't even know for certain that it'll take six weeks."

She hauled out a fistful of twenties. "Maybe so, but I'd

rather pay up while I'm thinking about it. I've got the cash now, and I'm not always so good with keeping track of my money."

She handed me the bills, and I gave her a receipt and thanked her, stashing the cash in my wallet and reasoning that I could always give her a refund if she had overpaid. "Were the men Sage barked at before wearing hats, in addition to raincoats?"

Beth said slowly, "I guess they must have been, when I think back. I just thought it had to have been the coat. I mean, who would notice such a little thing as a man's hat?"

"Dogs have excellent memories. While it's a little unusual to have a memory triggered by something visual and not a smell or sound, Sage was probably traumatized by a man wearing a hat."

"Yeah. Such as one shooting his owner in the head," Beth murmured.

"Maybe, but the trauma could have been caused by any number of actions." Which was why I was handicapped in not being able to ask Hannah Jones about Sage's personal history. Even so, it should be fairly easy to counter condition Sage not to bark at men wearing hats. "We've got a starting point now for working with Sage on Monday. But I'm afraid I'm going to have to take a rain check on breakfast. I've got a basketball game to go to."

"Oh. Okay. I'll walk out with you. I'd like to thank your little man with the enormous crush."

I grinned. "Let's not call him that, though. I have a feeling he'd take it the wrong way." I hesitated. With Russell's touchiness regarding dogs, I decided there was no point in asking him if we could drive Doppler home first.

If I was going to leave Doppler alone for over two hours, he needed a dog bowl. My coffee cup—which would taint the water with coffee flavor—wasn't going to cut it. I'd have to sacrifice my mayonnaise-jar-cum-flower-vase. I quickly filled the sink, put the flowers in that water, rinsed out the vase and filled it to the brim.

"Okay. Let's go. I need to leave Doppler here."

Seated in his car up ahead, Russell was getting the anxious look of a man who, though he might never be on time for anything else in his life, knew that the game's tip-off was growing near.

Beth glanced nervously down the street, barely managing a smile at me as she said good-bye.

Perplexed by Beth's change in attitude, I asked, "Are you going to walk home? We can give you and Sage a ride."

"No, I can use the exercise. Besides, that's one of the reasons I—"

A black car screeched to a halt. A male driver who was so tall his curly brown hair was nearly brushing against the ceiling of his car rolled down the window. "Beth!"

"Oh, jeez," Beth said under her breath, "It's Chet."

"I've been looking all over for you!" he called, thumping the side of his door through the window. "Figured you were out walking your dog. What the hell's going on?"

"You said you'd pick me up at ten. I gave up waiting for you."

To an outsider, Beth's decision not to wait sounded very reasonable, since it was now well after eleven. Chet, however, hollered, "Shit!" He got out of the car, still in the middle of the road. He was even taller than I'd first imagined. He looked to be at least six-foot-five. "I was a couple minutes late. Why make a federal case out of it!" He crossed the street, ignoring the honk of a pickup that had to drive around his car.

Beth took a step back and gestured at me. "This is Allida Babcock. She's working with Sage. She already—"

He shifted his glare onto me. "What the hell makes you think you can pull this dog-shrink shit on Beth?" He towered over me, clearly enjoying the intimidation factor.

"Because what I do *works*. I help dog owners learn how to eliminate the cause of their dog's behavioral problems. And what is your noble occupation, Chet?"

He crossed his arms and studied me at length. "You're one of those smart-mouthed pip-squeak types, aren't you?"

"To tell you the truth, I'm not sure. As soon as I meet enough smart-mouthed pip-squeaks to know what they're like, I'll let you know." I could hear Russell's footfalls as he approached from behind me and wished I could signal him to stay out of this.

"You know, Beth might fall for this dog psych garbage. 'Oh, boo hoo!' " he imitated in a high voice. " 'My dog's depressed.' But I don't buy it. I'm not letting you con Beth out of—"

"Are you having some kind of a problem here, buddy?" Russell asked.

Chet was a full foot taller and guffawed as he looked down at Russell. "You've got to be shitting me. What would you do if I did have a problem? Karate-chop me in the knee?"

Beth grabbed onto her boyfriend's arm and started to try to drag him toward the car. "Oh, please, Chet. Can't we just go?" Sage, in the meantime, started growling at Chet.

Chet leveled a finger at me. "You watch yourself, little girl. You try to swindle Beth, and you'll wish you didn't have to answer to me!"

The basketball game proved to be a welcome diversion to my unpleasant encounter with Beth's boyfriend, though the experience zapped my concentration during the first half. Chet had struck me as a total bully—the kind who wants to dominate "his woman." I was worried for Beth's sake, but was also determined not to discuss my concerns with Russell, who was too likely to jump on any chance to build on our relationship.

The Colorado Buffaloes had had a losing program when I left the state years ago, but now they had what announcers and sports writers would call some "real scrappy kids" who worked hard on defense. Offensively, however, they had a tendency to stand around the perimeter a little too much. They needed a big man or two to work the paint. This team didn't have that luxury.

Russell and I struggled to make conversation, and, to my annoyance, Russell stared at my face in profile throughout the game. The Buffs won, and my—lest I forget— dog-disliking date and I soon found ourselves in queue with thousands of other cars waiting to get out of the parking lot.

"The Buffs' point guard is terrific," I said. "His ball control is something to behold."

"So are you," Russell said, then blushed.

Oh, good grief! Nobody had ever even *inadvertently* called me "something to behold." Under the circumstances, I decided to stay away from the topic of balls entirely.

He cleared his throat, his cheeks crimson. "Traffic sure is backed up." After a moment, he seemed to regain his composure and, while staring straight ahead, asked me, "So, how come you're not married or anything?"

"I was engaged after college. Things just didn't work out."

"What happened?"

"He eloped with my maid of honor."

"Ouch. Having had friends like that, it's no wonder you like dogs."

I stared at Russell in surprise. "Dogs certainly do tend to be more loyal than certain people. Not to mention more trainable." This conversation was making me a tad un-comfortable. Privately I'd acknowledged that that par-ticular chapter in my life had taught me to be a little overly cautious about my choices in both girlfriends and in lovers. The last thing I'd expected from Russell Greene was insightful analysis into my psyche—not something I found enjoyable this early in a relationship. It was time to employ a time-honored technique for dealing with men—get them to talk about themselves. "How about you?"

"Haven't found the right woman. Yet." He tapped the steering wheel nervously. "Or at least, if I have, she doesn't know she's the one." His cheeks reddened once again and he shot me the quickest of glances. "Got any sugges-tions on ways I could sweep her off her feet?"

Well, so much for the get-'im-to-talk-about-himself tech-nique. Of course, if I were an expert on handling men, I wouldn't still be single and barely scratching out a living for myself at age thirty-two. "No, but I can give you one minor suggestion. Don't call her up when she's on the ra-dio and ask her out. We women tend to react badly to be-ing held up to public ridicule."

"Now she tells me."

There was an awkward pause, but then traffic started to move. When we finally emerged from the lot, he com-mented, "That little dog in your office was kind of cute. Was he yours?"

"Yes. His name's Doppler."

Russell smiled. "Maybe you can introduce us sometime."

"You want to meet my cocker spaniel?"

"He looks about my speed."

"So I take it you wouldn't want to meet my German shepherd?"

Russell laughed, then stopped when he saw that I wasn't joining him. "That, uh, that wasn't a joke, was it."

"No, I have a cute *big* dog, too."

"Oh," Russell replied, then fell into silence. As we neared our office, he said, "Are you going to invite me in for a cup of coffee?"

"No, our cups are otherwise occupied. Besides, I'm just going to tidy up a bit in my office and then head out to my next appointment." Actually, my appointment with the golden that was chewing up house and home was two hours away, but I still wasn't sure I should be dating Russell Greene, who was, after all, glaringly incompatible with me in at least one key aspect.

Russell nodded and pulled up along the curb by the steps. "Thanks, Allida. I enjoyed being with you today. I'm glad you let me force you into coming with me."

"I had a great time." It suddenly struck me that my automatic response had been the truth, and the realization made me uncomfortable. "Thanks for . . . forcing me." I stepped out, taking a deep breath of the rapidly chilling air. The weather was being a bit schizophrenic today, but so were my feelings regarding my officemate. He lifted a palm in a good-bye wave, then drove off pretty quickly for someone who'd claimed to want to meet my dog.

I went in, Doppler rushing over toward me then flopping at my feet for a tummy rub. "So, little guy. Did you take any calls for me while I was out?" I rose and pressed the button on my answering machine, but once again only a series of quick hang ups had been recorded. Doppler leapt at me, scrambling to get his front paws even waist high.

"Down! Just because you're small doesn't mean I can cut you slack. I don't get any special treatment 'cause of *my* height." Doppler picked up on my tone of voice and looked appropriately contrite, his head hanging below his shoulder and his big brown eyes looking up at me.

I had to get the bathroom back into some acceptable condition before leaving. Russell might take offense at finding the flowers he'd bought me floating in the sink.

Doppler started barking before I could transfer all the flowers into the jar. I went to see what was going on.

I gasped at the unexpected sight of Sage on the tiny cement walkway to my door. He appeared to have dragged his unattended leash with him. There was no sign of Beth.

I rushed to the door and opened it. Sage did not come in, but instead climbed two stairs, then stood looking at me, waiting for me to follow.

"Good dog. Wait." My heart was already pounding in what I could only pray was false alarm. The handle of the leash was right in front of me.

The green nylon weave was now dark. "Please, let that be mud," I said to myself. As I started to reach for it, the collie climbed another stair. "Sage, stay."

I grabbed the loop, but then dropped it in shock. The flecks that stuck to my hand were red. I stared at them.

My hands were flecked with dried blood.

Chapter 7

I scanned the street and called "Beth!" There was no answer. Maybe Sage would lead me to her. I glanced again at the leash and took a calming breath. The blood was probably from the cut on Beth's thumb yesterday. Sage could have tugged on the leash, which might have re-opened the wound.

"Sage, sit. Stay." He obeyed, and I dashed inside the office and grabbed a leash. Doppler was picking up on my excitement. He barked and hopped at my knees, expecting to go with me now that I'd picked up a leash.

"No. Down, Dop."

He stopped hopping and cocked his adorable head at me, relaying his confusion. I glanced through the glass door at Sage, who was waiting for me patiently.

I grabbed a lilac-colored sticky notepad, wrote: Beth— I have Sage, A., and rushed out the door, stuck the note on the glass, and locked the door behind me.

Doppler rushed to the door and put his paws on the glass. It killed me to have to leave him in my office again. I had a persistent and, hopefully, irrational fear that some evil person had tracked Beth through my office address that I'd given over the radio. If so, he'd come here next, and poor little Doppler would be unprotected. Yet I had no choice. If I were to have any hope of Sage's leading me to Beth, he could not be distracted by a second dog.

I removed the leash on Sage's collar, telling myself I was only doing it because I didn't want to hold on to something blood-soaked, not because Sage's leash might be evidence in a horrible crime. My hands shook nonetheless. I slipped over his head a thick-linked chain collar attached to a long, inch-wide blue leash. Nothing could get a dog's attention faster than the sound and sensation of a quick snap on this type of leash. If Beth was in serious trouble, I would need Sage's instantaneous response.

How did all of this get so out of control so fast? I was a dog psychologist, for heaven's sake! Now here I was, scared to death that my first Boulder customer had been murdered because of something some maniac had heard her say to me on the radio!

Unlike yours truly, the collie had calmed down in the few moments it took me to leave my office. He no longer seemed anxious for me to follow him. That had to be a good sign. Surely, if Beth was severely injured while the two of them had been out walking, Sage would be more agitated than this. Instead, he sat patiently while I switched leashes, one ear up and one down, and peering over that almost comical long, bumpy muzzle of his.

"Sage, find Beth," I told the collie. He trotted toward the busy intersection at Broadway and Mapleton. As we waited, I wondered how he'd managed to cross this intersection alone to get to my office.

I encouraged him to go quickly across the road—which meant we crossed at a dead run. As we trotted along the streets lined with enormous budding maple trees, I listened for sirens. Sage led me a block south, and I realized he was leading me back to Beth's house on Pine Street.

My heart was thumping as the two of us headed up the walkway to Beth's house. The screen door was shut, but the inner door was open halfway. "Beth?" I called as I opened the screen door. Sage trotted in ahead of me. He stopped just inside the doorway and barked at something in the kitchen, directly ahead of us. After three short barks, he looked back at me.

"It's all right, boy," I said quietly, not believing my words for a second. Dogs are so trusting, even when their handlers are quaking in their shoes. Keeping one hand on Sage's soft, long coat, I cautiously stepped alongside the large dog, not even sure what to hope to see.

It was Beth's boyfriend, Chet, just rising from the kitchen table, a cup of coffee and a newspaper in front of him. Indoors he looked larger than ever. He wore work boots, jeans and a black-and-white plaid shirt over a forest green T-shirt. His curly brown hair was uncombed.

"What are you doing here?" he demanded, glaring at me with unmasked menace.

A horrid thought occurred to me. Beth could be here, beaten to a pulp by this creep. If he were keeping her here against her will, what better way for her to contact help than to send her dog out a window with a blood-stained leash?

Considering our lousy first encounter, there was no sense in my trying to force pleasantries. I called upon my best professional facade—which was effective for dogs but not necessarily for humans—and said calmly, "I'm bringing Beth's dog back. He showed up at my office, dragging his leash. Is Beth here?"

"No."

"Do you know where she is?" I wanted to scream at him. I really, really didn't like or trust this guy, and my gut reaction was telling me Beth was in deep trouble.

"No." He maintained a snide, taunting expression on his face as he stared into my eyes.

"When did you last see her?"

"What is this? Twenty Questions? I don't know where she is. I'm waiting for her."

"But you went out to brunch with her a couple of hours ago, right?"

"No."

That did it. Unwilling and unable to continue false calmness, I dropped Sage's leash, whirled around on a heel, and charged down the hallway.

"Beth? Are you here?" I hollered. I threw open the first closed door—a bedroom that Beth apparently had been using as a storage room. There were no signs that anyone had been in here for days.

Chet overtook me. "Hey! What the hell do you think you're doing?" He grabbed my shoulder. His fingers dug into me.

I wrenched my shoulder free. "Look, Chet! I've gathered that 'no' is your favorite word and that you don't want to talk to me, but Sage's leash was bloodstained and there's no sign of Beth."

Chet's enormous hands were still fisted, but his expression turned from anger to surprise.

"I'm more than a little bit concerned here," I continued. "The last I saw of her was as she was getting into your car with Sage, and the two of you were arguing. So, have it your way and don't talk to me, because I'm calling the police!"

I got all of two steps toward the kitchen phone before Chet cried, "Wait." He still looked angry enough to hit me, but Sage had followed us and was now standing by my side in the hallway. Sage was growling and barking at Chet, who ignored the dog's threatening demeanor, took a couple of long strides, and grabbed the leash to inspect it. "What do you mean, Sage's leash was bloody? It looks fine to me."

"This isn't his leash." I tried to step around him toward the second room at the end of the hallway. This had to be

Beth's bedroom, and I could search for her while calling the police. "Excuse me, I need to get to the phone."

He grabbed me by both shoulders this time. "When did Sage get to your office?"

I leveled a glare at him, and he let go just as I was considering giving him a knee to the groin. "I left when you did, around eleven-thirty. I got back there around two. I didn't see Sage when I first arrived, but he might have been waiting for me on the lawn someplace."

"My God," Chet whispered, slowly paling. "Somebody could have . . . This is all my fault. We had a terrible argument. Beth and Sage got out of the car at . . . I don't know . . . must have been Arapahoe and Twenty-eighth Street. I ate alone, finally cooled down, and came here 'bout an hour ago, but there was no sign of her. Maybe somebody . . . ."

Chet seemed so worried that I found myself believing him and feeling the need to reassure him. If this was all a show, he was a fine actor. "She cut her thumb earlier. Maybe that's where the blood was from. She could have reopened the cut when Sage ran away from her. She might just be out searching for her dog, with no way of knowing he's with us."

As though he hadn't heard a word, Chet cried, "Shit. Her car's still here. But when the dog was gone and his leash, I figured she was just . . . out walking him or something."

"Were there any clues that she'd been back since you last saw her?"

"Clues?"

"Yeah, you know. The same clothes that she'd been wearing, her fanny-pack, something like that?" She'd had a great deal of money on her when she was in my office a couple of hours ago, I thought to myself. Perhaps she'd been mugged.

"I, uh, we'd better go check." He led the way into the room at the end of the hall, which was, indeed, Beth's bedroom. The king-size waterbed had been left unmade. Only one side was mussed, as though Beth had slept alone last night. I studied Chet's face in profile. There was a shocked glaze to his expression. By all appearances, his worry seemed genuine, but I was much more skilled at judging dogs' reactions than my fellow two-leggers'. I quickly searched the bathroom and closet for any signs of blood or, God forbid, Beth's body. There was nothing. I felt only slightly relieved.

"Shit," Chet said, which was apparently his second-favorite word. "Here's her fanny-pack. She had to have come here after she got out of the car." He held up the purple canvas fanny-pack, which did indeed appear to be the one she'd had on when she was at my office that morning.

"Maybe that's good news," I replied, not knowing what else to say.

He searched through the pack. "Her money's here, but her knife's gone. She must have taken that with her." He dropped the pack onto the bed.

"Why would she take a switchblade with her while she was walking the dog?"

He widened his eyes at me as if amazed at the stupidity of my question. "For self-protection. I told her never to go out without it." He glanced at the fanny-pack and rubbed his prominent chin. "Well, shit! I'm calling the police," Chet said, more to himself than to me.

I watched him as he punched 911 into the beige princess phone on Beth's nightstand. After a moment he said into the phone, "Yeah. My girlfriend's missing." He paused, then said, "Three hours or so, maybe." He shook his head at the dispatcher's response, then said, "Yeah, but her dog's leash had blood on it. See, she must have been out walking her dog, 'cause the dog showed up at this—" he waved his hand in my direction, then continued "—stupid dog-shrink's office she's been going to. Her name's Beth Gleason." He listened to the dispatcher's response, then jerked his free hand into the air in frustration. "No! Not the *dog-shrink's* name! My girlfriend's, you moron!"

Just in case Chet was only pretending to speak to a 911 dispatcher, I decided to pick up the other phone in the kitchen. I rushed through the house, and by the time I'd picked up the kitchen phone, I heard the woman dispatcher saying, "—normally wait twenty-four hours, but we'll send an officer out to take a report. You say her name is Beth Gleason, and she lives at—"

Convinced this was an actual call, I hung up. Sage had once again followed me to the kitchen. A few seconds later, Chet stormed into the room.

"The police aren't going to do jack shit!" he announced.

"They *are* sending somebody out to speak to you about this, though."

"A shitload of good that's going to do."

Maybe Chet could use some time alone to come up with some new words. "There's only one thing I can do to help in the meantime. Try to find her myself."

"How?"

"Sage," I answered simply.

"I don't know what you think you're going to accomplish that way. This is just a dumb mutt. We're not talking a bloodhound or anything."

"Sage is *not* stupid, and all dogs can track," I answered sharply. The latter half of my statement was only partly true. My challenge would be to get Sage to understand what I wanted from him. Getting a dog to follow a new command is always difficult, even if the action itself— such as tracking—comes perfectly naturally to the dog.

"Just . . . wait here for the police, in case Beth comes back, all right?"

I hoped to make my instructions as clear as possible. I picked up a black sweater off the floor by the front door where it had fallen off the coat hook.

"Is this Beth's?" I asked Chet.

He nodded. "She wears it all the time."

I held the sweater up to Sage's nose. "Beth," I said. "Sage, find Beth."

"This isn't going to work, you know," Chet said.

"Sage, find *Beth*."

Sage looked at me, then trotted out the door, his nose to the ground. I breathed a sigh of relief. At least he acted as though he knew what he was supposed to do. Could Sage already know exactly where Beth was? If she'd had Sage on leash when someone confronted her, he'd likely lead me to that spot; that was fairly automatic dog behavior—to go to the place the sought-for object last was.

On the other hand, if he'd been with Beth when she'd been attacked or injured or something, why hadn't Sage led me there directly? Why lead me to her house? Maybe, since he wasn't a trained tracker, he was confused by the leash. I removed the leash, wanting Sage to concentrate on following Beth's scent, not on his leash training.

Now my heart was really pounding hard. I had relinquished immediate control of a large dog, while sending him out to search for his possibly seriously wounded owner. He could well attack the next man in a hat he happened to see.

Sending up a quiet prayer, I quickly folded the length of leash into my hand and followed the dog.

Sage was tracking, his nose pressed to the ground, trotting along as if he'd forgotten my presence. We were on Mapleton, passing the mushroom-shaped building that housed a children's playhouse, when Sage stopped.

He sniffed at the ground and circled.

He crossed the grounds behind the building, clearly tracking something now. He leapt a two-rail fence and ran across a yard, and I climbed over the fence in chase. If the homeowners called in a trespassing complaint, I'd have to explain this to the police.

A much bigger concern hit me: Why would Beth have climbed a fence? Maybe Sage had run away and she followed. That was plausible. I tried to tell myself that was all there was to this—that she hadn't climbed a fence to get help or to escape.

Sage scrambled over a five-foot-high privacy fence that bordered this property. I started to look for a gate when something caught my eye. There was a dark stain on the cedar fence post near the section the collie had just leapt over. Please, dear God. Don't let that be blood.

My heart pounded wildly as I stared at the stain. I couldn't waste time rounding the property now. The flat railing at the top of the fence was just above eye level, but charged up by a mixture of fear and urgency, I hoisted myself easily over it.

Across the yard from me, Sage had stopped his search and was whining over Beth's motionless body.

Chapter 8

Ahead of me, just a few feet from the back door of a small, white house, Beth Gleason lay on her side on the wet grass. Sage was whining and nudging her limp hand with his nose.

Only vaguely aware of myself dropping the leash on the ground, I staggered toward her and called, "Somebody, help me." But help was already too late. I put a hand on her cheek. It felt as cold as the wintry blasts of wind that seemed to whip straight through me. Her eyes were closed, her lips were blue, and I deliberately refused to look at her blood-soaked T-shirt, sliced in at least three places. I pressed my fingers against her carotid artery. No pulse.

A woman's voice called over the fence to me, "Oh, my God. Is she all right?"

I didn't look up, but heard myself answer, "No. She's dead. Call the police." It felt as though my voice were coming from some distant tunnel—not really me speaking, not my words, none of this was really happening. I turned Beth over just in case there were signs of life, knowing full well this was senseless. So was everything that had happened to her since she'd gotten Sage.

Sage circled Beth and me as I knelt beside her. My mind was a torrent of thoughts and unanswerable questions, penetrated by Sage's childlike whimpers. How, in a town of Boulder's size, had someone managed to stab Beth Gleason in broad daylight with, apparently, no witnesses? Why hadn't anybody been around to help her? Even now, a steady stream of traffic passed by. Though my view of cars was blocked by the fence, the hum of engines and tires on asphalt was ever present.

I deserted my pretense of attempting lifesaving measures. I took off my jacket, draped it over Beth's face, and sat on the hard ground hugging my knees to my chest while I shivered uncontrollably. Sage came over to me and sat down beside me, pressing his body against mine. As I stroked his fur, I realized how hard I was fighting against breaking down.

Sirens in the distance grew louder. The police would soon be here. I would have to explain. How could I?

What did I even know about Beth? That she was too young to die and didn't deserve this fate. That she was supported by a trust fund, and that she seemingly had little common sense and atrocious taste in men. Yet she was wise enough to recognize the soul of a truly fine dog when she met him.

And what of Sage? My heart ached for him. I felt sure he'd been a voiceless witness to two violent deaths. Worse, both victims had been his owners. Could this dog identify the killer? How could I find out?

Police cars pulled up, their shapes visible through the slits in the fence. Sage rose, watching the approaching officers on the other side of the fence, then turned and looked at me in a plea for protection. I hugged him and whispered, "We'll get the bastard who did this. I don't know how, but we'll get him."

I heard the footfalls of the officers heading up the front walk of the house and called, "She's back here." I noticed the gate for the first time, which was within ten yards of where Beth had fallen. "She's been stabbed."

The officers entered through the gate, eyeing the collie and me as if primed to aim their guns at us if we moved. Sage barked wildly at them. The first officer said, "Do you live here, ma'am?"

"No, I—"

"The paramedics are on their way," the second officer told me. He gestured for me to come toward him. "Let's give my partner some room, okay?"

"She's already dead," I murmured, but got up and did as I was told. "The leash." I glanced back and saw where it lay on the lawn, equidistant between me and the fence. I started to head back to grab it.

"Stop right there," the officer commanded.

I looked up at him in confusion and realized both officers were poised to pull their guns at me. "The dog needs to be on a leash," I explained. "I dropped it back there in the grass."

"Just leave it where it is, ma'am, and step towards me."

I did as I was told, realizing the policemen were afraid I was about to retrieve a weapon. The first officer pushed his cap back on his forehead as he knelt by Beth. He tossed my jacket aside and felt her carotid artery. Sage's frantic barks turned to growls; he might go on the offensive to protect his owner from these strange men.

"Sage, come." He followed my instruction, but continued to bark. Sage was almost as frantic as he'd been in the PetsMart parking lot. I had to get him out of here.

The officer, an average-looking, middle-aged man with a receding hairline, led us to the sidewalk in front of the house. I glanced back at Beth, just as the grim-faced officer beside her slowly shook his head at his partner.

The officer introduced himself, but the name left my brain even while he was saying it. He asked my name and address. To my embarrassment, I couldn't remember my house number. I rambled about how I'd just moved back to Colorado after several years in Chicago, till enough of my mental faculties returned that I could remember my address. Two more patrol cars pulled up, along with a chartreuse-colored emergency fire department vehicle. One officer rang the doorbell of the white house, while another escorted the paramedics to Beth's body.

By now, pedestrians and people from neighboring homes were gathering, and the question, "What's going on?" kept being asked over and over by various voices. I had to steel myself against shouting, "Where were you when Beth Gleason was getting stabbed to death?" I tried to ignore the crowd and give the policeman as complete a picture as I could—what had happened in the last twenty-four hours or so since some stranger named Beth Gleason called into that damned *Tracy Truett Show*.

Behind us, mostly blocked from view by the cedar fence, the paramedics were working on Beth Gleason, which seemed macabre to me, since there was not a doubt in my mind she was already dead. In the meantime, the policeman with me asked more questions about what I was doing here and my "relationship to the victim." I did my best to answer him, but I hadn't felt this out of it since I'd been knocked unconscious by an elbow to the head during a high school basketball game. At once, things seemed to swirl around me in a flurry of motion and yet barely drag by.

A detective arrived and had me repeat my entire story. He was Hispanic with a trace of an accent and was softspoken, so much so that I had to ask him to repeat himself almost every time he said anything. I grew impatient to leave and check on Doppler, who was still alone in my office. Sage, too, was growing more restless as time passed, barking nonstop. Once again, I began to shiver uncontrollably.

The detective said, "Cold day to be outside without a coat." At least, I think that's what he said.

"I . . . covered Beth with my jacket. I don't want it back." I doubted I'd ever be able to look at my L.L.Bean without thinking of this day.

"Would you be more comfortable in my car?"

For once, I heard him the first time. I shook my head. "I'd really like to go back to my office. I need to get Beth's collie to a quiet spot, and my own dog is locked up there and needs to be let out."

The detective pocketed his small notepad. "Would you come to the police station and give a formal statement?"

I fought back a sigh. "Of course. I'll do anything I can to help. But can I meet you there in a couple of hours?"

He nodded. "Matter of fact, I'll be . . ." He looked over his shoulder toward Beth while mumbling. The next words I could make out were: ". . . hours yet. Can you meet me at the Boulder Police Station tomorrow morning?"

"Yes, I'll be there." That reminded me. My appointment with the golden retriever was fast approaching. I checked my watch. I was supposed to be at the client's house in ten minutes. "There's a guy named Chet . . . something-or-other who's waiting for the police at Beth Gleason's house. He called in about Beth being missing well over an hour ago. He . . . needs to be told."

"We'll take care of that, miss."

"The collie's leash is in the pocket of the jacket with Beth. It's a green nylon leash. There was blood on it. There's also a second leash back in the yard behind . . . It's between Beth's body and the fence. That's my leash and I'll need it to walk the collie back to my office."

The detective knelt on one knee, talking softly to Sage as he examined Sage's leather collar and ran his hands over his fur, in a tactile examination that apparently yielded nothing. "You're going to take the victim's dog with you?"

"Yes. He's traumatized. He needs my help."

The detective rose, staring at the dog. I worried he was going to tell me he'd have to take Sage for evidence. He finally nodded and muttered something indistinguishable, except for the word "wait." He headed through the gate and soon emerged, inspecting my leash in his hands.

He handed me the leash, eyeing me as he did so. "Be sure you're at the station house no later than noon tomorrow." His words were quite forceful this time.

"I'll be there," I said, battling my emotions as I slipped the chain over the collie's head. I hated being treated like this—as a possible suspect. Mustering as much confidence as I could, I said, "Sage, come," and patted my thigh. He came with me in perfect heel position on my left side. To his further credit, he managed to maintain this all the way to my office, despite my brisk stride.

I trotted down the steps and unlocked the door to my office. Fortunately, I'd stashed the keys in my pants pocket and not in my jacket. Ignoring Doppler's cheerful, bouncy greeting, I pulled off Sage's leash then headed straight for the phone, and the dogs turned their attention to each other.

My remaining appointment was with a golden and his owner, George Haggerty. George answered, and I explained that I would have to postpone my appointment until the next day. "I'm terribly sorry for the inconvenience," I went on, "but I just witnessed a terrible accident and couldn't possibly give you and your dog the attention you deserve."

"An accident?" he asked. "What happened?"

"Do you think I could possibly reschedule to one P.M. tomorrow?" I asked, ignoring his question.

"Uh, sure. That'd be fine. Rex and I will be waiting."

I thanked him and hung up. According to statistics, Rex was one of those perennially popular dog names, but this was the first time I'd heard of a dog in Boulder with that name.

Doppler was making it clear that he needed to go outside—all but crossing his legs as the whites of his eyes turned yellow. I took both dogs out, wondering what to do with Sage. Taking him to my house was out of the question. Kaitlyn would never consider having such a large dog at the house, and more important, being around Kaitlyn and all her emotional storm patterns wouldn't be healthy for Sage.

I did a double take at my car as we rounded the building toward the side lawn. Was it my imagination, or was my Subaru listing to the right? I bent over and inspected the tires, and sure enough, the right front was totally flat.

"Shit!" What next? And why now? The tire hadn't been leaking. Maybe I'd run over a nail or something and hadn't realized it. Was everything connected? Had someone let the air out of my tire after killing Beth? I glanced at the dogs, who were fine. I struggled to calm myself. I'd go crazy if I started to think every least little thing was linked to Beth Gleason.

We returned to my office. Doppler was in playful-dog mood while Sage was in such an anxious state that he might bite. Sage growled at Doppler and trotted into Russell's office and, to my surprise, hopped onto the couch. My little dog followed, not taking the hint. I ushered Doppler back into my office with me, closing Russell's door.

I grabbed my keys and went out to the car, letting Doppler come with me, only to put him in the backseat to keep him safe while I changed the tire. I'd just gotten the spare out of the trunk and was unloading the jack when a deep male voice said, "Hi, there. Can I help?"

Jumpy and out-of-sorts, I turned to face a nicely built, bearded young man, but my eyes were immediately drawn to his dog, a small mutt that appeared to be mostly terrier and toy poodle—a toodle. When I looked back up, the man was smiling at me. His dark, almost black hair was in need of a trim.

"No, thanks. I can handle it."

Doppler and the toodle spotted each other and barked— his giving a shrill yipping song, mine enjoying his superior position up high in my car.

"I'm sure you can, but odds are, I could do it faster."

That was tempting, as he was probably correct, and I would love to get Sage and Doppler out of here. Furthermore, it was probably a coincidence that my tire went flat around the time Beth Gleason was murdered, but I couldn't know for certain that this man with his toodle hadn't set me up. Just in case, I stared at him, memorizing the features beneath his dark beard.

"My name's Joel," he added. "Joel Meyer."

I forced a smile—being in a decidedly bad mood—and shook my head. "Thanks for offering. Really. But I don't mind taking aggression out on some lug nuts. Besides, you do something as macho as change my tire, and I'll feel obligated to do some unmacho favor for you—" I pointed at the torn pocket of his flannel shirt "—such as stitch up that tear in your shirt, and I'm not much of a seamstress."

He watched in silence—not counting his yapping dog— as I pried the hubcap off, then tried to loosen the first lug nut. Uh-oh. The blasted lug nuts had been machine tightened. I might need a sledgehammer to get them off.

"All right, then. Tell you what," he said. "How about I change your tire, then you buy me a cup of coffee."

Talk about not taking "no" for an answer. Does this guy wander around neighborhoods, searching for flat tires to change?

"Sorry. I don't think so." I kept my attention on the tire,

wondering how long I could stall. I'd changed enough tires with machine-tightened lug nuts to know what I was in for. I was going to have to stand and possibly bounce on the end of the wrench till the lug nut budged and I fell off my precarious perch. This was not the kind of dignified process for which I wanted to have a witness.

"Joel!" a deep yet feminine voice called from the bottom of the hill. "Don't be a dolt! Change the lady's tire!" I whirled around and spotted Tracy Truett heading down the sidewalk toward us.

Caught off guard by Tracy's unexpected appearance, I let Joel take the wrench out of my hand and replace it with the leash to his dog. He had the lug nuts loose by the time Tracy reached us.

Tracy was breathing hard and sweating profusely, despite the chill in the air, as she strode up the hill. She was wearing a navy blue knit top and matching pants, with a black cape around her shoulders that rippled in the wind. With her spiky hair and impressive size, she looked as if she might have come straight out of the comic pages—Batman's villain, Big She-Bat.

"We meet again," she said to me, smiling broadly. She pointed down at my small office window, which afforded me a little light and views of pedestrians' ankles. "That your office?"

"Yes, how did you know?"

"I got your address off your flier. Got any coffee?"

After finding the body of a murdered client, now I was supposed to have coffee with Tracy Truett? What was next? A game of badminton with Darth Vader? "I'm afraid you caught me on the wrong day. I don't have any cups."

"I'll drink it straight from the pot." She grabbed the leash from my hand and started to lead Joel's dog toward my office. She said over her shoulder, "Joel can come join us as soon as he's finished. Come on, Suzanne."

I thanked Joel, let Doppler out of my car, then said, "By the way, my name's Allida, not Suzanne."

"I know. Suzanne is the dog's name."

Joel's mutt yipped fiercely at Doppler, aggression which Doppler returned. He was squaring off, prepared to defend his space.

"Shut up, Suzanne," Tracy said, then looked at me. "Unpleasant little dog. Joel takes her everywhere."

I started coffee brewing, wishing I could just curl into the fetal position until Tracy and crew left. By the time I'd returned my attention to her, she was comfortably settled into my desk chair, pushing herself back and forth a quarter turn or so, while Suzanne sat in her lap and, from this safe perch, barked at Doppler. The racket was getting to me. I was off duty now and didn't want to deal with bark management. I swept up my dog, though he had every reason in the world to bark, and marched toward Russell's office. Sage was napping on Russell's couch, but opened his eyes as we entered. "Good dog," I reassured him, then left Doppler.

"I take it, Joel's a friend of yours?" I asked as I returned to my human visitor.

She nodded, then grimaced. "This is every bit as unpleasant as I imagined."

"My office?"

"No, my coming here. To apologize."

"You don't need to do that."

" 'Course I do. Why else would I be here, hung over as all hell?"

"I don't know. To coerce your friend Joel to change my tire, perhaps?"

"Nah. He wanted to come. In fact, we spotted you out there with your flat tire while I was looking for a parking spot, and he asked for a minute alone with you."

"Why?"

"He's got the hots for you."

I was too surprised to say anything.

"You'd be amazed how many men called the station yesterday to ask about you. Must have been at least five." She chuckled, then settled back in my chair. "Well, all right, two." She pressed her palms against her spiked hair and muttered, "Holy crow, what a headache I've got. Got any aspirin?"

"No. Sorry."

"Too bad you didn't land on my show a year ago. I could've run a radio dating service and been the hottest thing since sliced toast. Anyway, Joel's a real decent guy. Used to work for the station and now calls into my show everyday." She sneered and rolled her eyes. "Guess I need to remember to use past tense when referring to my show. But, the long and short of it is, he wants you."

The timing of this announcement was so bad that my stomach lurched. "Why? He doesn't even know me."

"Ask him yourself," Tracy said, gesturing at the door, where Joel was just entering. "Joel, dear, I was just telling our friend here how you want to ask her out."

Joel froze and gaped at her, then gave me a sheepish grin. "I'd planned to be charming and tactful."

"Aah, go ahead, Allida. Go out with the guy. He's a real peach. Just happens to go for the petite type." She put both hands on her hips and said in a husky voice, "Though I keep telling you, Joel, you don't know what you're missing."

Joel chuckled nervously and smiled at me. "It was never my intention to put you on the spot like this."

He was being so sweet that I smiled despite my state of inner turmoil. Russell came bounding down the outer steps and burst into my office. He stood back in surprise as he eyed Tracy and Joel, all the while slipping what looked like a greeting card into a pocket of his jacket. He shrugged in my direction. "Didn't mean to interrupt. You said you had an appointment with a golden retriever. I figured, you'd be out, making a house call." He stared at the white-and-gray mutt in Tracy's lap and muttered, "I decided I could get a lot of work done today, with no ringing phones and . . . ." His voice drifted off, and he met my eyes. "I don't know much about dogs, but aren't goldens normally a lot bigger than that and kind of yellowish?"

"I never forget a voice," Tracy said too loudly for the small room. "Tracy Truett," she said. She rose and stashed Suzanne under her left arm as if the little dog were a football, then pumped Russell's hand. "You called my radio show yesterday." She peered down at him. "You sounded taller on the phone." She turned toward Joel. "Well, guy, this is the Russell who asked Allida out on the show yesterday." She jabbed his shoulder and laughed with abandon. "Boys, meet your competition."

Sage was starting to whimper. I opened the door to Russell's office, half hoping Sage would start barking at Joel to demonstrate he might be the killer. Both dogs raced into the room. Sage did indeed start barking, but at Tracy and the small dog in her arms.

"Oh my gawd!" Tracy shrieked. "Is that the collie that the girl called in about?"

"Yes." I called for Sage, and he came right over to me, but maintained a rhythmic, nervous bark.

Tracy narrowed her eyes as she watched us. "I remember." She snapped her fingers. "Beth Gleason. Where is she?"

"She . . ." I paused, hesitant at the thought that, for all I knew, Tracy Truett would be on another radio station tomorrow, blabbing about Beth Gleason's death and running listener surveys. "She's dead. I'm sure you'll be reading about it in tomorrow's paper."

"Dead?"

"That woman who called your show yesterday?" Russell asked in shock. "She's dead? What happened?"

"I don't know. Somebody stabbed her. Early this afternoon."

"If it'd help, I'd be more than happy to watch after her dog for a while, provided my dog gets along with him," Joel offered.

"*I'll* watch him. Sage, I mean," Russell shot back, moving closer to me despite a nervous glance at the still-barking Sage. "I don't have another dog to worry about."

Joel, I noticed, had taken a step closer to me as well. They were posturing, acting as territorial toward me as a pair of male dogs to a bone. Good thing they *weren't* male dogs, or I'd have to shampoo the carpet.

"No, thanks, both of you," I replied harshly. "I'll take care of him. He's . . . been through a lot."

"Coffee's done," Tracy said. She thrust Suzanne into Joel's arms, snatched the Pyrex pot off its stand, tore off its lid, and sipped from it as if it were an oversized cup. Just watching her sip that hot liquid made my eyes water. Years of nonstop talking must have anesthetized her mouth.

She glanced around the room at us. "Excuse my lips, but does anybody else want some?"

"No, thanks," the three of us said in unison.

"My cup's underneath the sink, catching drips," I explained to Russell, who was staring at Tracy, utterly appalled.

Suzanne was yipping away at the other dogs, and Sage was barking sporadically and pacing around the room, badly stressed-out. Russell was looking more than a little uncomfortable at being surrounded by barking dogs.

I moved toward the door, hoping they'd all take the hint that I wanted them on the other side of it. "It was nice meeting you, Joel. Really. But I've got to kick everybody out. I have to take Sage home."

"Maybe I can call you for a date sometime?"

"Sure, that would be . . . fine," I answered, thinking under normal circumstances I'd be both flattered and tempted. Now, though, it was unlikely I'd accept any dates until Beth's murder was solved and my life began to make sense again.

"I gotta tell you, Allida," Tracy said, wagging her thumb in Joel's direction as she set the coffeepot on top of my file cabinet. "I'd take this guy in a second if I were you."

Russell crossed his arms and glared at Tracy.

She grabbed Joel's arm and gave him a tug toward the door. "Joel, you've got her number; call her sometime. And Russell, if I were you, I'd get myself a pooch if you want to win that chick's heart." She swept out the door, closely followed by Joel.

The resulting quiet seemed to turn the room into a vacuum. Russell turned toward me and asked, "How do you feel about goldfish?"

Chapter 9

I excused myself from Russell's company, ushered both dogs into my car, and drove to my mother's house. My mother absolutely loves large dogs, and I knew she'd be happy to dog-sit Sage for a while. I just wish I'd had the chance to call first. My unexpected visitors had distracted me.

I left Sage in the car so that I could prepare my mom. We went through a repeat of yesterday's routine on my mother's doorstep. Doppler was so eager to greet Pavlov that I stepped inside so he could come in, too. Then I said, "I have a bit of a surprise for you."

I went back out to the car and opened the door. Sage hopped out. My mother had followed me onto the blond brick front porch. She took one look at the collie and said, "Sage."

"His owner was killed and he needs a temporary home."

"But I thought she died several weeks ago."

"I don't mean Hannah Jones, I mean Beth Gleason. Somebody stabbed Beth to death early this afternoon." My mother gasped in horror, as I continued, "Sage came to my office and found me. I can't think of where else to keep him, at least not till I can find a new place to live." I winced, realizing I'd just blurted that I was shopping for new living quarters.

Mom, however, was so transfixed by the dog as she ran

her hands over him that she didn't take any notice. "My goodness, he has been through a lot, hasn't he? He's all skin and bones." She opened the door, and the three of us went inside.

"He's starting to eat again. If you can just feed him"— I hesitated as I tried to decide how I wanted this done— "the same amount you give Pavlov, he should be all right. It's the dog brand he's used to. But if he seems hesitant or afraid to eat it, you might want to hand-feed him the first couple of kibbles."

Judging from the sounds, Doppler was lapping water from Pavlov's bowl in the kitchen. Pavlov wanted to investigate Sage. The dogs circled one another, getting each other's scents. They trotted off shoulder to shoulder into the kitchen, and I silently congratulated myself on my decision to bring him here. A wonderfully even-tempered German shepherd was exactly the right companion for Sage after his traumatic day.

"They get along great," Mom said. "Good thing Pavlov was spayed. We'd have ourselves collie-shepherd puppies."

"Are you sure you don't mind? I don't know how long it will take till I can guarantee a good home for him. Could be as much as a month or two."

She smiled, patting some loose strands of her long braid. "Some mothers baby-sit their grandchildren. I baby-sit my children's dogs. It's better than nothing." She gave me a visual once-over. "You'd better hurry home, hadn't you, sweetie?"

"Why?"

"Don't you remember? You have a date with one of my flying students. Keith Terrington. We set this up two weeks ago."

"Oh, no! That's tonight? I'm not up to it. Do you have his number? I'll call and explain."

"Allida, I hate to force you to do anything you don't want to do, but—"

"Since when?"

Undaunted, she continued, "But I have to insist you go ahead and at least explain things to him face-to-face. Just like you and that . . . louse you were engaged to, his wife ran off with one of his best friends. In fact, he reminds me of you."

"Then why would I want to date him? I'd have to have some psychological problem to want to date a man my mother thinks is a male counterpart of me."

Mom met my eyes and said evenly, "Knock it off, Allie. He's a wonderful man. You're perfect for each other."

She'd called me "Allie." I probably had the only mother on the planet who addressed me by my nickname only when she was starting to get annoyed with me. "Not tonight, we're not. The only thing that's perfect for me tonight is a good book, a fireplace, and a dog at my feet."

"That may be true, Allie, but I had to do a lot of cajoling to convince Keith to . . . . This is not coming out right. My point is, after what happened to your client, I'd feel a lot safer knowing you were with Keith tonight." Mom looked puzzled for a moment. "Did you just say you were looking for a new place to live?"

"I'd better get going, Mom. Thanks for watching Sage." I started to open the door, then thought better of it. "I'd better check on him before I go."

Pavlov, I discovered, was patiently waiting to be let out back. Sage, however, was the epitome of the "hangdog" expression, no longer paying attention to Pavlov or Doppler but lying listlessly in the kitchen.

"Hey, Sage, that's a good dog," I said. He didn't look up, and I sensed he knew I was about to desert him. "You'll be happy here. Pavlov and Mom are great company."

"Thanks for giving me second billing," my mother said.

I smiled at her and opened the door for Pavlov, who took off at a dead run for the fence, letting out her guard-dog woofs.

There, a white sedan was just pulling away from the curb alongside the chain-link fence.

Leaving the door open behind me, I charged across the lawn to get the car's license plate, but soon realized the driver had had too much of a head start. Sage rushed past me and joined Pavlov in barking as they ran along the length of the fence.

"Mom," I cried as I rushed back inside, "there's a white sedan just now driving off." I waggled my thumb over my shoulder in the direction of the road and struggled to catch my breath. "It was parked by the fence till the dogs started barking. It was here yesterday around this time, too. Have you ever noticed it?"

She studied my features and said in a deadpan voice, "A white car was parked on County Line Road two nights in a row? Should we alert the National Guard?"

I gritted my teeth. "Mom, Beth Gleason was murdered today after claiming on the radio that her dog witnessed Hannah Jones's murder. I suspect I'm being followed, and Beth's dog is currently in your backyard, barking at the very same car I think has been following me!"

She paled. "When you put it that way, it sounds terrible. I think I liked my version better."

"Mom, you—"

She held up her palms. "Sheriff Millay is a friend of mine. I'll call him this minute, tell him about this, and ask that he drive by the house every so often. How should I describe the car?"

"A white four-door sedan. I never got a good look at it. But let me tell the sheriff that myself when I—"

"You've got to get going back to Boulder. I'll do the talking to the sheriff."

"But, I can't leave Sage here under these circumstances. I'll get one of my friends from high school to take him for a—"

"Sage will be fine. I'll keep him inside, in my bedroom tonight. Now quit stalling and get home so you can meet Keith Terrington while you're both still young."

"I'm not stalling! This is important! You and Sage could be in danger!"

"Fine. You've convinced me." She threw up her hands and marched to the phone. "I *will* go ahead and alert the National Guard. Just bear in mind, Allie, that I am still your mother and I am still in charge of making my own decisions."

"True, and *I'm* an adult and am in charge of making *my* own decisions!"

She gestured at me to leave with a flick of her wrist, but started dialing with her other hand. "So go make them, rather than dawdling around here. Sage, Pavlov, and I will be fine."

Doppler had trotted back beside me, and I realized that in my haste, I hadn't even shut the back door. I was too angry now to care. "Doppler, heel," I said, as usual not bothering with the leash. "Fine, Mother. I give up. I'm going, but don't say I didn't warn you." I strode out the door, Doppler a step behind me.

As I closed the door behind Doppler, Mom called in a cheerful voice, "Have fun on your date, sweetie."

I drove home in an indescribably foul mood, furious with my mother for treating me like a child. How dare she accuse me of trying to turn my spotting of the white sedan into a stall tactic to miss my date? That certainly wasn't true, at least not on a conscious level, and even if it were true, it was my business if I was late for a date. Whoever this Keith Terrington was, I was determined to hate him on sight.

My mother had never set me up on a date before. That's precisely why last week I'd agreed to do this in the first place, having reasoned that this guy must really have something going for him. Now, however, I was more inclined to attribute the whole thing to a strong force of mother nature: my mother's determination to have grandchildren nearby.

I drove below the speed limit the whole way to Boulder, seriously considering stopping. Maybe I should double back and drive around Mom's house, checking for suspicious white sedans myself. But what would I do if I did find one? Ram it?

Still pondering the issue, I arrived at my house. A blue sporty-looking Mazda was parked out front. I parked, checked my rearview mirror and messed up my hair a little, promising myself that no matter what, I would not apologize for being late, but would explain that the date was off, due to some troubles I'd experienced today that were beyond my control.

Resolved, I walked inside, followed by Doppler, and found my roommate flitting over the most attractive man I'd seen in ages. He had straight, light-brown hair about the same shade as mine, and the bluest eyes I'd seen this side of Paul Newman, with a body and face to match. He wore a sports jacket over a teal-colored T-shirt and faded denims. With his broad shoulders and tapered waist and hips, he could wear that same wardrobe on the cover of *GQ* and get no argument from me.

Kaitlyn's smile faded a little as she looked away from him—they shared seats on the couch, practically sharing the same cushion, as well—and said in a voice dripping with regret, "Here she is now."

The man endeared himself to my heart by meeting my eyes only briefly, then smiling at Doppler. "What a handsome cocker you've got there," he said. He called, "Here, boy." Despite years of training, Doppler leapt onto his lap in an amazing display of instant affinity for the man.

"You must be Keith Terrington," I said in a dazzling display of wit. "I'm Allida Babcock. I'm sorry that I'm so late."

"That's quite all right. Your mother's said a lot of wonderful things about you."

"Yes, but she feels genetically obligated." I searched my memory for what Mom had told me about Keith. As I recall, she'd said of his appearance that he was "reasonably handsome, with brown hair and blue eyes." She was right about the hair and eyes. But if this was "reasonably handsome," Albert Einstein was reasonably intelligent.

He gave me a killer smile and asked, "Are you ready to go?"

"Not quite." I turned to head for my room and heard myself say, "I just need a minute to freshen up." I rolled my eyes as I reached my bedroom. *Freshen up?* I sounded like an ad for a feminine-hygiene product. In record speed, I changed into a denim shirtdress and leather boots with sizable heels, then set about repairing the damage the day had done to my makeup and hair.

I'm insecure enough that I prefer to date men I consider either roughly equivalent to my looks or slightly more flawed. I hate to have waitresses ogle my dates and then tell other waitresses, "He must be on a blind date," which would be true tonight. That makes me sound paranoid, but I waitressed during college and partook of many a barb with my fellow employees about couples at the restaurant.

"All set," I said while I cinched my best belt around my waist and returned to the living room. I hoped that, despite my frenetic pace, I could refrain from panting.

Kaitlyn was still sitting inches away from Keith on the

couch, and Doppler grudgingly got off Keith's lap to examine my new outfit and see if he could shed on it.

"You're going to be proud to hear that I accepted a date of my own tonight," Kaitlyn announced to me, then focused on Keith. "My husband and I are separated, but Allida here doesn't think that a little thing like a broken heart should interfere with my social life."

Keith raised an eyebrow at me.

"That's not a direct quote," I said in my defense. In point of fact, my lone suggestion had been for her to think about seeing someone new, but no sense quibbling over semantics. "Anybody I know?" I asked Kaitlyn, just to be polite, for the only man she'd ever mentioned to me was her virtual-reality husband.

"No, I just met him today. Just after you left, in fact. I was sitting out on the porch, and he happened to be lost and asked me for directions. We hit it off, and he asked me out."

She met him *today*? Oh, blast it all! The hairs on the back of my neck were rising like miniature warning flags.

"He was driving by in his car?"

She nodded.

"It wasn't white, was it?"

"No, why?"

Both Kaitlyn and Keith were looking at me so intently that I doubted I could pass off the question with, "It's bad luck to date a man in a white car," so I said, "My new client, Beth Gleason, was murdered this afternoon. Since then, a white sedan has—"

"A client of yours was murdered?" Kaitlyn said in alarm, hands to her throat. "How do you know her death was murder?"

"She was stabbed. I found the body."

Keith rose. "This happened to you just today? Do you still want—" He paused, then said gently, "If you'd like to take a rain check on our date tonight, I understand. Or maybe we should just go someplace quiet, where we can talk."

"Yes, let's do that last suggestion," I said, perhaps a bit too eagerly. "If I just sit at home by myself tonight, I'll get paranoid."

"You'll have to excuse me," Kaitlyn said dramatically as she rose. "I have to get ready myself." She left the room, saying, "Have a nice evening, Allida."

"Thanks. You, too." I watched her for a moment. However biased I was by her personality, Kaitlyn truly was pretty, especially because of her luxuriant auburn hair. There was little basis for my fear that her meeting a stranger who asked her on a date was anything other than a coincidence. As was my car getting a flat today. Each day was full of incidents, and until something as significant as a murder happens, we don't consider their connections.

Keith, meanwhile, strode past me and held open the door. "Shall we?"

I grinned and started to waltz out the door, envisioning myself as the heroine in a romance novel. Until I realized that, even with my tall boots on, I was so much shorter than Keith I could easily have passed right under his arm as he supported the door.

My dog started to whine. "Bye, Doppler," Keith said. "Don't worry. I'll be good to her." He closed the door behind us.

He put his arm around my shoulder, but I froze in my steps. "How did you know my dog's name?"

"Your roommate told me." He removed his hand from my shoulder. "Why?"

"I'm sorry. Apparently I'm getting paranoid even when I'm *not* left alone with my imagination."

Keith opened the passenger door of his car, which was, indeed, the blue Mazda. I got in, silently chastising myself. Why hadn't I stopped to realize that Keith could easily have heard Doppler's name from either Kaitlyn or my mother? I reached over to unlock his door.

"So, how long have you been working as a dog behaviorist?" he asked as we drove off.

"Only a few weeks, but I've trained dogs at kennels for years, back in Chicago. I went to school there and stayed in Evanston afterwards."

"What brought you back here?"

"I just thought it'd be the perfect place to open this type of a business. Boulder seems to have more therapists per capita than any other city, and Boulderites feel so strongly about their canine population that leash laws make front-page news."

Keith gestured at the digital clock in the dashboard. "We've missed our reservations at Red Lion by quite a bit. Should we see if they can still fit us in?"

Feeling guilty that my late arrival had spoiled his plans, I shook my head. "Is there a less fancy place we can go to? I love that restaurant, but that's one of those places where they introduce you by first name to the maître d', the waiter, the wine steward, the chef, the busboy. Sometimes I feel like telling them I'm just there to eat, not to befriend their staff."

Keith laughed and said, "Burgers and beer at Tom's Tavern?"

"Perfect."

Tom's Tavern is located just west of the downtown pedestrian mall, and we had the predictable battle to find a parking space—so much so that we would have been better off leaving Keith's car at my house and walking. The long, narrow restaurant was crowded, but we eventually got a booth and ordered. It occurred to me that everyone who'd heard about me through the show had to know about Sage and was, until the police could show otherwise, under suspicion. At least Keith had made this date prior to Sage's entering my life.

I felt off-kilter throughout the evening. Every time there was a loud noise behind me, I jumped, half expecting to feel the point of a knife at the back of my neck. I may as well have had one of those "invisible fences" around me, operating in reverse to keep men away. And yet, ironically, this was my second date in the same day, and a third man had asked me out. Was I suddenly doing something right? Or was my I'm-not-interested-in-a-man-in-my-life-just-now philosophy drawing men to me faster than canines to a dog whistle? And how long could I keep up with these unspoken men-as-dogs analogies till I made some god-awful verbal miscue?

We finished our meals. I became unbearably antsy and excused myself to phone my mother. There was no answer. Her recorder kicked on, and I said, "Mom, this is Allida. Where are you? I'm really worried. I'm going to call back again in a few minutes, and if you're not there, I'll head out there or something."

My stomach was in knots as I hung up. Keith asked me what was wrong the moment I returned to my seat.

"Mom's not home. There's no reason for her to be out this late. I know she's a pilot and everything, but even so, she doesn't fly or drive at night anymore. She has too much trouble with her night vision."

Keith straightened. "What would you like to do? Should I take you home?"

"No. Not yet. I'll call again in a little while. I'm sorry about all of this. I'm really a fairly nice, normal person most of the time."

Keith grabbed my hand over the table and held my gaze, which was difficult for me, because I felt a bit swoonish—if that's a word—under the intensity of his incredible eyes and the warmth of his hand. "I have no doubt, Allida."

All of a sudden, I loved my first name, now that I heard it spoken by Keith. I felt my cheeks warming and knew my face must be beaming as bright as reindeer Rudolph's nose. He released my hand, which I immediately jerked back to my lap. "I'll go make that call now. Excuse me."

"Well, that was really smooth," I muttered under my breath as I crossed the room. Now I was feeling suspicious of Keith for acting more impressed with me than I thought he should be. Talk about a no-win situation. I dialed and sighed with relief when my mother answered. "Thank goodness you're there, Mom. I got really worried when you didn't answer before."

"For heaven's sake, Allie! I was out back playing fetch with the dogs and I didn't hear the phone."

"You were playing fetch in the dark?"

"Yes. *I* wasn't the one fetching the stick, after all, so the darkness really didn't spoil things for me. Did you cancel your date with Keith?"

"No, we went out. Keith is wonderful. He's everything you said he was, and more. Our date is still going on, as a matter of fact. I'm calling from the restaurant."

There was a pause. "When you were sixteen, you used to have a fit if I waited up for you. Now you're thirty-two years old, and you're calling your mother while you're out with a man you say is 'wonderful.' What is going on with you, Allida?"

I clenched my jaw and tried to count to ten, but only made it to three. "I'm not calling to chat, Mother! I'm calling to make sure you're all right and find out whether or not you've talked to the police yet!"

"The sheriff. Yes. No arrests have been made, I'm sorry to say." After a pause, she said, "Is Keith wearing his lucky hat?"

"Hat?" I repeated, immediately on edge at the mention of the clothing item that put Sage into frenzy.

"Yes, he has a beat-up hat he always wears for luck when he flies. I figured, if he's wearing it tonight, he's hoping . . . . Never mind. I don't like where this thought pattern is taking me."

"He didn't wear a hat tonight, Mom."

"Oh, good. I guess. Do me a favor and don't call me during any more of your dates, okay? You might be an adult, but you're still my daughter, and I'd just as soon not worry about how your date is treating you."

I glanced over my shoulder at Keith in the booth. He wasn't looking in my direction. "He's been what you'd call a perfect gentleman. I'll talk to you tomorrow." I hung up and returned to the table. "Mom's fine." Testing, I added, "She asked about your lucky hat."

"My lucky hat?" Keith repeated. "What about it?"

I studied his handsome features, trying to decide if his reaction was guileless. "She wanted to know if you were wearing it."

"I only wear it when I fly. It's too shabby-looking for anything else."

I breathed a sigh of relief, and we chatted easily as Keith brought me home and walked me to the front door. I decided to circumvent the first-date awkwardness and turned when I was still a step above him to give him a quick peck on the cheek. "Thank you, Keith. I'm so sorry all of this happened to me today of all days. Please call me again and let's make a new start of this."

"I will," he said, smiling. "Good night."

He waited while I started to unlock the door, but found that it wasn't locked. Kaitlyn's date must have been even more of a disaster than mine for her to have beaten me home. I said good night and thanked Keith again, and watched him from my doorway as he drove away. A floorboard creaked from the back of the house, and I headed down the hall to tell Kaitlyn that I was home.

As I started past my room, my heart leapt to my throat. I screamed at the sight of a man rifling through the top drawer of my dresser.

Chapter 10

"Don't scream!" he cried. He headed toward me.

I slammed my bedroom door and ran to the kitchen as fast as I could go, stumbling through the doorway. I snatched a long, heavy knife from the butcher-block holder by the sink and dialed 911 with my free hand.

The call didn't go through. The phone made a rhythmic shrilling in my ear. It dawned on me what the sound meant. Dammit! One of the phones in the bedrooms was off the hook!

Doppler had followed me and started barking his guard dog bark in the intruder's direction. I dropped the receiver and turned to see the man in the doorway. He froze at the sight of the long knife in my hand. Doppler growled and barked as loud as he could, inches in front of me.

"Don't come near me!" I held the knife poised, my heart pounding so hard I could barely breathe. "My other dog is a German shepherd!"

"Put the knife down," he said, with slow, careful enunciation. "I'm Bill Wayne, Kaitlyn's husband."

I stared at him, taking in the five-o'clock shadow on his lantern jaw, receding hairline, sunken eyes. He was of medium height and build. This was indeed an older, more haggard version of the groom in my roommate's wedding photos.

My brain tried to tell my senses that I was probably not

on the verge of having to defend my life, after all. My body refused to relax. Doppler, however, had toned down his barks to a woof every couple of seconds, not unlike a bag of microwave popcorn nearing the end of its cooking cycle.

"What are you doing here?" I kept a tight grip on my knife and indicated the useless phone with a tip of my head. "You have five seconds to explain yourself, or I'm calling the police."

"I have every right to be here. This is my house. Half of it, anyway."

"As far as I'm concerned, buddy, you're in the wrong half! How dare you go through my things!"

He held up his palms, his vision riveted to my knife. "I was just trying to locate your name and a work number. I needed to find some safe, neutral location where I could talk to you about my wife. She's not at all well, you know."

"What do you mean?" Aside from her acting somewhat manic at times, that is, but I wanted to hear *his* answer.

"Put the knife down and I'll tell you."

Unwilling to turn my back on him, I sidestepped over to the cabinet opposite the doorway he occupied and set the knife on the counter, within my immediate reach. I crossed my arms and awaited his reply, calculating that I could and would snatch the knife again if he made any sudden movements toward me.

"She's not stable. She wrecked my business by calling my associates and customers to locate me every five minutes. I got out before she could destroy what little was left of my life. I want her to sell this place. I'll personally refund whatever deposit you might have given Kaitlyn, if you'll agree to help me convince her to sell."

"Why do you need my help?"

"Because as long as Kaitlyn is soaking you for rent and insisting I come back to her, she's never going to sell. I want my half of the proceeds on this house, and I want out of this marriage."

"So, you felt you needed to convince me to help you. And the way you went about it was to break into my house and go through my private things and scare me half to death. I got to tell you, Bill, this has not been the best of strategies."

"Sorry I frightened you." He grimaced, in an expression that he, perhaps, thought made him look contrite. If so, he should look in a mirror, because the effect was more that of a smart-aleck sneer. "I didn't expect you to come back so soon."

I tensed. Had he been following me? Was he the driver of the white sedan? If he was, I didn't want to give away the fact that I was on the lookout for that particular vehicle. "What do you mean?"

He shrugged. "I was hoping to talk to you privately, later tonight. I was going to put everything back the way I found it and then call you."

He was a regular prince of decorum. I glanced down at my dog. Doppler had stopped his barking and was now lying on the floor before my feet. I'd like to think his intention was still to protect me, but he seemed to be nodding off.

"You got part of that right," I said. "You need to leave my house. Now. Kaitlyn's out, but she and her *date* will be here any moment."

Bill chuckled. "I wouldn't count on that, if I were you."

"What do you mean?"

The sneer on his face spread wider. "Let's just say I know all about her 'date' tonight."

Surprised and disgusted, I asked, "Her date was staged? She's going out with some friend of yours?"

"More like hired help. He's keeping her *occupied* till I

call her date's cell phone and tell him the coast's clear."
He ran his eyes the length of my body and raised an eyebrow. "Listen, you seem like a nice, sensible person. Get
out while the getting's good. Kaitlyn is nuts."

She *must* have been to marry this oily creep. If he proved
to be dangerous, as well, now that he'd masterminded
Kaitlyn's "date," there was little possibility of someone
coming to my rescue. I clenched my jaw and stared at him.
If I refused to talk to him, he might leave. Not that that
meant much to me in the way of protection, since he had
the key to the dead bolt.

He spread his hands in a flawed attempt to don a sincere posture. "I'm not exaggerating. Just before I left
Colorado, but after we'd separated, she used to injure herself, then turn around and claim that I was beating her.
She's a desperate woman. If I were you, I'd do what *I*
did. Pack up right now and move out." Doppler rose and
took a couple of steps toward Bill Wayne, who started to
bend down to greet him.

"Doppler, come!" I called in immediate panic. He
stopped instantly and circled back toward me. "Don't touch
my dog!"

"Whoa." Bill straightened and held up his palms. "You
sure are protective of your little mutt." He turned as if to
leave, then paused and said over his shoulder, "I wouldn't
trust leaving him, or any dog, alone with Kaitlyn, if I were
you."

I swept Doppler up into my arms.

Grinning, Bill Wayne watched me. I met his dark, sunken
eyes. He'd just found my Achilles' heel, and we both knew
it. I decided he was the ugliest man I'd ever seen.

"Ask her about our puppy sometime, if you don't believe me." He gestured with his large chin at the doggie
door built into the back door beside me. "I installed that

for our puppy. She sure didn't get much chance to use it, though."

Much as I didn't want to ask, I couldn't stop myself. "What happened to her?"

Bill grimaced and shook his head, his eyes focused on Doppler. "Like I said, you'll have to ask Kaitlyn. I still can't believe she would do something like that to a puppy."

A shudder of fear and revulsion ran up my spine. Kaitlyn had told me the former owners of the house had installed the doggie door, that she and Bill never bothered to put in a new door. His words had the disturbing ring of truth to them, but how could I tell? What if he was just trying to manipulate me and get back at his ex-ish wife? This was a man who'd just broken into my bedroom. I hugged Doppler closer to me and said as calmly as I could, "Please go."

He opened the front door and looked back at me. "Don't tell her I was here, okay? You won't be accomplishing anything. You'll only hurt her feelings when she realizes this so-called date of hers was hired help."

He shut the door behind him. Doppler wriggled in my arms, and I set him down, my stomach churning. I couldn't trust either of these people; not Kaitlyn, whom I'd already concluded was more than a little unstable; not her husband who seemed not only odd, but dangerous.

I marched into my room. How dare that bastard paw through my things! The thought of him violating my privacy like this both frightened and infuriated me.

One thing was certain. I was uncomfortable here, and I was not staying.

The handset of my phone had been placed off its hook on the nightstand. I replaced it, then began a thorough survey to see if anything was missing or out of place. I first scanned my bed; its blue-and-white quilt cover seemed to be in the same reasonably neat condition as when I'd left. I turned my attention to the top dresser drawer, which Bill had been rifling through when I surprised him.

Nothing seemed to be missing. Partway through my mental inventory, the phone rang. I answered, and a sexy male voice said, "Hi. Is this Allida?"

"Yes." I didn't recognize the voice and was trying to do so.

"It's Keith. You sound a little out-of-sorts. I'll bet you didn't expect to hear from me quite so soon."

My heart was racing with my pent-up anger at Bill Wayne. "It's not that. I just had a very unpleasant and un-expected encounter with my roommate's ex. Or rather, her separatee."

"Is everything all right?"

I took a deep breath in an attempt to calm myself so that I could enjoy talking to Keith, but it didn't work. "Not really. I doubt I'll be at this number much longer, but you can always reach me through my office phone or, for that matter, my mother's."

"You're moving out?"

"Yes. And I don't want to be here when my roommate gets back from her date . . . if you want to call it that. That jerk of a husband of hers set her up."

"What do you mean?"

"Oh, the sleazeball hired somebody to pretend to be interested in her and take her out just so he could get her out of the house."

There was a pause, and all I could think was how bi-zarre all of this must sound from Keith's perspective. He'd known me for all of three hours or so now. He must think he wound up with the all-time, loony-tune date. "I'm sorry," I said. "I shouldn't be dumping all of this on you. I barely even know you."

"That's all right." He chuckled. "Here I was, afraid we wouldn't have much to talk about."

I smiled and held the phone tight. "That's seldom a problem with me. It's one of the occupational hazards of working with patients with a vocabulary of less than a hundred words. You talk your fellow humans' ears off."

He chuckled again, then said, "I'll call you soon at your office. Good night."

"Good night," I repeated. I hung up, then stared at the phone for a moment, realizing I hadn't learned why he'd called.

I had to pack my essentials first, which meant Doppler and everything that belonged to him. His carrier/dog bed took up most of the space behind the backseat. Then I emptied the bathroom of my stuff, followed by dumping the contents of my top dresser drawer into my suitcase. I grabbed what I could out of the remaining drawers until the suitcases were so full I had to sit on them to shut them.

I grabbed an armload of clothes on hangers, took them out to the car and dumped them on the backseat, and put Doppler and paraphernalia in the front passenger side. I hugged myself to battle the rapidly chilling night air and made a visual appraisal of my packing. My suitcases and a couple of blankets would still fit in the back. There wouldn't be room for my full laundry basket, though. Maybe I could flip the basket upside down and tie it to the car roof. No, now that I was running my own business, I had to keep up at least the pretense of dignity.

Still making mental calculations, I went back inside. It was much too late for me to barge in on my mother. I'd spend the night on the couch in Russell's office and drive out to Berthoud in the morning. Wouldn't Mom be surprised? Her non-pilot daughter was about to throw up her hands and move back home. Life just didn't seem to want to get with my program, blast it all.

The phone rang again while I was lugging my two suitcases toward the front door. I hesitated. This could be my last chance to make a clean getaway before Kaitlyn returned from her phony date. Then again, it wasn't her fault that her "ex" had done this. I owed it to Kaitlyn to explain my departure face-to-face. Plus, considering the circumstances of her "date," I needed to stay and make sure she got home all right. I answered the phone.

"Allida Babcock?" said a male voice. "This is Dennis Corning. I believe you spoke to my wife yesterday about the collie, Sage, that used to belong to Hannah Jones. We were watching him after Hannah's death."

A little discombobulated at getting a business call at home this late, I muttered, "Oh, yes. Hello, Mr. Corning." Could he have gotten my home number from directory assistance? I wondered. He must have.

"I hope this isn't too late to call. We just saw a story on Beth Gleason's murder on the ten o'clock news. She was Sage's new owner, wasn't she?"

There was no sense in denying what he already knew. "Yes."

"We've changed our minds. We want Sage back. We'll give him a good home, and that poor dog has been through too much already."

"What about your other dog . . . what was his name?" I remembered Shakespeare's name, but wanted to make sure this really was the husband of the woman before I continued this conversation.

"Shakespeare. We'll work with him."

"What about your son?" The boy's name I truly *had* forgotten.

"We'll work through that, too."

"I'll have to give this some thought. I've placed the dog in a really good home, which could become permanent. I think for the short term he's better off where he is."

"And where is that?"

Surely I was being paranoid to find this whole phone call disquieting. I could see myself doing the same thing in his shoes. Even so, I decided, I would not have asked this last question. At the very least, it was presumptuous, and at the worst, it was suspicious. "With an experienced dog owner. Why do you ask?"

He said nothing for a moment. "Could you meet with us to discuss this?" he asked.

This would give me the chance to learn more about Sage's background. "I'd be happy to."

We made arrangements to meet tomorrow afternoon. I braced myself at the sound of Kaitlyn's footsteps on the porch. The door flew open and Kaitlyn dashed inside. She twirled as she shut the door, a move that made me dizzy just to watch. She leaned back against the door and gave an exaggerated sigh of contentment.

"Guess what, Allida?" I didn't hazard a guess, but she went on, "I'm in love, and I owe it all to you."

"No, you don't owe me anything. We're entirely debt free."

"If you hadn't told me to start dating again, I would have refused to go out with Jim, and I'd have never discovered how wonderful he is."

"So you had a nice time?"

"The best!"

There was always the possibility that this Jim truly cared about Kaitlyn. Not a very large possibility, however. Just so long as he didn't cut things short the moment he got a call from Bill, I'd find it a little easier to believe. "I'm surprised you're back so early."

"Oh, somebody from Jim's office contacted him on his cell phone and told him he was going to be making some big presentation in the morning."

"On a Sunday?"

"Lots of people work Sundays. *You* do."

I'd grown used to Kaitlyn's self-absorption, but I was finding it a little surprising that she had managed to miss not only my packed-to-the-gills car out front, but the pair of suitcases in the center of the floor not ten feet away from her. "Yes, I do. And speaking of which, did you used to have a puppy?"

"No. I've never had a dog. I thought I told you that already. Why?"

"The dog door was already here when you and your husband bought this place . . . what? Five years ago?"

"Six. That's right. Exterior doors cost hundreds of dollars." She studied my face and said, "What's wrong, Allida? Why are you suddenly asking me about dog doors?"

"I'm . . . going to stay at my mother's house tonight. I can't stay here until you change the locks, at the very least."

Finally, she noticed the suitcases, and her face paled as she stared at them. "What are you—"

"Bill was here when I returned from my date. He was going through my dresser drawers."

She gasped and touched her lips. "But, that's crazy. Why would Bill come here and go through your stuff? Are you sure it was him?"

"Yes. I've seen your wedding album." More than once, in fact, she had commandeered my attention to her album, not to mention the unavoidable fifteen-by-seventeen glossy of the two of them in the living room. "He said he was looking for information about me so that he could contact me privately to enlist my help in convincing you to sell. He also told me I couldn't trust Doppler around you, because of something that happened with your puppy."

She looked utterly confused. "But—" She stepped around the nearest suitcase and grabbed my arm. "Allida, I swear to you. I've never had a dog, or puppy. Neither has Bill. He's lying to you. I don't know why, but he is."

She slowly released her grip on me, letting her arms drop to her sides.

"I don't feel safe here, and neither should you, as long as Bill is willing to march in here whenever he pleases."

"Bill would never hurt you, or me!"

I scanned her angst-ridden face and could only wonder if it were even possible for her to see how much he already *had* hurt her. "Kaitlyn, please listen to me. You're crying all the time, and you've told me yourself that you're depressed. Why don't you find a therapist? Even if I'm wrong, what's the harm in giving therapy a try?"

Kaitlyn was staring at me with a wide-open jaw and now started to sputter, "Why . . . you . . . you're a monster! I was so wrong about you! I thought you were a nice person! How can you be so cruel?" She started to cry.

I felt sorry for her, but her reaction was too extreme to feel much more. I'd lived here for less than a month. She was acting as though I were her best friend—and judging from what I'd seen of her social life, that could be the case. "I'm not trying to be cruel, Kaitlyn. I'm truly not. I'm just telling you the truth."

"So that's it?" she shrieked. "You're all packed and you're leaving?"

"I'm taking what I can for now, and I'll be back for the rest before the end of the month."

"You're acting just like Bill did! I should do the same thing I did then and just . . . burn all of your stuff!"

I picked up my suitcases and shuffled toward the door. "Well, we all gotta do what we gotta do. It's mostly just laundry I've got left here anyway."

"I can't believe you're doing this to me!"

I sighed and said, "Kaitlyn, all I know is that I have to take care of me and mine. Look at it this way. Our deal was that I'd be here on a month-to-month basis until your husband returned, right? Well, Bill's back. So, good luck to both of you. I hope you can work something out."

She sobbed noisily, but said nothing and I made it to the car without her grabbing hold of one of my legs. My head and back muscles were aching as I drove to my office and pulled into my space.

Doppler trotted inside my office amicably, then I made a couple of trips to the car, collecting one suitcase, a blanket, and my dog's things. I put his carrier in the corner, along with his water and food dish. He lapped up some water, then curled into his bed and promptly fell asleep. Oh, to have one's needs so easily met. As for me, I used the bathroom's limited facilities—dripping sink and all— then draped a blanket on the couch. I could already tell that sleep was going to be a struggle. Though this was essentially a basement with small, below-ground-level windows, a streetlight outside poured light on the couch, and there were no curtains.

The phone rang, and I answered without thinking, anxious to stop the shrill noise. There was such a long pause that I was about to hang up, when a woman said, "My gosh. Is this Allida Babcock?"

"Yes, it is. Who's this?"

"I'm terribly sorry. Here it is nearly midnight. I thought I was calling your office number and I'd get your recorder."

"This *is* my office number."

"My gosh, do you ever keep long hours!"

I said nothing.

"This is Sarah Adams. Remember me?"

"Yes, and Mugsy as well." This must be an emergency for her to be calling at this hour. Mugsy must have bitten someone. "How's she doing?"

"Fine, actually. That's why I'm calling." I breathed a sigh of relief while she continued, "You know, ever since your visit, I've been seeing her in a new light. She really is just trying to find her role within the family. I was watching the news tonight and John had to go out, and you know what Mugsy did? She lay down on my feet, just like she always does with John when he's here. I spoke to John just now, and we've decided we want to keep her. Can you help us work it out?"

I smiled and felt a surge of gratitude at this well-timed reminder that my work had meaning. "I'd be delighted to. When do you want me to start?"

"Would tomorrow work?"

We set a time, then I set about trying to force myself to sleep. Every now and then, I'd glance at the illuminated clock just to verify that, yes, time was passing and, no, I was still not asleep. Finally, I shut my eyes and counted English sheepdogs.

Somebody was pounding on the door to my office. I sat up a little on the couch, considering what to do, too groggy to be quick about it. I blinked at the clock. A few minutes after one A.M. The pounding stopped. Suddenly, a pair of bare ankles appeared in the tiny semicircular window at ground level. Startled, I strained to get a better look. Those ankles seemed to be attached to feet wearing fuzzy pink slippers. But the only full-sized person I knew who wore fuzzy pink slippers was . . . .

I jumped and stifled a scream as a face appeared in the window. No! Please tell me this is just a nightmare! But it wasn't. Kaitlyn Wayne was outside my office. Even in the muted external lighting I could see how puffy and tearstained her features were. She must have seen me, for she clutched her hands together in mock prayer and pointed in the direction of the door.

Not knowing what else to do, I nodded and rose, and switched on a light to search for my keys. How did she know I was here? I told her I'd be at my mom's. "I'm in hell!" I muttered to myself. "This is the worst day anybody has ever had since the dawn of time!"

Doppler stepped out of his carrier and cocked his head at me. The sight of my beloved dog answered for me that my laments weren't accurate. Somebody I knew had had a decidedly worse day than mine—Beth Gleason.

I eventually found the keys, told Doppler to get back to bed and shut Russell's door behind me to encourage my dog to sleep. I stumbled through my office and to the front door, and unlocked it.

Kaitlyn appeared to be hyperventilating. She gasped for air, sobbing, shaking. Despite this, she managed to step inside and shove the door closed behind her. "Oh, Allida." She took a couple of deep breaths, unable to continue. I knew I should offer her a drink of water to help her calm herself. But I also knew that I'd be far too tempted to throw it in her face.

She finally collected herself enough to speak. "You've . . . got . . . to help me! I can't take this . . . not again! I saw it! The white car. There's this man . . . in a white car. He's following me!"

Chapter 11

"What do you mean?" I asked, immediately on edge and yet thoroughly confused.

Kaitlyn merely gasped for air, still sobbing.

How on earth could she have been "followed" at this hour, when here she was in her slippers and nightgown? "Kaitlyn, please. What did you mean when you said, 'I can't take this *again*?' Was somebody following you before?"

She shook her head and buried her face in her hands, leaning back against the door. This was like dealing with a histrionic teenager—and I wasn't up to the task. I'd had only ten minutes of sleep and had to work in the morning. If only she were a dog, I might be able to teach her to bark once for yes and twice for no.

I grabbed both of her upper arms and guided her toward my desk chair. "Kaitlyn, sit." She obeyed. I managed not to say, "Good girl." In the absence of a paper bag for her to hyperventilate into, I ran off to get her some water, remembering too late that I also didn't have a cup for her.

The moment I opened the door to Russell's office, Doppler leapt at me, his claws reaching only mid thigh, but since I was wearing only a T-shirt, this was decidedly uncomfortable. "Not now," I snapped. My feet were freezing from padding around on the office linoleum. Judging by the volume of my ex-roommate's sobbing, she wasn't going anywhere soon, so I yanked on some socks.

Doppler had picked up on my anxiety and was underfoot as I entered the bathroom—but then, I'm sure child psychologists' children aren't always perfect little angels either. I grabbed my coffee cup out from under the leaking pipe, rinsed and filled it. What Kaitlyn didn't know about where my cup had been wasn't going to kill her.

I juggled, pushing Doppler back with one foot while passing through the doorway and balancing the water, then thrust the cup into Kaitlyn's hands. "Drink this."

With trembling hands, she took a couple of dainty sips. Her auburn hair was unkempt and her eyes so red and swollen from this latest crying jag that—with facial fur and some floppy ears—she could have been a poster puppy for the SPCA.

The moment she settled into a normal breathing pattern, I said, "It's after one A.M. Why would anyone have the opportunity to follow you any place at this hour?"

"After you left, I remembered what you said about a white car. I happened to look outside, and I saw a car with a male driver slowly driving past our house not just once, but twice."

"Can you describe him?"

She shook her head. "It was too dark."

"Then how could you be sure the driver was male?"

"I could tell from his silhouette. He wore one of those old-fashioned hats. A fedora."

My interest piqued. "What time was this?"

"About a half past midnight, the first time. Then he drove by again fifteen minutes later. I got really scared, being home all alone with someone watching the place, so I tried to call you at your mother's house. She suggested I try—"

"You *called* my *mother* at *one A.M.*?" I grabbed my

hair in frustration. "Why? If you were scared by this car driving by, why didn't you call the police? Even if you *had* reached me at my mom's house and I'd had some means of helping you, I would've been an hour away."

Kaitlyn whimpered and rotated her chair around so that her back was toward me, but this was the final straw to an emotional, havoc-wreaking day. "You must have scared my mother horribly. I'm just surprised she hasn't—"

The phone rang, right on cue. I picked it up and said, "Mom? Is that you?"

After a pause, my mother said, "Would you believe me if I said 'no'?"

"Not really."

"Allie, what on earth is going on? First you and now your roommate are going bananas over sightings of white cars. Two women are dead who owned the collie now sitting next to me, which my daughter is currently training. Do you have any idea what it's like having your phone ring at one A.M. under these circumstances?"

"I'm sure it was very unpleasant. By the way, did Sage eat his dinner tonight?"

"Yes! Never mind that I'm so upset I may not be able to keep *mine* down, but both dogs are fine!"

"Sorry, Mom. If there's any way I can make this up to you . . . ."

"Not unless you'd consider getting your pilot's license. All this goes to show that you've chosen the wrong occupation."

"That's something to think about," I answered, rolling my eyes.

"Meaning, 'Mind your own business, Mom.' Well, all I can say is I'm glad you're still alive. And I'll make up the guest room for you."

"Thanks." I hung up quickly, because Kaitlyn had risen and was now heading toward the door. I didn't want her to leave without giving me some answers. "Kaitlyn, did you see the car at all when you drove here?"

She shook her head, sniffling, her back still toward me.

"Have you been followed before? You said something about not wanting to go through this again."

She nodded and turned to face me. "Three years ago. Just before Bill left me, I was sure I was being followed. I told him about it, and he acted so weird, I asked him if he'd hired a private investigator. He denied it, but from then on, the guy quit following me. But this time it couldn't be someone Bill hired. Otherwise, he'd be following *me*, not you, and Bill doesn't have any reason to hire a P.I. this time."

"*This* time? Meaning he *did* have cause the last time?"

She clicked her tongue. "Jeez, I don't know. Why do you have to take every little thing I say so literally?"

My first reaction was to growl at her, but that wouldn't be to either of our benefits. "Are you going to call the police?"

She shook her head. "They'd think I was nuts!"

I managed to hold my tongue.

She stared out the glass door. "You can't see the street from down here. He could be out there right now and we'd never know it." She clenched her hands and whirled on a fuzzy-slippered heel to face me. "Allida, you've got to move back in! You can't just have people you work with get murdered and then leave me all alone and defenseless!"

Nonplussed, I stared at her. One thing this experience had taught me was to be far more discriminating about my choice of housemates. "Kaitlyn, is there any chance that the driver of this white car you saw was Bill?"

"No!" she snapped, then she furrowed her brow. "At least, I don't think it was . . . ." Her voice trailed off thoughtfully. She gave a small shrug. "Maybe." She spun back toward the door and unlocked it with a sudden burst of enthusiasm. "I'm going home now. I'll see you later."

Oh, great. Now she was so hopeful that the white car was being driven by her husband, she was set to dash out onto the streets of downtown Boulder. Never mind that it was one A.M. and all she was wearing was a flimsy nightgown. "Wait! I'll walk you to your car. I just need to put something on."

Not having expected a wee-hour visitor, I had done a lousy job of unpacking the necessities. I grabbed Russell's khaki-colored cardigan from his desk chair. While I was putting my sneakers on, I saw a pair of slippered feet run past the window. She was so energized at the possibility she could see her husband again, she hadn't been willing to wait one minute for me. "Kaitlyn!" I called.

With visions of her running in front of the next white sedan she saw in the hope that her husband was its driver, I cried, "Please be careful," though I knew she couldn't hear me. "Blast it all!"

My choice of actions regarding Kaitlyn was either to stay put or to try and outrace her to her car and convince her not to do anything rash. I opted for the former. My body aching with exhaustion but my mind wide-awake, I dragged myself back to Russell's couch and slumped down. Doppler rushed over to me and put his paws on my knees, hoping I'd invite him to hop onto my lap. Lost in thought, I petted him.

The man following me was wearing the type of hat that Russell had worn and which caused Sage to bark at him. That same man could have killed both Hannah Jones and Beth Gleason. Or it could be coincidental that the driver happened to own a fedora. Russell owned one, and I certainly didn't suspect him.

The fact that Bill Wayne had broken into my bedroom tonight to look for information about me could have nothing—or everything—to do with the man in the white car. Was there any chance this was all connected? That Bill Wayne was the killer? That would make me the victim of an enormous coincidence—that I'd happened to rent from his ex *after* he'd killed Hannah Jones. Unless Hannah's death really *was* a suicide, and Beth's conversation with me on the radio had triggered some homicidal maniac who started to trail us. Which meant Bill Wayne could be as likely a suspect as anyone else I'd met in the last couple of days. Enough! I was scaring myself.

I ordered Doppler to return to his own bed, though I sorely wanted his companionship. Dogs thrive on consistency in matters such as their sleeping quarters, and it's unfair to confuse them by cuddling up in bed with your dog only when you feel insecure. Then again, the way my life was going, I could be in for a long spell of insecurity.

If I was lucky, that is.

The police interview first thing that morning was a depressing experience. I gave every iota of information about my last two days that the police could possibly want, and probably much that they didn't. I told about the white sedan, as well as my unsubstantiated theory that Bill Wayne was the driver.

If I hadn't known better, I'd have thought that I was their number one suspect. For one thing, after I'd told them what Chet had said about having instructed Beth to carry her switchblade wherever she went—advice so terrible it might have led to her having been stabbed to death with her own knife—the policeman asked me if I had any idea where the murder weapon might be. My answer was, "No. I never saw the killer nor the weapon. Why do you ask?"

The officer's response had been, "You'd be surprised the things people forget to mention till we ask them directly."

Afterwards, I headed off to meet my new client, George Haggerty, and his golden retriever, Rex.

Mr. Haggerty and Rex lived in east Boulder. Many of the lawns in his development had been recently sodded, and the trees were all just saplings. George was a slender man in his late fifties to early sixties. He wore thick glasses and had gray hair with a lousy comb-over that disguised his hair impairment from no one. When he opened the door for me, his dog nearly barreled over him. I stepped back to the edge of the porch. Rex was perhaps the largest golden retriever I'd seen.

"No, Rex! Down!" George cried as he tried to unplaster himself from the doorjamb. Despite his words, I noted that he'd lifted his hands over his head, which was inadvertently signaling "up" to the dog.

In the meantime, anticipating what was coming, I reached into the compartment of my purse where I keep a noisemaker. Sure enough, Rex tried to goose me, and I pushed the button on my noisemaker, an inexpensive electronic toy that let out a shrill beep. Rex backed away immediately and looked at me quizzically. "Good dog," I said, stroking him.

"What was that?" George asked, looking around as he stepped out onto the porch beside his dog and me.

"An aversion-training technique," I answered, showing him the device in my palm.

He glanced at Rex, who was still looking as though he didn't know what had hit him. "Sure seems to work fast."

"When possible, I prefer to use positive reinforcement, but this has its uses, too. In my line of work, you meet a lot of large dogs. I won't tolerate their getting overly personal or jumping up on me."

Slipping his hands in the back pockets of his baggy brown pants, George smiled and said with enthusiasm,

"Say. I've got a coach's whistle you can hear a mile off. Should I just blow that whenever I catch Rex acting up?"

"Probably not. Blowing a loud whistle near Rex's head could affect his hearing. Besides, if your major problem is that Rex tears up your house when you're gone, you're not going to be there to blow your whistle. Instead of learning to avoid his bad behavior, Rex will learn to avoid you and your whistle."

"Maybe so," George said, "but when I come home, he gets so excited he nearly bowls me over. I could use it then, couldn't I?"

I was a little surprised that George seemed to find the thought of coming home at the end of the day with a whistle in his mouth so appealing. Maybe he was a former basketball coach.

I answered patiently, "There are other ways to get at the root of Rex's problem more effectively. Also, one reason this handheld noisemaker works so well is the dog doesn't see me operate it, such as he would if I were to blow on a whistle. If every time Rex were to sniff me or a visitor, a buzzer he can't even see goes off, he thinks his action caused the noise. He quickly learns not to do it, and he blames the unpleasant noise on his own inappropriate action, not on me or my noisemaker. Nor does he get the opportunity to check for my whistle and act up whenever he doesn't see me with it."

George's eyes were getting the glazed-over look that warned me I was giving too much information too fast. "I'm sorry," I said. "I haven't even introduced myself. I'm Allida Babcock, though I'm sure you figured that out."

He chuckled pleasantly and held the door for me. Rex nearly knocked me off my feet as he raced past me. The two led me into a room with the standard newer-home appointments—white walls and tan wall-to-wall carpeting.

I'd seen dog-wrought destruction before, but this was impressive. Of the sparse furnishings in the room, there was not a single cushion or pillow with no tears in it or woodwork that was free from teeth or claw marks. The fabric on the arms and base of the couch was also torn through so that the wood framing was revealed. It was also badly gnawed.

George gestured at a cushion-less rocker. "Have a seat. I'd offer you a seat on the couch, but as you can see, the cushions are rather lumpy now."

"This couch was relatively intact when he started to rip it up?"

"That was the nice one, believe it or not. We have our junker in the basement."

"The 'junker' must really be something to behold."

I winced at my comment, which was too forward, considering I'd just met the man, but he laughed. " 'Fraid you're right. He's been tearing that one up for more than a year now—ever since he got to be eight months old."

So Rex was twenty months old—the adolescent stage for a dog in which so many behavioral problems emerge—though in this case, Rex had been at it awhile. George sat on the former couch, and I sat kitty-corner to him on the rocker, mentally reminding myself not to lean too far, as much of its base had been gnawed away. "Is your family here?"

"Kids are grown and scattered. My wife is too freaked out about what Rex has done to our house to want to talk about it."

"Is she here?"

"No, she's out of town for the week. I hope that doesn't make your job harder."

"It could lengthen the treatment phase a little," I told him honestly. "You and your wife are going to have to do the lion's share of redirecting Rex's behavior. Otherwise, you'll see him revert to his old patterns very quickly whenever I'm not around."

Rex leapt onto the couch and draped himself across George's lap. With his flawless, shiny yellow coat, Rex was a beautiful dog, yet this had all the makings of a textbook case of the dog mastering his owner.

We chatted pleasantly while I gleaned the necessary background information. During my note-taking, I slipped in the question, "What models and colors of cars do you and your wife drive?" Understandably, George asked what that had to do with his dog, but he accepted my bogus reply that "It gives me an indication of your dog's lifestyle outside the home." His wife drove a silver Toyota and he drove a white Jeep Cherokee.

To my chagrin, I had to struggle to concentrate. My thoughts kept wanting to return to Sage and my mother. I wished I could convince myself that there was little cause for worry. For one thing, Pavlov was a first-rate watchdog.

George paused, and I asked, "He hasn't started chewing on himself, has he? Some dogs move into self-mutilation, I'm sorry to say."

"No." George's eyes widened in alarm, and he stroked the dog faster. "Do you mean he might start chewing on his own leg or something?"

I wanted to move away from this topic before I alarmed him unduly. "I need to observe your dog's behavior when you leave. Let's start by having you go into another room, shutting the door behind you."

George winced a little and murmured, "This is going to be embarrassing." He tried to push Rex off his lap, saying, "Down! Down, Rex!" The dog half slid, half hopped to the floor as George rose. With a wide, four-paw stance primed at preparing himself for his owner's next movement, Rex stood in front of George, watching over his shoulder so that he could lead the way in whatever direction his owner chose to take. "Rex, stay. Stay."

The dog completely ignored this command. When George stepped to the left as if heading toward the kitchen, Rex dashed ahead of him. George followed, then reversed fields and tried to head down the hall. Rex stopped in his tracks and galloped ahead, but the moment Rex got far enough in front of him, George ducked into the first door he passed, which was a small coat closet.

What followed was a truly pitiful scene—Rex howling and scratching at the door and trying to tunnel through the carpeting. The dog made such a racket that George couldn't hear me call to come out. I walked up to Rex, growled, "No," and pushed the button on my noisemaker. Rex stopped and I immediately praised and petted him. This afforded me my first glance down the hallway, where every door bore gouges and claw marks, and each doorway was delineated with shredded carpet.

George Haggerty emerged from the closet, then had to fight off Rex, who was intent on licking his master's bright red cheeks. "He's not always quite this bad," George cried over the noise of Rex's excited barks at their reunion. "Sometimes he sleeps through it when the wife or I leave the room."

"I can see where we need to start."

I discussed my treatment plan and billing procedures, all of which he agreed to. His one bone of contention was when I suggested he purchase a Gentle Leader collar, which George thought was a muzzle. I explained that the collar actually works just like a horse bridle; one strap fits behind the dog's ears and the other loops around the dog's muzzle just below the eyes. The dog's jaw is unrestricted, but the handler can control the dog's head position.

I keep a spare Gentle Leader in my glove box and showed George how to slip it on Rex while enticing him with a treat. At first Rex pawed at the collar and tried to rub it off, but by my encouraging Rex with treats and pats during basic leash training, he eventually accepted it. As soon as I showed George how effective a word of warning followed by a firm pull on the leash was when discouraging Rex from jumping up, I'd made a sale.

During the bulk of my initial hour-long treatment, we focused on having George stand up then sit down, Rex repeatedly rising and trying to lead the way. We gradually wore the dog down to the point that he would allow George to leave the room briefly and then return.

As I was about to leave, I assured George that he needed to continue to work on this and not to make such a big fuss out of leaving and returning. I thanked him for being such a good sport, as I was certain his knees had to have been killing him by then.

He gave me a weary nod. "I was thinking, wouldn't it be easier if I just bought another dog to be Rex's companion?"

"You want to get a second dog?"

He scanned my face as he accompanied me to the door. Rex, to my—frankly—considerable credit, stayed put. George half shrugged, half nodded. "What about the collie that belonged to that woman who was killed yesterday? Could I just borrow that dog, do you think?"

"Sage?" I gaped at him, completely taken aback by the suggestion.

"I figured Beth Gleason had to be the 'accident' you told me you witnessed yesterday. Her death was all over the news this morning. I figured, her collie probably needs a temporary home, right?"

"Um, the collie's fine. And while it might well help Rex if he had a canine playmate, we need to work with him first. I suspect Rex would have jealousy issues if you were

to get a second dog at this time. However, if you're thinking about preventive measures for his house-wrecking,
you may want to consider building a high-quality pen and
doghouse in your yard."

He nodded and combed his fingers through what was
left of his hair. "See you tomorrow evening. We're meeting out front on the sidewalk, and you're going in my
house *with* me, right?"

"Yes, and I'll show you how to reprimand him when
he jumps up."

George furrowed his brow, but nodded.

I drove to my appointment with Mugsy, feeling horribly uneasy. George's question about Sage had been an
unwanted reminder that all of my new clients knew about
Beth Gleason and Sage. There was no way I could guarantee that I wasn't being set up—their dogs' problems a
convenient method for getting to Sage through me.

Chapter 12

John O'Farrell answered the door. He reached out to me on the porch, took my small hand in his beefy one and shook vigorously. "Thanks a lot for coming on such short notice." He held the door open for me. The shrill din of screaming children, barking dog, and squeaking wheels inside was sonic-ear-shattering.

Though his wife, Sarah, greeted me with more enthusiasm than she'd shown upon our initial meeting, her red hair appeared to be standing on end. The tufted hair combined with her thin, beak-like nose made me think of a cardinal. "I'm so glad you're here," she all but shouted. "We're having a hard time with Mugsy's barking."

The source of Mugsy's nervousness was abundantly clear. The children were racing in circles from room to room. Someone had fashioned a wagon out of roller skates and twine, on which little Emmy sat, giggling away as her brother, Ben, pulled her across the hardwood floors at a dead run, Mugsy chasing after them.

"Hold it right there, partner," John said during one of the revolutions, stepping in front of his son and laying his hand atop the boy's red hair. Ben giggled and tried to squeeze past, but John grabbed him good-naturedly and flipped him over one shoulder. Ben squealed, and Emmy immediately hopped up and held up her arms, crying,

"Me, too," while Mugsy maintained her relentless high-pitched bark.

Though Sarah wore a bit of a frazzled expression, she had an amazing tolerance for noise and commotion, far surpassing my own. Over the background noise I asked her, "Has Mugsy nipped at anyone since yesterday?"

"No, though she's been barking like this ever since we got up this morning. It's d-r-i-v-i-n-g me c-r-a-z-y."

I wasn't sure why she spelled this. It wasn't as if Mugsy could have understood the reference to her behavior. Maybe Sarah was overly conditioned to spell as a means of parental communication.

To my immense gratitude, John shooed the kids into the TV room, while Sarah and I took seats on the sectional couch. Our brief time alone was spent on my declining her offers of various beverages. John returned, took a seat next to his wife, and said to me, "What's happening with Beth Gleason's murder? Are you the one who found the body?"

"How did you know that?" I asked, giving away my answer.

"There was a mention in the papers that the woman who found the body was an acquaintance who trained dogs."

"Yes, that was me." I watched for his reaction, wondering whether this was typical human curiosity, or something more.

"What happened to her dog? Did a family member adopt him?"

I sat there in silence, mulling my answer on the one hand and alerted to the fact that he'd just leapt with suspicious quickness onto the issue of the collie that could potentially identify the killer.

"John," Sarah said, giving a bit of a forced giggle, "we are paying this woman by the hour to work with our dog, aren't we?"

"Yeah. But that doesn't mean we can't chat with her, does it?"

"No," she said through her smile, "but we can chat with lots of people without having to pay them for it."

I cleared my throat to cover a smile at her comment. John, however, shot a surprisingly hostile glare at his wife when she wasn't looking. Not married myself and having grown up in an essentially single-parent home, I couldn't begin to guess at the depths of emotion that might run under their still waters. However, I happened to agree with his wife. My meter was running, and besides, Beth Gleason and Sage were none of John's business. I'd had nothing but admiration and pleasant feelings for John, but was beginning to wonder if I needed to reassess my opinion.

"All right. You've decided to keep Mugsy, so we need to work on her understanding and accepting her relatively new role as a family dog, rather than just John's loyal canine companion."

"Yes," said Sarah.

"Which of you feeds her?"

"I do," John said, which I'd expected.

"I'd recommend you alternate those duties between the two of you and that you consider allowing Ben to set the bowl down and call Mugsy to dinner. This brings up another point we need to address immediately. Ben and Emmy need to be taught the basics of how to approach and handle dogs safely. You can hire me to do this, or you can save some money by letting me recommend a video or two on dog safety, which you can rent. You can watch it with your children and go over the lessons with them afterwards."

I paused. John gave the briefest of glances to his wife, then said, "Let's have you work with the kids. Money's no object."

Money's no object! Yippee! My favorite phrase! "Fine," I said somberly. "That's what we'll begin with, then. Even though much of what I'll be teaching them will be common sense to the two of you, it'll be best to have you listen in, so that you can reinforce my instructions after I've gone. Okay?"

They nodded in unison, and John said to Sarah, "Well, honey, you go get our hellions in here, and we'll let Allida here show 'em what to do and what not to do."

We both watched her leave the room, and John promptly turned to me and asked, "Where is Sage now, Allida?"

I gritted my teeth. What was it with this question? Just last night Dennis Corning had asked me the very same thing! He and George Haggerty had inquired about adopting Sage. I could see maybe *one* dog lover immediately wondering about the whereabouts of a deceased stranger's dog—but *three*? "Why do you ask?"

"He's a fine dog, that one," John said with a shrug. "I'd just like to know that he's being taken care of."

"He is. How did you meet Sage?"

The kids came galloping into the room—though Emmy stopped just inside the doorway. "Through his original owner." John turned his attention to Ben and cried, "Come here, sport." Mugsy hopped up on all fours and started barking as Ben did a flying leap toward his step-dad, trusting that he'd be caught. Fortunately, John was well-coordinated and strong enough that he caught the six-year-old with ease. Then John rose and started doing airplane-like swoops, with Ben providing sputtering—and spitty—propeller noises.

"You knew Hannah Jones?" I asked.

"We're not on that subject *again*, are we?" Sarah asked as she neared. Her daughter grabbed hold of her leg, forcing Sarah into a Frankenstein's-monster limp till she reclaimed her seat.

"Nope," John answered mid-flight pattern. "We're onto

the subject of how to treat Mugsy right so she won't bite us no more."

"*Any*more," Ben corrected.

John set him down on the floor. "Why, by gosh, you're right! It *is* 'anymore,' ain't it?"

"*Isn't* it!" Ben said, giggling infectiously.

Sarah was watching her husband and son with such obvious pride and love that it was touching to witness. What was going on with this family? Why the constant tension before and the lovey-dovey attitude now? Sarah looked my way, and I felt my cheeks grow warm. I felt guilty about my suspicions regarding John. Much as I wished that being a dog lover and a good family man exonerated a person from all possibility of having committed a heinous crime, they didn't. Otherwise, our judicial system would have undergone some radical adjustments long ago.

I'd taught dog safety classes to large groups of children back in Chicago. Having just one family in a class was a pleasure. It took me twenty minutes to get through the basics, then we worked at changing some behavioral patterns on John and Sarah's part. This is often the fun part of this job—getting people to change their own habits while they think you're adjusting only the dog's behavior.

As I was leaving, I said my good-byes, then John came running out of the house toward me.

"Thank you for helping us, Allida."

"My pleasure." Not to mention that it was my job and I was charging him. Once again, I was leery at his ditching his family to stage this conversation, and hoped that he wasn't yet again about to harp on Sage.

"As one fellow dog lover to another, I'm sure you understand why I'm concerned about that unfortunate girl's dog."

"Believe me, John," I said, maintaining my smile, despite my unease and disappointment, "Sage is in good hands and is doing fine."

"Did you see to that yourself?"

"Pardon?"

"Did you place the dog somewhere?"

I studied his face, honestly not sure if I was being paranoid, or if the question truly was out of line. "I'm really not at liberty to discuss any details about the case."

He nodded. "Of course. I understand."

"How well did you know Hannah Jones?"

"Hardly at all. Ate at her restaurant a lot, years ago. I'm a vegetarian."

"Really?" I instantly felt a touch of chagrin at my surprise. He was a solidly built man, and I'd rarely met a non-thin vegetarian—yet to make the assumption that he couldn't be a vegetarian was every bit as silly as assuming I couldn't play basketball. "But how did you meet Sage? Surely she couldn't bring him to her restaurant, right?"

"Oh. No, that's true. Not at the restaurant, but on other occasions." He took a step back and held up a palm. "Gotta get back to my monsters. See you next time." He pivoted and went back inside, leaving me in the same state of mild discomfiture as before.

As I drove off, I decided that the past couple of days had taught me two important life lessons I hoped I'd never forget: 1) Check out your prospective housemate thoroughly before you agree to move in. 2) Never find a dead body. The ramifications of number two were all-encompassing.

Next on my agenda was a visit to Dennis Corning's house. He lived in west Boulder, next door to Hannah Jones's house. Sage's old residence. My office was somewhat on the way, so I planned to have lunch with Doppler there first. Too bad I'd forgotten to clear out my half of the groceries from the house. Funny that I'd remembered Doppler's food, but not my own. Though I never publicly admitted it, I like the taste of Milk-Bone—but not as the main course. I couldn't bring myself to try kibble, though, and Doppler probably wouldn't want me sharing his food anyway.

I grabbed a sandwich from the deli section of a grocery store and then headed to my office. Russell's car wasn't there, which was not surprising on a Sunday. But lately, I wouldn't have put it past him to be waiting with Doppler for my return.

There was an envelope on my desk, which I now remembered spotting when I'd first arrived last night, but I'd had so many things on my mind then, I didn't open it. Besides, I'd suspected it was a note from Russell, and I still wasn't in a mood to be flirted with. "Allida" was printed on the envelope in neat block lettering.

I pressed the playback button on my recorder and opened the envelope. My mother's voice said, "Morning, Allida. Call me as soon as you get this message. This is your mother, as you probably realized."

I skimmed the rhyming note on the front—getting to know you, yada yada, wanting to show you my world, yada yada. I have very little patience for mushy rhymes. I opened it and saw that the card was, indeed, signed "Love, Russell."

You're sweet, Russell, but I've kind of got my hands full right now, I thought as I dialed my mother's number.

She said, "Oh, good. I'm glad you finally called. Is now a good time for me to see your new office?"

"Now?"

"A book I ordered finally came in at a store just a mile or so from you, and I thought I might as well stop by."

I just wasn't up for having Mom in my office at the moment. Her wanting to visit right now seemed contrived—

as though she wanted to check the place out to make sure I was safe here. All the while, *I* was still worried whether or not *she* was safe as Sage's caretaker. "Thanks, but I have to come out there anyway later this afternoon. My car's still full of stuff, and I need to stash it in your spare room, if that's all right with you. How about I just pick up the book for you before I leave?"

"Is there some reason you don't want me to see your office?"

"No, of course not," I replied in a partial untruth. "I just thought it'd be more convenient for you if—"

"I want to see my daughter's office," Mom said. "The book was just an excuse."

"Okay, Mom," I immediately replied. Why did I ever attempt to out-worry my mother? She had two extra decades of worry experience on me. "Come on down. I have one more appointment, but I'll meet you here at two o'clock. Do you know where the place is?"

"Yes. Can I bring Pavlov and Sage?"

"I don't see why not," I said slowly, surprised at Mom's suggestion. I hated the thought of her being with Sage in Boulder. Beth Gleason had died that way. Then again, nobody would threaten her if she was with both a collie and a German shepherd.

The Corning residence was nestled into the foothills at the end of a wildly winding, mountainous road. It was one of those palatial homes that always make me wonder how anyone can earn enough money to afford them. I knew the answer with regard to Hannah Jones, whose house I identified as the only one next door, but the Cornings' place was even larger. Plus, these folks had to be young enough to have a two-year-old. Maybe they were the same Cornings that made the casserole dishes.

I didn't think, "How did you get to be so filthy rich?"

would be an appropriate introductory question. So, when a handsome, thirtyish man answered the door, I said instead, "You must be Dennis Corning. I'm Allida Babcock."

He shook my hand. "Nice to meet you. Come in." He was wearing jeans and a light blue shirt with the sleeves rolled up, but he also had a white cable-knit sweater loosely tied over his collar. He was inside his house, for crying out loud, so I saw no excuse for wearing a sweater draped on his shoulders, other than for giving off the full yuppie effect.

Despite my uncharitable thoughts, I said, "This is quite a place you've got here." If anything, that was an understatement. Dennis was leading me down a hallway toward a kitchen that could easily hold my entire house. Kaitlyn Wayne's entire house, I should say.

"Thank you. So you believe me when I tell you we could afford to have another dog."

"Yes, but that's really not the issue. By the way, do you own a white car?"

"No, why?"

"There's one just around the corner with its lights on," I lied.

"Ours are in our garage, of course."

I nodded and ignored his haughty, you're-such-an-idiot tone of voice. This was the price one pays when one can only come up with an inane excuse for asking an inappropriate question.

A salt-and-pepper shih tzu that I knew must be Shakespeare ran up to me, claws clicking on the hardwood flooring. Shakespeare started with his shrill bark. Being barked at reminded me of such a stupid omission I had to restrain myself from striking my forehead. I hadn't warned my mother about Sage's reaction to men in hats! If she took him anyplace but straight to my office . . . .

A two-year-old boy ran up as well, with a huge grin that seemed to take up most of his face. I couldn't help but notice that the grin was all he was wearing.

"Brian! Bri! Get back in here! And put some clothes on before I—"

I'd forgotten Dennis's wife's name, but she was certainly an attractive woman—blond curly hair and blue eyes. She could have been a professional model. She stopped mid-sentence as she saw me.

"Sorry," she said. "We're in the perpetual stage of potty training. We sometimes reveal more of ourselves to guests than they want to see."

"That's okay. I'm not that easily embarrassed."

"Good, but I am." She grabbed her son underneath the armpits and scurried off with him.

Dennis eyed me at length. We stood in the center of his immense kitchen, and he made no move to offer me a chair. "Let's get right to the point. I want Sage. How can I convince you to give him to me?"

"I'm not sure that you can," I told him honestly. "And while your directness is a refreshing approach, not to mention a time-saver, it's a little off-putting."

He gave me a smug grin and gestured at the cherry-wood kitchen set. "In that case, Ms. Babcock, do sit down. Can I offer you some fresh-squeezed juice? Have you eaten yet?"

"No and yes, thank you." Even as I was telling myself what a complete jerk this guy was, I took a seat, largely because I really wanted some background information on Sage, and he and his wife were now the only remaining people I could ask.

I held Dennis's gaze, and he finally pulled up a chair across from me. As he did so, he yanked the sweater off his shoulders and draped it over the empty chair between our seats. "You say Sage is staying at a good spot, for now, but you didn't say if this was going to be a permanent situation."

In that moment, I realized that I very much wanted to keep Sage myself. This meant I would need to find a place in Boulder where I could keep all three dogs. "That's right. I'm going to do what I can to make it a permanent home for Sage."

"We're really fond of Sage ourselves. As you know, my wife is occupied at the moment with my son; however, we've agreed that it'd be in the dog's best interest to let him move in here with us."

"Let me be frank, Mr. Corning."

"Dennis," he interrupted, flashing me a full-wattage smile. "Tell you what. You be Allida, I'll be Dennis, and neither of us will be Frank."

It was a little too late for me to be charmed; otherwise, I might have laughed. "The thing is, Dennis, I simply can't let *anyone* I don't know well have contact with Sage until Beth Gleason's killer is locked up. I'm sure you understand."

"No. I don't understand that at all. You can't possibly think we had anything to do with that, or with Hannah's death."

His wife entered the room just then, saying, "I've got Brian down for his nap, at last."

"Susan, Miss Babcock here thinks we had something to do with Beth Gleason's death," Dennis told her, by way of getting her up to speed with our conversation.

"What?" Susan said, eyeing me as if my body were morphing into a hairy beast.

"I never said that, Mr. Corning. Dennis, rather. I have to be cautious, so I'm not going to reveal the location of the dog to you or to anyone."

"I see," Susan said, taking a seat next to her husband.

"Maybe you can help me clear up a mystery surrounding Hannah Jones," I said. "I don't understand why the dog food that we got from you, at least indirectly, was tainted with a dog repellent."

"What are you talking about?" he snapped.

I launched into a brief explanation of the condition of the dog food and how I'd gotten possession of the slip of paper with his name and number on it.

Dennis frowned. "I did donate the bag of dog food I found in Hannah's kitchen, and I also stuck a slip of paper on top of it in case the new owner had any questions. Donated a box of dog treats, as well. But Sage wouldn't eat that food at all when we brought him home with us. Remember, honey?"

Susan nodded. "We fed him Shakespeare's food. He ate about ten times as much as Shakespeare." She paused, her pretty, blue eyes staring directly into mine. "But why would someone have done that to Sage's food?"

"That's the question of the hour," I replied. "Could Hannah have done it? Could she have been trying to change Sage's eating habits and want to train him to dislike dog food?"

"Christ, no," Dennis said, shaking his head. "Hannah loved that dog more than anything in the world."

"Absolutely," Susan said. "She would have given her life to protect him."

"Is there any chance that she did do just that?" I asked.

They looked at each other. At length, Susan shrugged. "As I said before over the phone, Hannah had cancer, so suicide wasn't out of the question. But to be honest with you, I've never fully accepted that. I *would* believe someone shot her as she tried to protect Sage. Nobody could ever convince me she'd ruined his dog food."

"Same here," Dennis said.

"Did you happen to notice if she had any visitors the night she died?"

Dennis shook his head. "I was out of town on business that night. Hon?"

Susan shook her head. "Brian and I stayed at a friend's condo in Vail that night."

Dennis pushed back from the table and stood up. "I can certainly understand now why you're reluctant to let that dog out of your care." He picked up Shakespeare. "If he were mine, I wouldn't let him out of my sight."

I rose as well and thanked both of them, feeling much better about Dennis at the end of the visit than I had at its start. Yet I drove off in a state of more confusion than ever. If neither Hannah nor the Cornings had tampered with Sage's food, who had? And why? What possible motive could somebody have to kill both Hannah and Beth?

Everything seemed normal when I reached my office, though Doppler was unusually nervous. Chet Adler barged in just as I was calming him.

" 'Bout time you got here. Shit. I've been waiting for hours."

"I'm sorry about Beth."

"You're sorry? You're sorry! It's your damned fault she's dead! If it hadn't been for you and that call-in show, nobody'd even know about her and that stupid, mangy mutt of hers!"

Doppler had been trained not to bark at visitors, but he justifiably began barking now. Chet pointed at him. "Speaking of mutts, if you don't want me to kick yours through the door—"

"Doppler, cease!" I cried. The dog immediately stopped barking and looked up at me. "Mr. Adler, just—"

"Don't try 'n' bluff me! You know full well you're responsible. What I want to know is, why her? Why didn't the shithead kill you and the collie if he thought the flea-bag could recognize him?"

"I don't know the answer to that question. I wish I did."

"The police wouldn't tell me shit. Where did you find her? Did she say any last words?"

"No. I found her in a yard on Spruce Street."

"And? Did the house belong to a customer of yours?"

"No. I think she might have climbed the fence into the yard to try to get away from her attacker. That's all I can tell you."

"I want the names of all your customers."

"Why? What possible good would—"

The veins on his forehead were bulging. "Some bastard got to Beth through you. I want to find the shithead. I'm gonna kill him!"

I took a step back. "Calm down, Chet."

"Just as soon as I get what I'm after." He crossed his arms and stepped to within a couple of inches of me, my chin nearly touching his chest. I could smell liquor on his breath.

I had far too much experience staring down growling dogs to fall for this power-assertion technique. I stayed put and said, "Back off. I'm not giving you my client list. Even if I did, what possible good would it do you? Do you plan to bully each person on the list into confessing?"

He glared at me, then finally said, "Shit, I don't know," and took a step back.

"Chet, let the police handle this."

"Lot of good you are," he snarled, then he stormed out the door.

I was shaken by the confrontation. He struck me as a loose cannon, and I wanted nothing to do with the man. Deciding to make use of the few minutes I'd have until

Mom arrived, I typed up notes on my customers and made out bills, checking my watch periodically.

I shut off my computer afterwards and stared forlornly at the door. As a child, I'd once asked her who the people at the time-and-temperature number called when *they* needed to set their clocks. She'd answered, "Me." It took me the longest time to realize she'd been joking, largely because my mother was compulsively prompt.

Why, then, was she nearly an hour late?

Chapter 13

By the time another half hour had passed, I was all but frantic. I'd called her four times. I'd also called every friend I could think of whom she might have dropped in to visit, all to no avail. What was this? Get-Even-with-My-Daughter-for-Scaring-Me-Last-Night time?

Leaving the office unlocked and my answering machine on, I took Doppler on a walk to check for any signs of Mom wandering around lost. No luck. I was sitting on the top concrete step of my entranceway when she finally drove up in her covered pickup and parked next to my car in Russell's space. She didn't seem to see me sitting there, but both Sage and Pavlov greeted me with great enthusiasm the moment she opened the door to the truck bed.

Her jaw was clenched and her lips pursed. She marched with such evident anger that even her braid seemed to be taut.

I rose, still petting both of my big dogs. Doppler, too, was so excited at the sight of his canine friends he tried to engage them in a game of tag, despite the leash I still had a hold of. Surmising that this was not the time to go on the offensive with my mother, I merely greeted her and asked what had happened.

"Some dog hater who thinks he's a big deal police officer gave me a ticket for having the dogs in the mall."

"Well, Mom, dogs aren't allowed in the mall."

"It's a stupid rule!"

"Not really. It's a pedestrian mall, period. They've got all this expensive brick, and they have to have certain rules to protect that and the pedestrians, such as 'No animals, no bicycles, no vehicles.' "

"I was just walking the dogs. It's not as though I were riding through on a horse-drawn cart constructed out of bicycle wheels! The ticket was for fifty dollars. Fifty bucks! The city of Boulder has it in for dogs."

She put her hands on her hips and glared at me.

"There was somebody walking a black lab right in front of us, and *she* didn't get a ticket. The officer singled us out because Sage started barking at him."

"Was he wearing an officer's cap?"

"Of course, but that hardly makes his ticketing me and not the labrador owner any more acceptable! It wasn't fair, Allida! I went down to the courthouse to make a formal protest."

I was so tempted to repeat her oft-heard refrain, "Who says life is fair?" that I had to bite the inside of my lip.

"You can't just ticket one dog owner and let the next one stroll on past without a word! And did I happen to mention that the unticketed dog owner was a pretty young girl? I'll tell you, Allie, I am not going to pay this. I'll fight them with my dying breath, but I refuse to sacrifice my ideals for an arbitrarily enforced law."

I couldn't resist leaping on that last remark as I ushered her into my office. "Just because the enforcement of the law is arbitrary doesn't give you the right to ignore it. Couldn't you just have left the dogs in the car till you were done shopping?"

She gave me an angry visual once-over. "I don't know how I managed to raise such a conformist for a daughter, but it's damned annoying."

"On that note, this is my office." I held my arms out to demonstrate—Mom's mood too sour to let me give in to the temptation to say, "Ta Dah!"

"Oh, yes." She turned in a slow circle. "It's very nice, dear."

It's pretty hard to take someone on a tour of a one-room office, so I wound up including the bathroom, forgetting that I'd neglected to replace the cup under the leaking pipe last night, so the floor was wet. Mom slipped and nearly fell, but I managed to catch her. Despite our acrobatics, she noticed the flowers and asked, "Who gave you those?"

"They're from Russell Greene, my officemate."

"Is there any reason they're floating in the sink?"

"It's been a hectic two days since he gave them to me." In a flurry of motion, I swept the flowers out of the sink, shook them off, and returned them to their jar. "I had to use the vase for Doppler's water dish, and I forgot to replace it. There."

Mom crinkled her nose at the mayonnaise jar. "I've got a lovely applesauce jar back home if you want to upgrade the vase."

I snapped to attention at the sound of my outer door opening. All three dogs barked and galloped toward the sound. If this was merely Russell trying to get to his office, the poor man would need therapy for posttraumatic stress disorder.

Mom and I no doubt shared the same concern for my unsuspecting visitor and raced into my office. Pavlov and Doppler stopped barking almost immediately, as Joel Meyer, sans his good buddy Tracy Truett, greeted them. Sage, however, continued to bark.

Admittedly, I'm somewhat warped, but there's nothing sexier in my estimation than a man petting a dog. No sooner had this thought formed in my brain than I disagreed with myself—but still, Joel looked a zillion times more handsome now with one hand out to Doppler and another scratching Pavlov's ear than he had yesterday with a tire iron in his hand. Also, his dark hair and beard had been neatly trimmed since yesterday, and he was wearing a cotton plaid shirt instead of the torn flannel one.

Though Joel had seemed to win over both Pavlov and Doppler, Sage was keeping his distance and barking. The collie looked back at me and then returned his attention to Joel in what was dog language for, "Take a look! This could be trouble!"

"Sage, no," my mother said firmly. Sage let out a couple of more sharp woofs, then quieted. But he stayed at attention, staring at Joel. As I appraised the situation, I had to say that Sage wasn't acting nearly as threatened by Joel's presence as he had the other day when Russell entered wearing a hat.

"Hi, there. Who's this?" Joel said, offering his palm to Sage to sniff.

Sage barked and then growled. Joel put his hand down and stayed put. Few people realize that the best way to approach a strange dog is to come around to the dog's side. If you simply hold your hand to its nose, for all the dog knows, he's about to get slapped. At least Joel had offered his hand palm up.

"I'll just put him in this other room, all right?" Mom asked, already tugging Sage toward Russell's office.

Now I really was uneasy. Sage hadn't acted this defensive, even when he was next to his dead owner. It could be a very understandably anxious state for him to be in, but it made me nervous.

"I see your tires are all nice and round. The spare must have been good."

"Yes, thanks. Nicely done."

"Everything going all right?" he asked.

"Just fine, thanks." I could pad my answer a little to be more friendly to him, but what could I say? No dead bodies? No rabid canines? "You?"

"Doing fine, thanks. I see you have a client, so I won't keep you."

"I'm not a client," Mom said as she returned to my side. "I'm her mother. What kind of dog do you own?"

Joel gave her a charming smile, and I remembered what a sucker Mom was for men in beards. "A little mutt. Her name's Suzanne."

"You should bring her to Allida. She's the best. And all dogs have some behavioral things that could stand improvement. Allida's services are worth every penny she charges, and then some."

His attractive dark eyes sparkled as he shifted his vision to me. "Hey, that is a good idea. What do you say, Allida? Can you fit Suzanne into your schedule this week?"

"What would she be seeing me for?"

This question gave Joel pause, but only momentarily. "For one thing, she's terrible around other dogs—never stops barking, tries to bite them. I've never worried about it too much, to be honest with you, but Tracy pointed out to me the other day that she's going to start a fight with a bigger dog one of these days, and she won't stand a chance."

"I can help train her out of that," I said, perhaps overly confident in Mom's presence. Having been a trainer of what was often large groups of dogs of all shapes and sizes, this was among the first behavior problems I'd helped dogs to overcome.

"Great!" Joel gave me a downright eager glance. Next thing I knew, we had set an appointment for him to bring Suzanne here the next morning, since we would need to start by working in a neutral territory. Unless trained otherwise, all dogs bark at other dogs when on their own property. He left in great spirits.

Mom immediately turned to me and said, "I got you a new client. You need to be more aggressive in your marketing. Act like a pit bull, not an elderly basset hound."

I searched my mind for a dog-motif comeback line, but I was too sleep-deprived. Anxious to put at least a temporary halt to my nomadic existence, we drove our separate cars to her house—the three dogs in her truck bed, most of my possessions in my backseat. It took me little time to clear my things out of the backseat and into the closet of her guest room. Afterwards, I found her seated at the kitchen table enjoying a cup of tea, mine already poured and occupying the place mat across from hers.

"I take it you shared my appreciation for my favorite flight student last night?" she asked as I sat down.

"Keith Terrington?" I took a sip of the tea. It had a pleasant, tangy flavor that I recognized. Cranberry Cove, from the local Celestial Seasonings factory.

"Yes. He really is my favorite student, you know."

"From what little I saw, he seems terrific. Thanks for introducing us. I just wish things had been a lot less harried yesterday, so that I could have made a better impression."

"Oh, don't underestimate yourself, my dear. I just hope he's good enough for you. I was worried you wouldn't find him attractive."

I chuckled at the thought of my not finding Keith attractive, who was one of the most handsome men I'd seen on this side of a movie screen. "See, you're supposed to think that way. You're hopelessly biased because you're my mother."

"I am not!"

I raised my eyebrows and she added, "Biased, that is.

Well, okay, I *am* biased, but I'm also a good judge of people."

"What did you think of Joel Meyer?"

"He seems nice enough. Are you thinking of dating him, too?"

I shrugged. "It made me a little nervous the way Sage wouldn't stop barking at him."

"Joel was only there for two minutes or so. Sage probably would have stopped on his own momentarily."

"I meant to tell you, Mom, I haven't had the chance to condition Sage out of barking at men in hats."

"He barks at men wearing—" She paused, then said, "Oh, that's right. The men in raincoats thing. That was actually directed at hats?"

"Oddly, yes." I sipped my tea and considered the matter. In point of fact, barking at raincoats would have been much more common. A long raincoat would likely make a swooshing noise, and its wearer would be considerably bulkier looking to a dog. Either sensation could have easily upset Sage. The hat, however, was admittedly odd.

"Which is something I wanted to talk to you about," my mom began in a non sequitur. "There's something special about Sage. Don't take this the wrong way; I'm very fond of Pavlov, too. It's just that . . . maybe it's because Sage is so homely."

"Homely?"

"In a classical sense. He's got this one ear up, the other down, the bumpy, Roman nose. But really, it's the fact that he's . . . so noble, despite being an orphan. Anyway, what I'm trying to get at is, I want to keep Sage."

I sat up in surprise. "Really?" I mentally readjusted. I'd been thinking of finding a place for all three dogs and me, not wanting to see Sage go, either. But this was a better solution—and one that allowed me to go on seeing

Sage in the future. "The offer's come up many times, of late. It's as though Sage is the most adoptable pet in the city of Boulder. That's what concerns me. I'm not sure it's safe to own him."

"What do you mean?"

"Both of his former owners were killed. What if that's because some creep forced Sage to swallow a diamond or a packet of cocaine or something. You hear about things like that on the news sometimes." I snapped my fingers and hopped to my feet. "Wait a minute. That's it! Some smuggler wanted to get something in or out of the country in Sage's stomach. So he or she destroyed Sage's dog food, so that he'd be hungry enough to swallow the contraband!"

Mom furrowed her brow. "You think that over a month ago, somebody force-fed Sage contraband? The dog would poop it out the next day."

That was a good point. Although gross. "But maybe it was a regular thing. Every month or so they'd force-feed Sage the contraband, and it was working so well, they didn't want to have to start all over again with a new dog."

"Why would anyone take the risk of doing that to another person's dog?"

"If it was Hannah's business partner, who got greedy . . ." My thoughts raced ahead of me. What if Hannah was not as sweet and scrupulous as everyone thinks? She and a partner use Sage to smuggle. That could explain Hannah's flying lessons at her late age. She intended to pilot the plane for their illegal operation. The partner kills Hannah, but doesn't want to draw attention to himself by taking the dog immediately.

As if reading my thoughts, Mom shook her head. "Remember, I knew Hannah Jones. It simply isn't possible.

She lived as a law-abiding citizen all her life. She had more than enough money, no dependents, and not much longer to live. She would never risk injuring Sage."

"Maybe the food wasn't actually tainted till Beth Gleason got it, then. It could have been a coincidence that Sage took to preferring Shakespeare's dog food. Maybe that's what gave Beth's boyfriend the idea to taint the dog food and feed Sage the contraband."

"Shakespeare?"

"The dog owned by the people who gave Sage up for adoption after Hannah was killed."

"This is all very farfetched."

"So's everything regarding Sage. I'm calling the detective in charge of the investigation and telling him my theory."

"I'm sure he'll be appreciative."

Ignoring Mom's sarcasm, I dialed and spoke at length with the detective. Though he was very polite, it struck me that he was exceedingly so. I got the uncomfortable feeling that the moment we hung up, he announced to his peers, "I got me a loony, guys! This crazy broad's got a theory about smuggling and wants me to pressure some poor slob who's just lost his girlfriend!"

Mom was listening to my end of the conversation and undoubtedly noticed my pink cheeks. Nonetheless, she said, "You didn't answer my question about my taking permanent ownership of Sage."

"As far as I know, no one else has a legitimate legal claim to him, so unless one surfaces, he's yours."

"That's wonderful."

"That doesn't mean I won't keep him with me or at yet another place till whoever did this is under arrest, though."

"Now that that matter's out of the way, let's head back to your house and get the rest of your things, shall we?"

We drove to my house in her truck, this time leaving

the dogs at home so we could use all of the covered truck bed for my stuff. En route, I filled her in at great length about Kaitlyn and my troubles with her. When we reached the house, I got my key ready, but the door was open, though I didn't spot Kaitlyn's car out front. My senses immediately leapt to red alert. Was Bill Wayne trespassing again?

To my surprise, Kaitlyn was seated in the living room. Her smile faded a little at the sight of me and my mom. "Hi," she said. "Are you moving back in?"

"No, I'm here to finish moving out."

My mom stepped in between us.

"This is my mother. She's going to help me pack the rest of my stuff."

"Hello, Kaitlyn. I'm sorry things didn't work out between you and my daughter. You have a nice little place here."

"It's nice to meet you, Mrs. Babcock," said Kaitlyn, demonstrating the charm and self-control that had duped me in the first place. "This is so ridiculous. I need a roommate, and we got along great. Tell her not to do this."

Mom took a seat on the opposite side of the couch from Kaitlyn, but reached over and patted her knee. "You and I need to have a little talk, woman to woman."

Kaitlyn shot a desperate glance my way. Not about to help, I asked, "Where's your car, Kaitlyn?"

"I parked in the back alley. In case Bill comes by, I wanted to surprise him."

"That's what I want to talk to you about," my mom began. "Is it true that you haven't even changed the locks since your husband moved out almost three years ago?"

"Yes, but . . . why should I change the locks? I'm hoping we'll reconcile."

"You need to protect yourself. You have no idea what

changes your husband might have gone through since he left you. What if he's become violent?"

"Bill? That's ridiculous!"

"Was it ridiculous when he implied to my daughter that you badly injured a dog the two of you owned?"

"No. I mean, yes. I . . . don't know. We never owned a dog. I still don't know what Bill meant. Maybe Allida just . . . misunderstood him."

"Or maybe Bill was lying. Regardless of your personal history, do you really want to trust a man who would accuse you of something like that to have the keys to your house?"

Kaitlyn seemed to deflate. She mumbled, "No, I guess not." Mom had her over the barrel. If Bill was telling the complete truth about her and their dog, she couldn't admit it. I felt a little sorry for her. In dealing with my mother, she was hopelessly overmatched.

Wanting to take the coward's way out and not have to witness anymore of this, I started to head for the kitchen to begin packing my things. The doorbell rang. "I'll get it," I cried.

My heart leapt at the sight of Keith Terrington at my door. Good Lord, he was handsome, wearing tight, faded denims and a forest green turtleneck. "Hi, Allida. I'm sorry to come over uninvited."

"How did you know I was here?"

"I don't live all that far from here and thought I'd swing by, just in case. There's something I have to talk to you about right away."

"Come on in. We're in the midst of moving my stuff out." This was convenient, I thought. I'd give my mother a chance to see Keith and me together now, instead of during the more socially awkward situation of picking me up for a date.

My mother rose and smiled broadly at her "favorite

flight student." Then to my utter shock, she stepped toward him and offered him her hand to shake. "Hello. I'm Allida's mother. Are you a friend of hers?"

Chapter 14

Keith stood there, looking at me as if he were the dog who'd just been caught with his nose in the kitchen garbage can. I was too stunned and hurt even to move.

"That's what I wanted to talk to you about," he said to me quietly, sounding a little upset, but nowhere near as bad as I felt. "I'm not Keith Terrington. I'm Alex Ferron, his best friend."

My mother recoiled, withdrawing her proffered hand. There was a flash of anger in her eyes directed at The Man Formerly Known as Keith Terrington. Her expression changed to one of sympathy as she looked at me. "Guess I'd better leave you two alone." She turned to Kaitlyn, who was still seated in the living room and watching us with slackened jaw. "Why don't you help me separate what's Allida's from what's yours in the kitchen?"

Kaitlyn gave a little appreciative smile at Keith—or rather, Alex—as she went into the kitchen with Mom. My mother's notion of sorting kitchen items was not the best of all plans, if she truly intended to give Alex and me privacy. There was no kitchen door to shut and they would be able to hear every word we said. Nevertheless, I was not about to risk trusting Keith/Alex enough to step outside with him. I headed to the living room and slumped onto the nearest chair, my ego having taken a massive beating.

"Allida?" Keith/Alex said quietly. "This all must seem unforgivable right now, but I truly am sorry. What happened was, Keith told your mother he'd go out with you only because he didn't want to hurt her feelings."

Wonderful. I had been a pity date to appease my mom. That made me feel so much better.

Keith/Alex continued, "Then a friend gave him a ticket to a Nuggets' basketball game last night, and he couldn't stand the thought of calling you up and telling you he'd rather do that than go out with you."

"How considerate," I growled. His words were moving me rapidly out of a state of self-pity and into anger. Kaitlyn had left a copy of the *Boulder Daily Camera* sitting on the coffee table, and I envisioned myself rolling it up and whacking him with it.

Keith/Alex paused to assess my mood. Wisely, he rose and distanced himself such that the coffee table was directly between us. "I owed him a huge favor, so he pleaded with me to fill in for him and, well, let you down gently."

"Is any of this supposed to make me feel better? Because if it is, I gotta tell you honestly, it's not doing the trick."

"I know. I'm sorry. See, Keith was just going to back out of his date with you, but then I happened to have been listening to the *Tracy Truett Show* during my lunch break on Friday. I was intrigued and wanted to see what you looked like, so I asked Keith if I could stand in for him. He made me promise I'd pretend to be him at first, treat you to a fancy dinner, and then tell you who I really was."

"At which point, I'd tell my mother what you and he did to me, and she'd force Keith's lucky hat down his throat."

My suspicions that Mom was listening in—fueled by a lack of "sorting" noises coming from the kitchen—were confirmed at this last remark, when I heard what sounded rather like a proud chortle.

Keith/Alex paused and glanced in the direction of the kitchen. He lowered his voice and said, "I don't think he was thinking ahead very clearly. Not only because of that, but because I . . . I want to keep seeing you, and now—"

"Is that why you called me last night after our date? To tell me over the phone who you really were?"

"That, plus to beg your forgiveness. Only then you immediately told me about your roommate's date being a setup, so I—"

"What?" came a shriek from the kitchen. Kaitlyn charged around the corner, my jar of peanut butter and can of chicken-noodle soup in her hands. She pointed at me with the index finger of her chicken-soup hand. "What do you *mean* my date was a setup!"

I sighed. She looked set to fling the food items at me if she didn't care for my answer. I could likely fend off the peanut butter, which was in a plastic jar anyway, but if Kaitlyn decided to throw the soup can at me, I'd better hope her aim was off. In the meantime, Keith/Alex winced and watched us in shock.

Mom rushed into the room. "Could you take me on a tour of the backyard, Kaitlyn?"

Kaitlyn glared at Mom, then said to me, "Well?"

"Bill asked me not to hurt your feelings by telling you that . . . your date Saturday night was with someone he knew. He wanted us out of the house so he could search for something."

"Bill wouldn't do that! And Jim's a terrific guy! He wouldn't have agreed to such a thing, either. You're lying!" Kaitlyn cocked her arm. I dove off the couch and onto my knees. Keith/Alex and my mom were a second too late as they both tried to grab her. Kaitlyn flung the chicken soup with so much force the can crashed through the window behind me—right where my head had been. We all stared at the shattered glass in stunned silence for a moment.

And friends wonder why I sometimes prefer the company of dogs to humans.

Kaitlyn dropped the peanut butter and brought both hands to her lips. "I can't believe I just did that."

"Are you all right?" Mom asked me. Her hands were fisted, and she appeared ready to slug Kaitlyn if my answer was no.

I nodded and rose. Glass fragments were on the back of the couch and seat cushions, but none had hit me, as far as I could tell. "So much for chicken soup being good for the soul," I muttered.

Kaitlyn was hugging herself.

"I'm very sorry you overheard my conversation with Keith. Alex, I mean. I'm telling the truth about what Bill told me, but you can believe what you want to believe."

Kaitlyn's lower lip trembled, but she refrained from crying. She lifted her chin, whirled on a heel, and marched back into the kitchen. Mom's eyes were wide with alarm. She told me in a whisper, "Sorry. Did you know Kaitlyn can listen to someone else's conversation in another room *while* she's speaking herself?"

"I heard that!" Kaitlyn called.

"Maybe we should forget getting the rest of my stuff and just leave now."

Mom nodded. "I'll grab whatever's left in your bedroom, and we'll write off the rest."

I returned my attention to Alex. He had paled and was looking at the broken window in disbelieving silence, his hands deep in the pockets of his tight jeans. He was as handsome as ever, and part of me still wanted to be open to the possibilities. I wasn't sure whom I should be angry at—him? The real Keith? Myself?

Just then, he turned and caught my gaze. "This has been . . . a nightmare," he said. "Everything I say has resulted in . . ."

"I'm going to need some time to sort through my feelings."

He handed me a business card. "Could you call me? Whenever you want, I'll . . ." His vision drifted to the broken window behind me. He shook his head. "I can't believe how badly all of this went." He headed out the door.

I watched him, wondering if I'd ever really speak to him again. And, if I did, whether or not I'd remember his name was Alex Ferron. In any case, Keith Terrington had just exited my life forever.

Mom came out of my room with a full laundry basket in her arms. Judging by the nervous look in her eyes, she wanted just as much as I did to get us out of there before Kaitlyn could attack me again. "C'mon," she said. "There're a couple of ugly towels in the bathroom that might belong to you, but we'll go shopping tomorrow."

Mom gasped in a rare display of nerves as Kaitlyn emerged from the kitchen, a full carton of jars and canned goods in her arms. Mom looked as though she were ready to drop the basket and step between us to protect me, but Kaitlyn said softly, "Here, Allida. I think this is everything. I owe you a can of soup."

My only objective was to get the possible projectiles away from her. "That's quite all right." I grabbed the box from her. "Good luck with everything." And *please* don't ever contact me again!

I doubted this wish would be granted.

Mom and I shoved everything into the back of the truck and took off, heading north to her place in silence. It was so embarrassing to think of the emotional scene my mother had just witnessed. I knew she had to be sitting there wondering how on earth she'd managed to raise a daugh-

ter so naive as to wind up living with a woman that was
out of control.

After a minute of silence, Mom gave me a reassuring
smile. "Well, dear, all I can say is the next time I see the
real Keith Terrington, I'm going to kill him."

The next morning, I woke up disoriented, finally remembering that I was in Mom's guest room. She'd left a
note that she had some early morning lessons and was already at the airport. For his sake, I hoped none of those
lessons were with her "*former* favorite student, Keith
Terrington," as Mom was still furious with him.

I had a delightful breakfast with our three dogs, debat-
ing which of the three I should bring with me to introduce to Suzanne as part of her treatment. She'd already
met Doppler, with whom she'd exchanged barks. Pavlov,
however, was generally too dignified to indulge in verbal
exchanges with such a small dog. She so vastly outsized
the little toodle—terdle? pooier?—Suzanne would be well-
taught not to bark at such dogs.

Keeping Pavlov in my car till I could warn my dog-
fearing officemate, I entered my office. To my surprise,
Russell was just hanging up my phone. "Good morning,"
he said, smiling brightly. He was dressed neatly as usual,
his pin-striped shirt hugging his short but nicely propor-
tioned frame, and his dark hair shimmered as though it
had just been washed. "You just got a weird phone call."

"Oh?"

"Yeah. I, uh, it happened to be ringing while I passed
through your office." That made little sense, as Russell
likely arrived at least two hours earlier, but I let it pass.
He went on, "I picked up, and a deep voice said, 'Who's
this?' And I said, 'Russell Greene. Who's this?' and he
hung up."

"I seem to be getting quite a few hang ups lately."

Russell glanced at the desktop where I'd already found his card, then gave me a nervous grin and rocked on his heels.

"Thanks for the card. I'd give you a thank you card for it, but then you'd feel obligated to give me a thank you card in return, and we'd find ourselves trapped in a never-ending Hallmark circle."

"Ah, yes. That could be problematic. I'm glad you liked my card, though."

"I have both a warning and a confession for you."

Russell wiggled his eyebrows. "This has potential. Go on."

"I have my very large German shepherd in the car, and in a few minutes, I need to bring her in to work with my next client."

Russell's face fell. "That would be your 'warning,' right?"

"Yes. The confession is that I slept on the couch in your office Saturday night. I had some trouble with my roommate. I tried to put everything back the way I found it, but if you find any odd items, they're probably mine."

"Haven't come across anything new. Just some dog hair," Russell said pleasantly.

"Those would only be mine indirectly. I went over your couch with the handheld vac, but I'll bring in my Kirby and—"

"No, it's fine. Please don't bother. Are you looking for a new place to live?"

"Yes. Know of anything?"

"Not anything you'd agree to." He glanced nervously over his shoulder, in the direction of my parking space. "About this shepherd of yours. Does he like men? Do I have to be sure not to wear a hat around him or anything?"

"Her. Pavlov's a female. Yes, to men, no to hat sensitivity."

To my surprise, Russell's face had paled and beads of

perspiration were rising on his forehead. I hadn't expected him to react quite this strongly. Even so, he replied, "By all means, bring her in. I want to meet both of your dogs."

"I'll understand if you want to wait in your office till after Pavlov's gone."

"No, no. I mean it. I want to meet your pets. It's just that I'd hoped to start with getting to know the cocker spaniel and work my way up. But this way's faster. We'll start with the abject terror part and see if we can move toward mild discomfiture later."

I was caught between wanting to chuckle at his over-reaction and being annoyed at his thinking he had anything to fear from my extremely well-trained, highly intelligent shepherd. "On that note, I'll go get her." As an after-thought, I grabbed the long leash attached to the training collar. "Listen, Russell. I'll put this on Pavlov just so you can be assured I'm in complete control of her actions. The best way to approach a dog is to walk steadily and confidently, then turn so that you're side by side."

He nodded. "Sideways. Got it." He gave me a small salute. "No problem."

I smiled at him, then left for the car. The poor guy. He was acting as though he'd had some sort of traumatic past event involving a dog. If so, he'd never shared it with me. Before I signed the lease, we discussed at great length the fact that my occupation meant I'd have dogs in my office very often. He'd told me he was "not a dog person," but that this wouldn't pose a problem.

Pavlov was patiently waiting for me. For Russell's sake, I slipped the chain onto her neck and told her to heel. We came down the steps and I pulled opened the door. Russell smiled at me, but I noticed he was gripping the counter behind him with white knuckles.

"This is Pavlov," I said, unable to keep the pride from

my voice. Pavlov was a beautiful shepherd—medium-sized by the usual standards, in the classic Rin Tin Tin brown, black and gray markings—though Rin Tin Tin's brown tones were lost on those black-and-white televised reruns.

Russell was actually shaking. For some reason, he seemed to find his meeting my calm German shepherd much more frightful than even the slightly larger collie who'd been barking viciously at him. To my equal surprise, Pavlov had tensed and was taking an aggressive stance.

Before I could warn him otherwise, Russell reached a quaking hand out toward Pavlov, as if he intended to pat her on the head—or poke her in the eye. She let out a loud *woof.*

In one fluid motion, Russell jerked his hand back, spun around, and leapt onto the counter. Then, plastered against the wall, Russell turned to look down at us. Pavlov and I stared back up at him in surprise, Pavlov cocking her head.

"I thought you said she liked men!"

"She does! You're acting so fearful, though, you made her nervous. Dogs pick up on that kind of thing!"

"So, you're saying I look like a cornered, edible bunny rabbit to her right now."

"No, I'm saying *you* need to establish your position as her superior. You're not going to be able to do that from up there. How about I take Pavlov back outside, and in the meantime, you—"

I stopped as the door hinge creaked behind me. Joel Meyer was entering with Suzanne in his arms. The little dog started yipping at the top of her lungs at Pavlov, who simply looked at her.

Meanwhile, Russell hopped down and said, "Hey, Joel. We met Saturday." He wiped away the sweat from his brow, then turned to me and said, "I was right. I can reach the ceiling from up there. We won't have any trouble changing the overhead lightbulb." Ah, yes. Humiliation in front of another male. The one thing that's far more terrorizing to a man than even his worst phobia.

"Your bulb's burned out? I'll get it," Joel offered, ignoring the grating noise of his dog's shrill bark. "I'm tall enough."

"It's fine," Russell answered sharply. "I was just testing for future reference."

"Suzanne, hush!" Joel said. She had no inclination to obey.

I grabbed a box of miniature dog treats and gave a handful to Joel. "Here. Put a few of these in your pocket. Take Suzanne back outside. Set her down. The instant she stops barking, tell her, 'Good dog,' and give her one. Then lead her back inside, but don't pick her up. If she starts barking while she's still outside, let the door close—carefully, of course—on the leash with her still on the other side of the door."

Joel said, "Can do," and winked at me. He was looking especially handsome with his neat dark beard contrasting with his white dress shirt.

The moment Joel and his noisy dog were on the other side of the door, Russell grumbled, "Like he's so tough. I've got gym socks that are bigger than that mutt of his." He cast one quick glance at Pavlov, whose back was turned to watch for Joel and his dog's return. "I've got a lot of work to do. See you later." He went into his office and shut the door. His face was still red, but he managed to put a bit of a swagger into his step.

A minute or two later, Joel returned, and as I could have predicted, Suzanne started barking fiercely at Pavlov. He followed my instructions and stepped inside anyway, leaving the leashed Suzanne outside barking away.

"What now?" he said, smiling.

"This could get a bit tedious, frankly."

"I doubt that very much," he said, giving me a visual once-over that made me bristle. This was my *job*, not a chance to flirt.

I instructed Pavlov to lie down, then I told Joel, "Stay put till Suzanne stops barking. The moment she stops, go back outside with her, give her a treat and praise her, then try to lead her inside again. Repeat those steps till you can get her in here without any barking. Just remember: Don't pick her up, don't reassure her while she's barking, do praise her and give her a treat when she isn't barking."

It took Joel many tries and half a box of treats, but by the end of the session, Joel was able to lead his dog in and out of the room, with her complete indifference to Pavlov's presence.

"You're a genius," Joel told me. "She's completely cured in one session."

"Not that I'm trying to drum up repeat business here, but this is only a good start. I can virtually guarantee you that if I were to bring out another dog from a back room, Suzanne would start barking just as nonstop as ever, all over again."

"Good," Joel said. "That gives me all the more opportunity to see you. Would you consider an evening session tonight? Say at my place, during the dinner hour?"

"Not tonight."

"What's the next step?"

His coy, flirtatious demeanor was so annoying to me that I answered, "Assuming you're referring to your dog, that's up to you. I would imagine you want to at least get her trained not to confront other dogs when you're walking her, right?"

"So, the next step is a walk in the park, right?"

"Right."

"Cool. Sounds like a date to me. I'll bring the glasses and the wine." I started to object, but he held up a palm and said, "Just kidding." He talked me into a follow-up session the next morning. He winked, then said, "See you next time."

Just as he was leaving, John O'Farrell entered. If I'd expected this much unannounced drop-in business, I'd have installed a revolving door. Mugsy wasn't with him, nor was his wife or children. "Hi, Allida. I was just canvassing the neighborhood."

"Canvassing?"

"Putting fliers on windshields, actually. I own a health-food store, and I'm sure you know how tough it is competing for customers in Boulder. Thought I'd drop by and tell you again how much I appreciate your helping with my wife and Mugsy."

He stared at Pavlov, who rose and stepped between us. I was slightly surprised at her taking such a protective stance. She generally had an infallible sense of when I felt nervous in someone's company. Yet I was completely at ease now and felt not threatened in the least.

"Is this your dog?"

"Yes, her name's Pavlov." I bent over and patted her sleek fur.

"Does she get along with Sage okay?"

I tensed, as did Pavlov. "Sage?"

"Yeah. I'm assuming you're watching him, too, now, right?"

"I'm a little puzzled by your curiosity with regard to Sage. Tell me again how you came to meet him."

"I used to eat at Hannah's restaurant a lot and got to know her there. Then we ran into each other when we were at the park one day walking our dogs. That's all there is to it. Not a very interesting story, I'm afraid."

"How's Mugsy been doing since I left?"

"Just fine. Like I said, I just dropped by to say thanks." He was already backing out the door in a hurry to leave. I couldn't begin to fathom why he'd wasted the time on a trip here. To ask one more time about Sage? He had to realize I was beginning to get suspicious of his interest. Why, then?

At the moment, I had enough to think about. I wanted to get Pavlov home, but first wanted to check on my office-mate's state of mind.

I instructed Pavlov to lie down in the corner, then tapped on Russell's door. He called for me to come in, and I leaned through the doorway. "I'm taking Pavlov home to my mom's. I don't have another client for a couple of hours, so I'll be a while."

"You're not just taking her for my sake, are you?"

"No. Not at all," I lied. "She's happier out in my mom's big backyard where she's got room to roam around. That's one of the reasons I had to settle for this arrangement in the first place."

"I need to explain something to you." He searched my eyes. "Got a minute?"

"Sure." I shut the door on Pavlov, who seemed fine.

Russell took a seat on his couch, and I sat down at the far end. He sat with his elbows on his knees, staring at his fists instead of meeting my gaze. At length, he said, "When I was three and my brother was five, we were play-ing out in the backyard. The neighbor's German shepherd attacked him—bit his face. That's my earliest memory."

"Oh, my God! Russell, why didn't you tell me this when I first told you what my type of business was?"

He shrugged, but looked at me with a longing in his eyes that spoke volumes. "I didn't realize then that it'd be this difficult for me. I've just always kind of avoided dogs. It hasn't been much of a problem as an adult."

"Was your brother all right?"

"Yeah. He had to have a batch of stitches, but he's fine

now. Lives in Michigan. Works for IBM. You can barely even see the scars."

"Still, though—"

"Do you believe in love at first sight?"

I stiffened. "No, Russell, I don't."

He scooted toward me. "Don't you believe it's at least possible that there was a reason you walked in my door, needing an office just as I was needing a new officemate?"

"Sure. It's called classified ads." My fight-or-flight warning flags were going berserk. An insidious realization popped of its own volition into my head—that if Russell had been a dog lover, I'd be every bit as much attracted to him as he was to me.

"You know that's not what I mean," he said quietly, searching my eyes.

"Well, if you mean, do you think our meeting each other was fated, I'd have to say no. Dogs are my life. You're afraid of dogs. I personally don't believe The Fates have that perverse a sense of humor."

He leaned over and kissed me.

Chapter 15

I cut the kiss short, then shot to my feet, my heart beating rapidly for more reason than simple surprise. This was the last thing I needed in my life—finding myself more and more attracted to a man who was pathologically afraid of my beloved German shepherd.

Deliberately keeping my back turned so my resolve wouldn't weaken, I said, "Russell, there is no sense in starting something between us that can't possibly work out."

"You don't know that. If I can get over my lifelong fear of dogs, we might be perfect for each other."

That was a very large "if." My emotions seemed to be in an utter state of confusion, and I honestly wasn't sure what I felt anymore. I'd been wildly attracted to Keith, until he turned out to be Alex. I had Joel Meyer hanging on my every word, and I'd yet to decide if I even liked him. There was something compelling and decent about Russell. He was so "cute"—though I hated that word—and his obvious affection for me was flattering. The truth was, I didn't want to have feelings for Russell Greene just now. I was too busy trying to sort through the shambles my day-to-day existence had become.

"Russell, the thing is, even if I weren't under as much stress as I am right now, I own a German shepherd. That isn't going to change."

"I'll get therapy for my phobia."

"That's sweet. Nobody's ever offered to get therapy on my behalf before." Pavlov let out a warning woof to signal that someone had entered my office. I headed to the door and said, "Let's just . . . forget this ever happened, okay?"

I left before he could reply, but caught a glimpse of his disheartened features as I closed the door behind me.

A man I'd never met before stood in the center of the room, holding a green vase full of red roses. He and Pavlov were regarding each other with interest. His large, crooked nose reminded me of a human version of Sage's. He wore a bomber's jacket and gray slacks with brown wingtips peeking out from below his cuffs. He appeared to be in his mid-thirties.

He gave me a half smile. "I'm Keith Terrington. The real one."

As opposed to the handsome actor who played the part during our date, I thought. "Hello, Keith. Nice to meet you, finally." I was unable to keep the bitterness out of my voice. For the sake of his friendship with my mother, though, I felt obliged to be at least somewhat civil. "I can't believe you stood me up for a Nuggets' game. They're terrible this year."

"I know. The game was just an excuse." He sighed. "After what I did, nothing short of a face-to-face apology seemed appropriate. Truth is, Marilyn showed me a picture of you she kept in her wallet. Ever since my wife left me, I haven't had much luck with dates—certainly not with ones who haven't met me yet. I . . . can't stand to see the expression of disappointment on blind dates' faces when they first see me."

The self put-down struck me as sincere, yet a martyrish overstatement. He was not especially good-looking, but the sight of his face wasn't guaranteed to disappoint a prospective date, either. "I wish you'd given both your-self and me more credit than that."

He frowned and nodded. "You're right. But Alex was so anxious to go out with you after hearing you speak on some radio show or something that it seemed like the best solution." He held out the flowers to me, which I ac-cepted. "I brought you these, by way of an apology."

His words had highlighted a concern that now gnawed at me—Alex was yet another man interested in me only after he'd learned about my connection to Sage. "Thank you. Apology accepted. And flowers certainly weren't nec-essary, but I appreciate them."

Again, he nodded and seemed to be on the verge of weighing his next words. "It was nice meeting you, Al-lida," Keith said, then turned toward the exit. "Again, I'm really sorry. I'll do my best to apologize to your mother, as well."

He left, trotting up the cement stairs without hesitation. This might just be a sign that this odd little wave of men at-tracted to me was about to enter ebb tide and return me to my usual long stretches between dates. I set his roses alongside Russell's in their pathetic mayonnaise jar and felt my heart lurch. Whatever happened to those pseudo-statistics that had me—in my thirties—more likely to be taken hostage than to find an eligible man? The way my life was going, the terrorist would ask me out—then shoot me when I declined.

All of these guys had—coincidentally, I could only hope—entered my life at the same time as Sage. At least I'd met Russell weeks before Beth Gleason had turned my life upside down. Russell had let his attraction to me be known from the very first.

I stared at his door and entertained the notion of burst-ing in and returning his kiss. Then good sense took over, and I collected my things to return Pavlov to Mom's. I'd planned to keep her with me all day—but that was before I knew about my officemate's justifiable fear of shepherds.

Before we could get out the door, the phone rang. The deep voice on the other end identified himself as Dennis Corning. "Listen," he said. "I know this is unexpected, but we need to hire you to work with Shakespeare. Right away."

"Shakespeare?" Warning signals went off in my brain. The Cornings' dog had seemed quite well-behaved yesterday. His parting words to me had been that if he were Sage's caretaker, he "wouldn't let that dog out of sight." This from someone who'd taken Sage to the Humane Society. Perhaps he was trying to get to Sage through me. "What's your dog doing?"

"He's got garbage-itis again. This is the second time. Yesterday, after you left, he got real sick, and we took him to the vet. He'd eaten a batch of Brian's crayons. He's much better today, but he's leaving multicolored presents all over our yard, if you get my drift."

I breathed a sigh of relief for my own sake, but was immediately worried for the dog. "Garbage-itis" was not the sort of problem that could be easily faked. Nor was it easy to cure. "I take it, then, you want me to train him not to eat nonfood items?"

"To stop being a garbage disposal, yeah."

This was an interesting connection. Shakespeare had eaten bad "food" at the household that had possessed and then passed along Sage's tainted food. Maybe, while treating Shakespeare, I could learn the cause for Sage's troubles. My instincts were telling me that the tainted food was somehow the key to both Beth's and Hannah's murders. Until those crimes were solved, I'd be unable to put my life in order. "I'll work with him. How soon did you have in mind?"

"As close to *now* as you can swing. I don't want Shakespeare to put himself through this sh— this junk again."

I glanced at my watch, then at Pavlov, who was pacing as if she were a caged animal. I needed to get her back to my mom's, where she could roam around the fully fenced acre. "I could be there in two hours. Can you meet us at your place?"

"Me? I didn't think I'd needed to be there. I'm at work. Susan and Brian and, of course, Shakespeare are going to be there, though."

"If you can't make it, that's fine, but it'd be best if the entire family was there at once."

"This is really Susan's problem. She's the one who hasn't trained Brian not to leave his toys around. Nor the dog not to eat them. But, whatever. I'll come home and meet you on my lunch break."

Big of you, I thought sourly, disliking his reference to his wife being solely responsible for "training" their son and dog. Nonetheless, I managed a pleasant, "See you then," and hung up.

I made good time driving to Berthoud during this off-hour. All three dogs were happy to see one another. I let them into the yard, indulging myself by watching them romp outside and stage their top-dog battles.

This was nice, I thought, leaning against the cool glass of the back door. Much better than living in my little house with my little maniacal roommate. If I stayed here, the dogs could be together. Then again, there was now that dreadful drive ahead of me . . . which would grow truly tedious by winter. After fourteen years of independence, was I seriously considering living in Mom's house again? No. I had to find a place of my own in Boulder soon. Within the next few months, at any rate. I made myself a sandwich, grabbed a can of soda, and headed back to Boulder to eat while behind the wheel.

* * *

Susan Corning ushered me into her elegant living room. Even with no makeup, barefoot, and in jeans and a pale blue angora sweater, she fit in this room with all its pricey appointments. As opposed to how out of place I felt here, despite my reasonably nice black slacks and beige blouse. Brian was on the floor at his mother's feet, hammering pegs into a block. The process had the little two-year-old thoroughly mesmerized.

"Let me ask you this," I said to Susan, once I'd collected the rest of the pertinent background information about the gray-and-white shih tzu. "If your son were to, say, spill some of his . . ." What did wealthy people feed their children? Escargot? Caviar? ". . . macaroni and cheese on the kitchen floor, do you allow Shakespeare to eat it?"

Susan chuckled. "Sounds as though you've been eating supper with us. That happens all the time. Is that bad?"

"I wouldn't necessarily call it 'bad,' but it can lead Shakespeare to think that he's *supposed* to eat whatever Brian drops, including crayons."

"Oh, I see. But I simply can't collect every last item that Brian drops. The thing is, Allida, I'm just not sure how much more of this garbage his little system can take."

It took me a moment to sort the pronouns in her statement and realize she was referring to the dog's literally eating garbage. "There are two ways I should be able quickly to break Shakespeare of the habit of eating off the floor. The fastest method is to use a long, light lead and a choke collar, which one of us would tug whenever Shakespeare tried to eat something off the floor."

Susan shook her head. "I don't want to hurt him."

"Of course not. But bear in mind that a brief pressure on Shakespeare's trachea is considerably less painful than the indigestion he's been causing himself."

She furrowed her brow. "What's the second choice?"

"Sound aversion therapy."

"Which is?"

I explained that I would press the button on my noise-maker every time Shakespeare tried to eat a treat off the floor and praise him each time he'd eat something I offered to him. This was the method she chose, and Shakespeare proved to be a quick study. Then I expanded the lesson to include food offered by the family, and especially to avoid inedible items that Brian dropped.

Dennis never showed up, but he finally called just as I was about to leave. Susan handed me the phone, and he immediately explained, "Something came up at work. How'd it go?"

"Fine. I'll just need you and everyone else in the family to reinforce the message that Shakespeare is only to eat the food that is directly offered to him."

"No *problemo*."

His haughty tone of voice annoyed me. Was I just being touchy here, or was Susan infinitely classier than her yuppy husband?

"Say," he went on, "I hope this little incident hasn't made you decide against us getting Sage."

I squared my shoulders. My nervous system was now tensing as if the very mention of the collie's name were as grating as nails on a blackboard. "I'm sorry, but since the last time I spoke with you, I've decided to give Sage to somebody else."

"What do you mean?"

From the corner of my vision, I saw Susan react and give me her full attention as well. "Exactly what I said. I already found a good home for Sage."

"Damn you! How can you decide something like that without waiting to see if we'd make you a better offer?"

His shouts rang in my ear. Out of deference to his wife

and son who were still nearby, I kept my voice level. "This isn't a public auction. Through no choice of my own, I've found myself in charge of finding a good home for a dog. That's what I've succeeded in doing."

"Have it your way. We'll find ourselves another collie. In the meantime, you're fired!" He hung up on me.

I set the receiver down and looked at Susan, who was now hovering beside me, no doubt having surmised the rancor between her husband and me. "Is everything all right?" she asked.

"Except for the fact that I've been fired, yes."

She lifted her chin and said pleasantly, "Oh, you have not been."

"Your husband was quite clear. He said, 'You're fired.' That's pretty hard to misinterpret." Along with his having cursed in my ear.

"In that case, you're rehired, by me." I started to protest, but she brushed my concerns aside with the explanation, "I'll handle things with my husband. He's always made it clear that he thinks I'm in charge of Shakespeare, so that makes this my decision."

I couldn't argue with her logic, though Dennis probably could. The friction between Dennis and me reminded me that I had yet to attempt to learn more about Sage. "By the way, did you or your husband ever meet Beth Gleason?" I asked on the off chance that this could lead me to a clue.

To my surprise, she sighed and nodded, combing her fingers through her blond curls. "That young woman was quite a nuisance, always hanging around Hannah. At first, I used to think she wanted Hannah to adopt her or something, till I found out that her father could have bought and sold all of us put together."

I was so confused by this my thoughts were reeling.

Beth had given me the impression that she only knew Sage and Hannah Jones through the cooking class.

The hammer and peg board long since deserted, Brian had been darting from room to room, but now entered and asked, "Mommy?"

"Not now, honey," she replied.

"You knew Beth's father?" I asked, trying to work backward to make some sense of this.

"Just by reputation. He's the CEO of a major computer company. Beth, however, latched on to Hannah after taking one of her cooking classes. In the last few weeks before Hannah died, every time I'd drop by for a visit, there was Beth. The minute Hannah died, Beth was on the phone to us, leaving message after message asking if we'd give her the dog. Dennis and I decided Sage would be better off with someone else—anyone else—as an owner. We took him down to the shelter and . . ." Susan lifted her hands in a gesture of surrender ". . . the joke was on us. She'd left her name there as wanting to adopt a collie, and she got Sage within a couple hours of our bringing him in."

That didn't jibe with what Beth had told me. She'd said she called *Hannah's* machine to inquire about adopting Sage. That once she got him, she called the number Dennis had left in the kibble, but wouldn't tell the Cornings where she lived.

"What did you do when you learned that Beth had adopted Sage?"

She shook her head and lifted Brian, who'd begun tugging on her sweater for attention. "Nothing. What could we do? We spoke to her only once after that and—"

"When she called the number Dennis had left in the dog food?"

"Right. We wished her well and asked her to keep us posted as to how Sage was doing."

"How did she know to call you prior to that?"

Susan furrowed her brow and turned her attention to her son, who said in no uncertain terms that he wanted "Juice!" She carried him into the kitchen, asking me over her shoulder, "You mean . . . when she was trying to get us to give her the dog?"

"Yes."

She filled a Winnie-the-Pooh cup with what looked to be fresh-squeezed juice and sent Brian on his way again. Watching her, though, I got the strong feeling my question had upset her. It had apparently never occurred to her to wonder about this. "I don't know. Dennis must have said something to her at some point about how we watched Sage whenever Hannah was out of town." She wasn't meeting my eyes. "Or maybe Hannah had told her that." After a pause, she brightened. "That must be it. As far as I know, she never even met Dennis. I mean, he's always gone during the day, when Beth tended to be at Hannah's place. Of course! Hannah would have told her at some point that we watched her dog."

She looked positively relieved at having come up with this answer. Why was the thought of Dennis and Beth having spoken prior to Hannah's death so unsettling to her? Only one answer to that question came to mind, which would mean Dennis Corning was every bit as big a jerk as I'd felt he was. Bigger, even.

At five P.M., I was waiting, as planned, on the curb outside George Haggerty's house, listening to Rex's pathetic howls within. A classic case of separation anxiety. This was one bored, lonely dog who considered himself master of his pack and couldn't understand why his pack members— George and his wife—were deserting him during the day.

George pulled into his driveway, and we agreed to have

me go into the house first. We further agreed that I would put a leash with a gentle leader on Rex, which George would give a quick yank on and say "No," while I activated my noisemaker. I went in through his garage, surprising Rex, who was all poised to leap on his owner. To Rex's great credit, it looked as though he was tempted to goose me, but remembered what had happened yesterday. I slipped the collar over his head and glanced around, seeing no immediate signs of destruction.

George came in, the dog pounced, George snapped the leash and said, "Down," instead of "No," but otherwise everything went according to plan. Rex stood there blinking as if wondering what had happened.

"Let's see how many more of my possessions he's laid to waste during the day," George muttered, surveying the place as he strode past me.

Normally, after having destroyed parts of the house in the owner's absence, a dog cowers when his master does this—not because the dog knows he's done wrong, but because the dog has learned that Master Plus Damage Equals Punishment. Rex, however, trotted happily by George's side, which told me that George wasn't punishing Rex. Maybe, I silently mused, I'd been misspelling Rex's name all along. Maybe it was *Wrecks*, as in what he did to the house.

George returned with a small, unrecognizable object clenched in his hand. He promptly threw it in the trash. "Well, it's a little better, anyway."

"Don't get discouraged." I removed the leash while speaking. "This has been going on for more than a year. It's going to take more than one or two sessions till he's learned new habits."

George ran his palm across his baldpate, his shoulders sagging. In a major non sequitur, he said, "The papers said they were reopening Hannah Jones's murder case."

"They're calling it murder now?"

"Actually, the coroner still says it appears to be a suicide, but they want to look into the possible connection between the two deaths." He plopped down onto his dilapidated couch and looked up at me. "Maybe Hannah's dog is cursed, like Jimmy Dean's car."

"Excuse me?"

"You know. That young actor. He was probably before your time. Everybody who owned even a piece of that car he crashed in would get into a terrible accident. Maybe it's the same with Sage. If I were you, I'd give him to somebody you don't like very much."

This conversation was giving me the willies. Was Mom safely back from her flight lessons? If not, Sage and the other dogs had been all alone most of the day.

"Could I use your phone?"

"Sure. In the kitchen near the sink. It's slightly gnawed, of course, but it still works."

My mother answered on the first ring. I greeted her, then said, "I'm at a client's house now, but I'm going to be leaving in—"

"You need to get a cellular phone or at least a beeper."

"I know. I will. It just seems so . . . Boulderish. Why? Have you been trying to reach me?"

"Pavlov is acting really strange."

My heart started pounding, but I managed to ask relatively calmly, "What's she doing?"

"She won't come when I call. She's in the far corner of the yard, and whenever the other dogs come near her she barks. It's as if she's guarding something."

"Oh, shit!" I blurted, realizing what was likely going on with my dog. "Mom, drop the phone and go out there now! See if she's near a piece of meat on the lawn!"

"A piece of meat? I haven't given her any—"

"I know! That's my point! Somebody could have tossed poisoned meat over the fence!"

"Oh, dear Lord," my mother cried. There was a *thunk*, then a long silence after she dropped the phone.

Chapter 16

"You were right," Mom said, breathless from her dash across the lawn, her voice strained with barely checked emotion. "Pavlov was guarding a big chunk of hamburger."

"Are there any bite marks in the meat?"

"No. I don't think the dogs ate any of *this* meat. I just hope there weren't any other pieces that Doppler or Sage . . ." She let her voice trail off.

"They're probably fine," I said to reassure both my mother and myself. "What you found had to be all of it, or Pavlov wouldn't have been acting so territorial."

Though my statement sounded good, it was overly optimistic. I'd taught Pavlov to eat only what was specifically offered to her by me or her caregiver. With her natural guard-dog instincts, she'd taken it upon herself to prevent the other dogs from eating the hamburger—probably because she was hoping Mom or I would later give her permission to eat it. Her behavior in no way guaranteed that Sage or Doppler hadn't already gobbled down hamburger chunks from other locations in the yard.

I fought down a rising sense of panic. I was too far away to get there fast enough to help the dogs if they'd eaten poison. My mother was going to have to take care of this.

Antifreeze was by far the most common source of poisoning for a dog. After showing signs of drunkenness, a poisoned dog would pass out, at which point it became a desperate race against the clock; the earlier the dog's stomach got pumped the better.

"Mom, do you know what antifreeze smells like?"

She paused. "No, not specifically."

"Go into the garage, find a bottle of antifreeze, and see if the meat smells similar. If so, watch for signs of alcohol poisoning—disorientation, staggering, and all other signs of drunkenness."

My own stomach was in knots. I looked at George, who was blatantly listening in on all of this with considerable interest. I didn't want to have to reschedule yet another appointment with Rex if I could avoid it. Mom returned to the phone and told me that the meat did seem to bear the same odor as antifreeze. I covered the mouthpiece and asked George, "Is it all right if I give my mother your phone number? We've got a problem that could escalate."

"Of course," he said. "Did someone try to poison your dogs? Is this about Sage?"

"No! Sage is fine!"

His face fell. He probably was every bit as nice a man as he seemed to be, concerned about the condition of an innocent dog. But how could I know for sure? I deliberately had not spoken Sage's name. Had George simply *guessed* that Sage was at my mother's house? Dammit! This was all so out of control that I didn't even know what to say to my clients!

I turned my back on George and gave Mom his number, with the instructions to race the dogs to the veterinary hospital upon even the slightest symptom of poisoning, and then to call me. I hung up, took a calming breath, and returned my attention to George. Rex, I noticed, watched us from a short distance behind George, as opposed to standing between us as he had on my first visit. This was another sign of progress toward improved behavior.

"Sorry I snapped at you. Some bastard barely missed killing one of my dogs."

George held up his palms. "Hey, don't think twice about it. I understand completely. Are all of your dogs okay?"

"It appears so," I answered, but once again, was confronted with the thought that, if George Haggerty was the killer, I'd just done him the favor of letting him know that his plan had failed. He would have already gathered that much from what he'd overheard, though. Extending that rationale, I added with considerable pride, "My German shepherd not only didn't eat the meat herself, but guarded it so the other dogs wouldn't eat it."

"I've never heard of a dog refusing to eat meat. How did you train her to do that? And why?"

"Back when she was a puppy, there were a few reports of dog poisonings in the papers. I worried that, since her breed occasionally gets bad press, she might be a target someday." Not to mention the fact that my own dogs had been my "proving ground" for work with others' dogs and therefore were trained in all kinds of potentially useless ways. However, this being one of those rare opportunities when I'd actually been *asked* to blow my own horn, there was no sense in my deliberately playing off-key. "I just used my usual basics—sound aversion if she started to eat something I hadn't offered her and positive reinforcement when she did as instructed."

"Huh," George said, casting a long look Rex's way before returning his gaze to me.

I forced myself to work with George and Rex as best I could manage despite the tremendous distraction. Rex was making considerable progress. By George's asserting himself as alpha dog, Rex was beginning to accept basic commands and was allowing George to leave the house for brief periods without whining. Nevertheless, my thoughts and my heart were elsewhere. Afterwards, I drove home as quickly as rush-hour traffic would allow.

Mom showed me the hunk of hamburger she'd collected from the portion of the yard that Pavlov had diligently been guarding. The two of us agreed that the meat indeed had a characteristic smell to it—antifreeze. She'd brought the dogs in, and we kept them in the kitchen with us while we watched for signs of their having consumed any. The dogs were fine. Mom and I were nervous wrecks.

We took out our fears and frustration in the good ol' method that has stood the test of time among dysfunctional families the world over: yelling at each other. Mom would no doubt have recalled our conversation differently, yet the fact was, *she* started it.

Just after we'd relaxed enough to take seats at the small, oak kitchen table, she said, "I thought you were trying to keep Sage's location quiet. How could the hateful, cowardly scumbag even know Sage was here? Did you tell your customers I had the dog?"

"Of course not, Mother! How stupid do you think I am?"

She tightened her jaw. "I don't think you're at all stupid, Allie. Just so stubborn that you get in over your head."

I furrowed my brow and glared at her. "If I'm stubborn, guess which side of the family I inherited it from?"

"In my case, it's known as determination. And believe you me, I'm determined not to let anyone get within ten feet of these dogs again."

"Good. Which is why we need to move out of here for a while. We should all just . . . move into a hotel or something."

"Allie, that's ridiculous! What kind of a 'hotel' would accept a collie, a German shepherd, and a cocker spaniel?"

"I don't know," I snapped. "There has to be some fleabag place around here somewhere."

Mom crossed her arms and glared. "This is my home, and I won't be chased out of it."

I clicked my tongue. "God, Mom! If I had said that, you'd accuse me of being stubborn, and you'd be right! Now that you're saying it, you're merely 'acting determined'!"

She maintained her cross-armed countenance. "Call it what you will," she answered in clipped tones. "In any case, I'm not leaving my house. You can take Doppler and Pavlov and go, if you'd like."

"You've got to listen to me, Mother!" I rose for emphasis and leaned against the kitchen table to stare into her eyes. "The killer's after Sage. That's his one link to the murders. We have to go someplace. What would have happened if I'd kept Pavlov with me this afternoon? Sage would have eaten that poisoned meat and possibly died."

"Maybe so, but that was before I fully understood the danger Sage was in. Now that I *am* fully aware, I can protect him."

I sank back into my chair, suspecting that my arguments were only forcing Mom to dig her heels in more. When could this have happened? Pavlov had acted normally when I let her out, and she has such an exceptional sense of smell, I highly doubted the meat was here when I dropped her off late morning.

If worse came to worst, we could always put the dogs in a kennel, but the thought of the dogs exposed to tons of contaminants and unable to exercise properly was truly unpleasant. Plus, Sage would also be vulnerable to the killer in a kennel, and he'd be totally out of our range of influence. In any case, I needed to mend fences with my mother, as fencing was about all we had going for us in the way of protection.

Forcing my voice to sound as relaxed as possible, I asked, "Did you see anything at all around the time the meat must have been tossed over the fence?"

"I didn't see anything, but, come to think of it, there was a strange door-to-door sales call. It was from some man who claimed to be selling 'organic dog food,' which he claims he 'makes fresh and delivers to your doorstep.' I told him I wasn't interested, and he left."

I tensed with alarm. "That's too much of a coincidence. Maybe he was going to try to poison Sage in person, then when you wouldn't let him in, he tossed it over the fence. What did he look like?"

"He was a big, strong guy. Mid thirties or so. Wearing a bad-quality hairpiece. German accent."

"A hairpiece?" I repeated.

"Looked as though he'd bought it off an Elvis impersonator. Phony sideburns, the whole nine yards. He kept insisting if I'd just let him demonstrate, I'd see how much the dog loved his product."

"Wait a minute. If he was the killer, he had to know that Sage would start barking at him. Did Sage, or either of the other dogs, see him?"

"No. They were all in the backyard when he came to the front. I remember one thing. He was wearing really strong cologne."

"Maybe he was trying to disguise his scent from Sage. Did you get his card or a brochure?" Mom was already shaking her head, so I continued, "Was he driving a company car?"

"No, just a plain, white four-door."

I grabbed my head in frustration, mostly to stop myself from reaching across the table to grab my mother. She'd teased me about my fears regarding a white car, then she missed our best chance to identify it! "Mom, a *white* car? Didn't you get the license plate or anything?"

She shook her head. "I didn't make the connection then. I was tired. I'd just gotten home, and it was broad daylight and everything. I didn't think there was anything sin-

ister about him—just one more pushy door-to-door salesman. He said his name was George Heidenburg."

George Haggerty was my only bald client who might
be inclined to wear some sort of toupee. The names were
bizarrely similar. But there was no possibility of the
Georges being one and the same. George Haggerty had
been with me when the salesman was visiting Mom. Besides which, it now dawned on me that during my last conversation with *my* George, I'd stupidly blurted out that
Pavlov had protected Sage from the tainted meat. If this
bogus salesman worked for George Haggerty, I'd given
them instructions on how to pull off their nefarious plan.
Mom was right! I was every bit as stupid as Mom claimed
she didn't think I was!

Returned to my previous level of anxiety, I renewed
our argument regarding how we had to hide our dogs, and
preferably ourselves, too. Mother retorted that she would
"sooner keep watch over Sage with a rifle in her hands"
than move into a hotel or a friend's house.

"In that case," I argued, "I'll just move Sage to a friend's
house."

"No! The poor dog has been orphaned twice. It would
be too traumatizing to Sage after all he's been through."

"After we get him back, I'll work with him. That is my
job, after all. Remember all that stuff you told Joel Meyer
about my being 'worth every penny' I charge, 'and then
some'?"

"Oh, please." She flicked a hand at me. "That was a
prospective customer. I'm your mother."

I fisted my hands. The heck with "mending fences." I
know when I've just been insulted! "Which means that
you know me too well to give me any credit?"

"I didn't say that. Sage is my dog now, and I'm not going to let him out of my sight."

The words had a chilling effect on me. They were the

exact same ones Dennis Corning had used when advising me how I should treat the collie. "Mom, moving Sage could prove to be the only way to keep him alive!"

"Don't you use that tone of voice to me, young lady!"

Oh, good Lord! My teen years all over again. Was this nightmare never going to end?

"I am going to stay in my own home and watch Sage and that's final." She rose from the table.

When my mother says, "that's final," she means it. Short of kidnapping Sage myself, all I could do was vow to help keep watch over both Sage and Mom, and to step up my own pace toward doing anything I could to help the authorities solve the crime. "What did the police say when you called them?" I asked.

"Oh, shoot!" She snapped her fingers. "I never did get around to doing that, I was so concerned with watching the dogs every second."

I sighed and grabbed the phone. The Boulder Police had been very professional and courteous in their dealings with me, and yet I had a hunch that they'd concluded I was an utter flake. By now, they'd likely tagged me The Dog Lady, intent on sticking my nose into their investigations.

A female answered the nonemergency number I'd called.

"My name's Allida Babcock. Somebody tried to poison my dog. I need to speak to someone assigned to the Beth Gleason murder case." There was a pause, which I interpreted as confusion over my request, so I quickly added, "My dog was a witness to the murder."

"I see. Just a moment, please." Her voice had an overly animated lilt to it, which indicated that I might as well have claimed there was a spaceship on my roof. Nonetheless, I eventually reached an officer who agreed that a trip out to Berthoud was warranted to collect the hamburger as evidence and interview my mom.

An hour later, Mom gave the same description of the dog-food salesman to the uniformed officer that she'd given me. Unfortunately, since the salesman had been standing on one of the porch steps but she couldn't say for certain which one, she was only able to give a range of height within six inches—between five foot ten and six foot four. The description was so vague—especially since it appeared that his hairpiece was a deliberate disguise—it could have been most any youngish, Caucasian man.

I had so many unanswered questions. Why was Sage's dog food tainted? What was Beth's relationship with Hannah Jones? Who was driving this white car that kept showing up? What was Bill Wayne really searching for in my room—and was his search somehow related to the murders? I felt as though I could jump out of my skin, and yet there was nothing I could do.

Of my own personal list of possible suspects, Chet Adler was so remarkably tall that I very much doubted she could mistake him for possibly five-ten. That left Dennis Corning, Alex Ferron—aka The Man Formerly Known as Keith Terrington—Bill Wayne, George Haggerty, John O'Farrell, and Joel Meyer—but only if he'd shaved his beard today, which seemed unlikely. Because I couldn't believe Alex was involved, that left Dennis, Bill, and John—provided there was one man, acting alone, who'd committed the evil acts, and that this was not a completely innocent door-to-door salesman. And, anyway, an "innocent door-to-door salesman" was an oxymoron.

It was after seven P.M. Mom and I ate dinner, but now that she was used to me as a house guest—after all of one day—she agreed to let me cook, so I made lemon chicken and rice. Both the chicken and the rice were dry and unexciting. Though our antagonism toward each other had, thankfully, faded, my thoughts were in such turmoil that I was lousy company.

If only I could explore the link between Hannah Jones and Beth Gleason, I thought, pushing some grains of rice around my plate. But how could I, when all that remained of the link was the collie? A second connection between the two women occurred to me then—one that was so obvious, I was tempted to whack myself in the head.

"Mom, do you know anything about this cooking class that Hannah Jones used to teach?"

Mom peered up from her plate at me. "Why? Looking for guidance?"

"Just trying to learn more about Hannah and Beth, really."

"It was through one of those adult education classes you see offered all the time. I took a class ten years ago, and they still send me schedules every six months or so. I might have an old class schedule around here someplace."

She rifled through a stack of papers on top of the refrigerator until she found what looked like a small newspaper. "Here it is." She paged through the catalogue, then flipped it back over and glanced at the cover. "They even have a class going now. I didn't realize that."

"I'm sure they cancelled it and gave refunds or something when Hannah died six weeks ago."

"Not necessarily," Mom said, looking at the paper. "It says here she had a co-teacher named Naomi Smith. She might have kept the class going."

"Let me see." I snatched the class catalogue away from her. Mother was right. "Hot dog," I muttered under my breath, feeling as though I was finally on to something.

"Vegetarian ones only, I'm sure," Mom replied, still overly focused on food.

At eight A.M. the next day, I arrived at my office. During my drive into Boulder, I'd come up with the idea of calling all the Smiths listed in the directory until I could happen across Naomi's number. I tossed my purse down, dropped into my chair, grabbed the Boulder phone book, and paged through to "Smith." The entry was surprisingly large. I made an estimate. Approximately four hundred and fifty Smiths in the directory—none of whom were listed as Naomi Smith.

Time for Plan B. I called the registration number for the school, asked if I could please speak to the director of education there, then inquired whether the class was still going on. It was. Better yet, she gave me Ms. Smith's number without my even having to make up an excuse for wanting it.

I dialed this number, and Naomi Smith answered. "My name is Allida Babcock," I told her. "I'm calling to ask about the cooking class that you teach."

"Oh, yes. Our last class of the semester meets tonight, but you're welcome to drop in and audit, to see if you'd be interested in signing up for the next class. That one starts in four weeks."

"Great. Thank you so much," I said and hung up, slightly appalled at how deceitful I'd just been. Upon further reflection, however, I decided that a little dishonesty went a long way. Trying to learn more about two murdered women from the same cooking class was not phone-conversation material.

Energized with the admittedly false sense that I was taking some action to find Beth Gleason's killer, I drove to Joel Meyer's house with a renewed sense of purpose. My jaw dropped when he came to the door.

He was clean-shaven.

"What happened to your beard?"

"I'm contemplating making a career change and thought

the beard might not be projecting the right corporate image." He held his chin high and turned his head slowly from side to side. "What do you think?"

What I *thought* was that he was now number one on my list of suspects. The whole strange thing about insisting on changing my tire and being in the neighborhood when Beth had been stabbed—and now his shaving right when my mother had gotten a bizarre visit from a clean-shaven man who later may have tried to poison my dogs. A thought pattern best kept unsaid.

"Personally, I like beards, but you might be right about having better luck in the corporate world without one." He opened the door, and I noticed a distinct absence of yipping little dog. "Where's Suzanne?"

Joel looked puzzled. "Gee. I really don't know." He turned and called for her, to no avail. "Wait here," he told me and strode off in search of her. Moments later there came a loud, "Oh, jeez!" from the kitchen. "Suzanne! You miserable little rug rat!"

Out of curiosity, I followed Joel into the kitchen. He was just slamming a closet door, Suzanne barking her protest from his arms. He blushed at the sight of me. "I forgot to close the pantry door and she got into the cereal."

I nodded, but scanned the floor in surprise. "Where's her dog bowl?"

"Oh, it's, uh, in the dishwasher right now."

He acted so disconcerted at this that I grew extremely suspicious. "What kind of dog food do you use?"

"I, uh, gee. Can't remember the brand name. It's that kind with the paw prints all over it."

Iam's I silently realized, but, to test him, asked, "Ion's?"

"That's it." He swept up a leash that was lying on the kitchen counter and clicked it on to the dog's collar. "Off to the park, right?"

"Yes," I said, needing time to think. I was now ninety-five percent certain that Suzanne wasn't even Joel's dog. And I had a pretty good idea to whom the dog truly belonged. However, I didn't want to show my cards too early.

"You and Tracy Truett met at the radio station, right?" I asked by way of wanting to explore their ties and surmise what was going on with Joel's having conveniently shaved.

"That's right. I used to be a tech at the station, till I got a higher-paying job."

"How long did you work there?"

"Couple of years."

So the two of them could know each other quite well, I thought. My belief that Tracy was totally innocent was all that was keeping me from running from him. There were only three possible explanations for why Joel and Tracy Truett had set me up like this. One: I had just found the killer; two: Tracy was using Joel to find out if I was on the trail of the killer in some bizarre attempt to save her radio career; or three: Tracy and Joel had paired up in some equally bizarre attempt to encourage me to go out with him.

We started by walking the dog around the block and doing basic leash training, which Suzanne was sorely lacking. She was also showing the fascination for sights, sounds, and smells a dog has in a relatively unexplored neighborhood.

I immediately discarded the thought of using any kind of aversion techniques to discourage Suzanne's barking—such as spritzing her with water—because this is something I would only want to do after first discussing it with the dog's owner. A block from Joel's house, we encountered a Boston terrier in a fenced yard. Both dogs barked wildly at each other, and we stuck to the basic positive reinforcement training.

We made some progress during the hour-long session—probably all wasted effort on my part, considering Suzanne was not in the presence of her owner, and how well any dog will behave for a trainer is irrelevant if the lessons aren't reinforced at home.

Joel praised me lavishly and asked me out again, which I declined. I left, got into my car, drove around the block, then parked just beyond the view from Joel's windows.

Not even fifteen minutes later, a sporty two-door that looked like a Corvette came zipping around the corner and pulled into Joel's driveway. Tracy Truett emerged. Leaving the engine running, she trekked to Joel's door and let herself in.

I got out of my car and peered into hers, just to see if I could verify my suspicions. Dog hair was all over the passenger seat.

Tracy came back down the steps a minute later, with Suzanne under her arm. Her jaw dropped at the sight of me standing by her bumper.

"Hi, Tracy. Can we have a little talk about you and your dog?"

Chapter 17

"I knew you'd figure this out, sooner or later." With Suzanne balanced on a hip under her arm, she marched past me. She was wearing a bright, solid yellow outfit that all but screamed "Big Bird" to me. "I have no idea how I wound up letting Joel convince me to lend him Suzanne in the first place." She unlocked the passenger door and held it open for me. "Get in."

I shook my head and gestured at my vehicle parked at the far end of the block. "I've got my car—"

"My feet are killing me. We either sit down in my car to talk, or we can head back inside and yak with Joel for a while. I figure you probably want to hear this from me first, or you wouldn't have ambushed me here in the first place."

I toyed with the notion of pointing out to her that she was in no position to accuse *me* of ambushing *her*, but it struck me as wasted breath. I sighed and got into the little car, Suzanne eagerly hopping onto my lap.

"See, it's like this," Tracy said as soon as she plopped into her own seat. "My God but these new shoes are killing me." She pulled them off as she spoke and chucked them onto the rear window ledge. "Why on earth I had to go out and spend my savings on shoes when I don't even have a job and—"

"Tracy, could you just explain why Joel wanted to pretend Suzanne was his dog?"

"You probably already figured this out for yourself, but it was so he could have an excuse to see you."

"And, if we had started dating, what? Didn't he think I was going to notice the absence of his dog?"

"He planned to tell you that now that you'd done such a great job improving his dog's demeanor, he felt he could give her to someone who had a more flexible schedule. Someone who could be with her more and who really wanted her."

"That would be you?"

She threw up her hands. "Hey, don't look at me like that. This was all Joel's idea. I told him way back you'd never fall for it, but did he listen?"

Her story was plausible, but did nothing to allay my concerns about Joel's having shaved at such an inopportune moment. "Why did Joel shave his beard?"

She let out a guffaw. "Hate to disappoint you, honey, but *that* he didn't do for your love. He's willing to pretend he's a disobedient-dog owner . . . or whatever I meant to say. But he didn't shave to impress you. He's been working the night shift on some production-line hoozy-fradgit place, and he's trying to clean up his image to impress the head muckamucks. He wants a promotion so he can join the white-collar, silk-tie wearers of the world."

If only I could find out that he hadn't shaved till after four P.M. or so yesterday, when the suspicious, clean-shaven dog-food salesman came to Mother's door. "Do you know what time he shaved it off? I saw him yesterday morning, and he still had it then."

She shrugged. "He's been talking about taking it off for a while now, but I didn't see him yesterday, except to drop off and pick up Suzanne in the morning. Why?"

"I just . . . I'm afraid he might be involved in all of this mess with Beth Gleason's murder."

"Joel?" she shrieked. "Hah! He wouldn't hurt a fly. I mean, yeah, he tried to pull the fur over your eyes to get you to be interested in him, but that's just Joel. Every week, he falls in love with a different strange woman he happens to pass in the street. Which is not to say that you're strange, or a streetwalker, or anything. Just that . . . well, you know what I mean. Then he concocts these elaborate schemes to run into her again. They never work, but they don't harm anyone, either."

If this was the whole story, I hadn't been "harmed" by his subterfuge, either. Not so long as I got paid for my work with Suzanne.

"So how do you like my dog? She's extremely intelligent, isn't she?"

"Yes," I said with sincerity, though that was one question I never said "no" to; admitting a client's dog was not the brightest thing you'd seen on four paws was the fastest way to lose a client. "And that's all the more reason to train her well. Intelligent dogs are much happier when they know what their owner expects from them and can be challenged accordingly."

"Well, then. That settles it." She patted my arm. "Let's just keep this little meeting to ourselves, shall we? The least we deserve out of all of this is for him to pay you, and for me to get a well-trained dog out of the deal."

"Except that much of my work is with the owner, not just the dog, so I need you—"

"Aah, we can work that out. I'll just insist on joining the two of you on all your training sessions. Joel's in no position to object. Hate to boot you out, but I gotta jam."

"Jam?" Was that radio lingo?

"I gotta find a job." She grinned and leaned toward me,

her wide, square-jawed face just inches from mine. "Say. I've been meaning to tell you. I worked for a couple of years as a dog groomer. I was pretty good, too." She poofed up her own wet-poodle-like hair spikes as she spoke. "Want to hire me as a combination receptionist-slash-groomer?"

"I can't afford to hire a receptionist, and I don't include dog grooming in my services."

"You've got to expand your vision, Al. Think about it. You could call your new business 'A Whole New Woof.' I could clean up their fur; you could clean up their behavior. It can't miss. And, it'll make your work a whole lot easier. See, if the dog looks better, the owners will enjoy being around their dogs more, so they'll naturally think the dog behaves better, too."

"I'll give the matter some thought," I grumbled as I got out of the car.

"Hmm. Well, sounds as though I'd better not hold my breath." She gave me a wave out the window as she took off.

Tracy was nothing if not energetic. And, in this case, perceptive. Much as I admired her humor and spunk, a little of her went a long way. The thought of working every day in the same room with that woman made me shudder.

I drove back to my office. Much to my consternation, there was a silver Mercedes convertible in my parking space. I continued up the hill and found a space on the street, then marched toward my building wondering what kind of ignoramus could miss the reserved-parking sign.

When I arrived, a man was seated in one of the two chairs I'd placed by the entrance. He'd rotated the chair to face away from the glass. Judging by his dark hair and gangly frame, I thought it was Chet Adler. He turned and rose as I opened the door. Bill Wayne, Kaitlyn's husband.

He gave me an uneven—and unappealing—smile. My day was complete. And here it was, not even noon.

"Hello, there," he said. "I found your office."

"So did I. Is that your car in my parking space?"

"Next to the green Volvo?" he asked. To my nod, he replied, "Sorry, but it was the only off-street parking I could find."

As if owning an expensive vehicle necessitates special parking privileges. "What brings you here?"

He chuckled. "Dog troubles. Seems as though I'm still married to one."

I made no comment and held his gaze.

"I see that you've moved out. You told Kaitlyn about my fixing her up on that date, didn't you?"

"You've spoken with her?"

He shook his head. "Her new 'boyfriend' called her to ask her out again last night. He got quite an earful. I wish you hadn't spilled the beans. I told you she'd just be hurt."

This conversation was more than a little annoying. Did he think I had nothing better to do than to worry about his relationship with my ex-housemate? "You got what you wanted from me. I moved out. Why are you here?"

"I drove by my house this morning. Kaitlyn's pretending to be sick so that she can keep guard on the place. Noticed she had cardboard up in one of the windows. Did the two of you have a fight?"

"Mr. Wayne, I'm busy. Please tell me what you want, then leave."

"All right. Here's the deal. Kaitlyn's got some new hiding place for her important papers. I need to know where that is. Before I left town a couple years ago, I had over sixty thousand dollars in a savings account. We'd agreed we wouldn't touch that money. First thing this morning, I went over to the bank to check the balance, and I found out she's been taking two thousand out of the account every month. It's now down to nothing."

He paused and studied me as if to assess the effect his words had had on me. If so, I hoped he could tell that I didn't care. This was Kaitlyn's and his divorce and was of no concern to me.

"I've already served papers on her, and whether she wants to attend or not, the divorce hearing's coming up next week. If I can't find some legal documents to prove she's still got that money, I'm going to lose all of it. Even if I find it, the judge'll split it down the middle, and I'll lose half. But that's better than nothing. I'll pay you a hundred dollars if you can get me the bank statement that can show what she did with my money."

"What makes you so sure she has the money in another account? Maybe she spent it."

"No way. I checked the closet. She hasn't bought so much as a new sweater or done anything to fix up the house since I left."

"Maybe she went on a cruise or two, though. In any case, Mr. Wayne, I am not going to get involved. This is between you and her. She's no longer my roommate. I returned my key, and I have no desire to see her again."

"Five hundred dollars. That's my top offer. I've looked every place I can think of. If I have to go in there again, I'll have no choice but to completely trash the place." He pulled out his key chain while he spoke and removed a brass-colored door key. "Tell you what. I'll give you this, my only copy of the key to the dead bolt."

"I'm not going to help you, regardless of how large you make the fee."

He gave me that smart-aleck smile of his that I so detested. "Don't get involved, then. Let her get away with stealing all of my savings." While he spoke, he pulled a business card out of his pocket. "But, by not helping me, you are helping a woman who once beat an eight-week-old puppy to death for peeing on her bedspread."

While I stared at him in revulsion, he slammed the key and his business card onto the top of my filing cabinet, pivoted on a heel, and strode out the door. In the meantime, alerted by Bill's raised voice, Russell opened the door to his office and stood in the doorway. He looked at me. "Jeez, Allida. Is he telling the truth?"

I shrugged. "I don't know." The image of her throwing that can at my head last night made me shudder. It was possible she'd killed a puppy. Damn Bill Wayne to hell, but now I had to know the truth.

But how? If the puppy had been only eight weeks old, they could only have owned the puppy for a few days at least three years ago. I could talk to the neighbors and see if they remembered the Waynes' owning a puppy, but if they said no, that was no guarantee. Bill had said *he'd* installed the dog door. I might be able to find out if that part was true.

I was not about to accept blood money from him, but if I could find out that Kaitlyn had lied about the puppy, I would gladly turn over to the authorities whatever documentation they needed to make her pay financially. Besides, finding out whether any of his story was true could go a long way toward allaying my fear that he was somehow tied to Beth Gleason's murder. If there really was a ton of money missing from his account, I'd be more inclined to believe that his searching my room the other day had been unrelated to Beth's murder.

The more I thought about it, the more I was certain I knew where Kaitlyn's important documents were hidden. That meant I had to get her out of the house, somehow, while I searched.

I looked at Russell. "You've never met my ex-housemate, Kaitlyn Wayne, have you?"

He shook his head. "No, why?"

"Have you made any plans for lunch?"

Somewhat to my surprise, Kaitlyn's blue Plymouth was not out in front of her house. She might have parked a distance away to lure Bill here though, as she'd done the other day. I slid down in Russell's car so she wouldn't see me and said, "If we're lucky, she's gone in to work. If she's home, tell her Bill Wayne said to meet him at the Food Court in Crossroads Mall."

"Got it, chief," Russell said as he left the car. He rang the doorbell. There was no answer. After waiting a suitable length of time, I came out. Russell, hands cupped over his brow, was peering through the window closest to the door. "Nobody's home," he said as I neared.

I used Bill's key. Russell followed me inside. I went straight to the kitchen and slid the table away from the wall. I'd once noticed that the three-by-six foot section of paneling on this wall was almost falling off. When I'd mentioned it to Kaitlyn, she'd blushed. Russell helped me pull the nails out, which we could manage with just our fingertips, then we removed the section of paneling. As I'd suspected, a section of the Sheetrock behind the paneling had been cut out, forming a sizable—if inelegant—cubbyhole between the studs. I grabbed a brown, manila file folder stashed there.

"Your roommate used to have to move this section of paneling every time she wanted to access her papers?"

"Like I told you on the way here, she's a bit odd." I spread the contents of the folder on the kitchen table. I soon located what I was looking for: the closing papers from the sale of the house.

"I'm in luck. The names of the former owners are Stuart and Linda Perlyon." I'd been worried the former owners would turn out to have the last name of Smith. "If they're still in the area, which is probably a pretty big 'if,' there won't be many Perlyons for me to call."

Russell got me the Boulder directory, and, to my delight, I found the listing for Stuart Perlyon. An elderly sounding woman answered on the third ring.

"Hi. My name is Allida Babcock. I'm a dog psychologist here in town. You don't know me, but—"

"Then why are you calling me?" she snapped.

I winced and tried again. "I'm renting a room at the house you used to own on North Street, and I need to know if you had installed a dog door at that residence."

"Oh, yes. I thought when you said you were a dog psychologist, you meant there was a problem with my poodle."

"No, I haven't met your poodle. Did you install a dog door at your former residence?"

"I already told you. Yes. Heaven knows we've had enough of this particular conversation with the people who bought the house from us."

"With Kaitlyn Wayne?"

"No, with her husband. After they bought the place, some squirrel got into their house through the door. Her husband hounded us for months, saying we owed them a new door. He said he couldn't stand animals and didn't want the door. Even though we legally didn't have to, we finally got so sick of his calls, we sent him a check. You know what? Our friends that live behind the house told us he never replaced the door."

"Huh. That's very helpful information. Thank you so much for your time." I hung up, feeling greatly relieved.

Russell had been fishing through an inch-thick stack of bank statements. "Know what?" he asked. "Bill Wayne's lying. Looks as though he cleared out their joint accounts when he left. She did have a batch of money in a savings account under the name Kaitlyn Feroska, which she moved to another bank right around the time all of her joint accounts were being depleted."

"Let me guess. Three years ago?"

"Right."

I scanned the documentation myself, my jaw clenched in anger at Bill's having manipulated me. "So, he's trying to get half of what little he left her—money she came into the marriage with. What a scumbag. And he wound up tricking me into sinking to his level."

We returned everything to its hiding place. "Now comes the hard part," I said. "I need to tell her about my sneaking a look at her private papers, and warn her about what Bill's been up to."

"Didn't she throw a can at your head the last time you tried that?"

I'd shared that story with Russell on our way over here, but ignored his warning now and dialed Kaitlyn's work number. I told her where I was and that I had "something important to discuss" with her. She agreed to meet me at the house in half an hour, telling me to "make myself at home." That was something I hadn't managed even while living here, but I thanked her and hung up. She must've forgotten that she now had my key and should've wondered how I'd let myself inside.

Russell's stomach growled. He glanced surreptitiously at his watch, then at the refrigerator. "I'd better wait here with you."

"Thanks, but why don't you go get yourself some lunch? I'd rather talk to her alone. This is going to be painful enough for her without witnesses."

"Don't you think you might *need* some witnesses, in case she lashes out at you again?"

I shrugged. "I'll be fine. I'll see you at the office later."

"How? We drove here together in my car."

"I'll get a ride from Kaitlyn, or I'll walk. It's only two miles."

After insisting, despite my protestations, that he was going to come back in half an hour and give me a ride, Russell left. Kaitlyn arrived not five minutes later. I had already cleared any obvious hurlable objects from reach. I sat her down at the table and told her about Bill's visit, and how I'd located her papers in reaction to his assertions. For once, she didn't burst into tears or shout at me, but rather, listened in stunned silence.

When I'd given her the full story, she stayed silent for a long time. Finally, she said quietly, "I can't believe any of this."

"It's the truth, Kaitlyn. I'm sorry."

She sunk her head in her hands and stayed motionless.

"Kaitlyn, why are you trying to hang on to him?"

She straightened, the flash of anger back in her eyes. "He's my life's partner! I need him!"

"No, you don't. You've gotten by completely on your own for three years now. You made the house payments by yourself all that time. You supported yourself completely. You made a life for yourself. You don't need to take this abuse from him."

She averted her eyes and sat with her lips pursed for a minute or two. Finally she said, "You're right. I've wasted years of my life on a man that sees me as a meal ticket. That money was mine, and it was all I had left. He wiped out all of our joint accounts. Next he's going to force me to sell, and I won't even have a place to live."

As she spoke, I remembered something. "A couple of childless friends of mine got divorced last year in Colorado. She told me that the judge split all of their assets right down the middle. If he emptied out your checking account to buy himself a new car, that car counts toward his half of your mutual assets."

"But . . . he always said cars were a waste of money. He drives some beat-up old Chevy Nova."

"Not anymore. He's driving a brand new Mercedes convertible."

Kaitlyn smiled broadly and reached over the table to squeeze my hand. "Oh, my God! That's worth almost as much as my little house!"

"Which would mean, depending on equity, you get the house, he gets the car."

"If what you're saying is true, I might not have to sell my home!" She leapt out of her chair and punched a fist into the air. "Oh, Allida. This is the greatest news I've gotten since Bill moved out! Know how I'm going to celebrate?"

So now Bill's moving out had been *good* news? Quite the emotional reversal on her part, but I learned to expect as much from her. "By calling a window-repair service?"

"No, I already did that. I'm going to buy myself a puppy! One that looks just as much like your Doppler as I can find. And guess who I'm going to hire to train it?"

In a moment of truth, I realized that I really did believe Kaitlyn. For all of her idiosyncrasies—bizarre as they may be—I truly could not believe she would hurt a puppy. "I'd be happy to help you train your puppy, but, Kaitlyn, they take a lot of patience. You can't just, oh, for example, hurl a can at its head when it does something wrong."

"I know that. I've done some thinking, and I realize I really do need some help getting control of my emotions. Do you have any fellow psychologists you'd like to recommend?"

I smiled at the thought of referring her to a dog psychologist. "Not offhand, but don't let that stop you. Also, please remember you have to wait until after the divorce is finalized. Otherwise the puppy will be half Bill's."

"No way I'd let that animal hater near my puppy. I'll tell you that much right now."

That evening, I drove to the senior center where the vegetarian cooking classes were held. I arrived early and got the chance to speak with Naomi Smith, who was already in the kitchen, chopping celery and some long, green vegetable I couldn't identify. Naomi was a pretty woman with a ready smile. She was not much older than I and her hair was about my shade of light-brown, but she was considerably taller. No surprise there.

I introduced myself and explained how I'd come to meet Beth Gleason. "I'm concerned about the possible connection between Hannah Jones's death and Beth Gleason's, who took this class from Hannah a few months ago."

"Ah, yes. I remember Beth. I was saddened to learn about her senseless murder."

"What was Beth's relationship with Hannah?"

Naomi gave a small shrug. "Oh, Beth seemed to want Hannah to mentor her. Beth was a flake, but a reasonably nice one. Hannah liked her more than I did, probably because Beth was so complimentary about Hannah's dog, which was the fast lane to Hannah's heart. Beth was just so spacey, I could only tolerate her in small doses."

That didn't tell me much, except perhaps to verify Susan Corning's version of Beth and Hannah's relationship. "What about Hannah? What was she like?"

Naomi gave me a sad smile and resumed her chopping. "She was one classy lady, believe me. Though she did have a terrible temper. You should've heard the way she screamed at a student for whapping her dog on the nose one time. Hannah booted her out of class and nearly slapped her."

"Really?"

"I don't know if I believed she took her own life. I mean, you can't know a person well enough to be certain about something like that. But I do know that Hannah had a lot to live for. She told me she was investing in a start-up company; her leukemia was in remission. Nothing could have surprised me more than her so-called suicide."

Others had begun to file in, greeting Naomi as they took places around the long kitchen counter. I thanked her and sat in the corner of the kitchen, my mind drifting as she worked with eight students of a wide variety of ages. The oldest students were in their late seventies, at least—a couple—him tall and thin, her short and not thin. They argued ceaselessly about who was to do the chopping versus the measuring and actual cooking.

Afterwards, while we all shared a small portion of the output of the class—ratatouille—I chose to sit at the elderly couple's table, largely because I noticed several long, dark hairs on their pant legs that looked suspiciously like dog hair.

I introduced myself, and the woman gave me a big smile. "I'm Eudora Finch, and this is my husband, Harry Finch."

"You don't need to give both full names like that, Dora," Harry growled over his plate. "You could've just said, 'We're Eudora and Harry Finch.' She'd 've figured out which of us was which."

Eudora sat with pursed lips till he finished, then said pleasantly, "My husband, Harry, is the grouchy old man sitting across from us. What do you do for a living?"

"I'm a dog behaviorist."

Her eyes widened, and she glanced at her husband, who had stopped eating to stare at me. "Did you hear that, Harry?"

" 'Course I heard that! I'm two feet away, for cryin' out loud!"

Undaunted, she beamed at me with slightly yellow but perfectly straight teeth. "You are a godsend!" She wrapped both of her dry hands around my forearm. "We need you to help us. Our dog has stopped eating."

Chapter 18

Every nerve ending in my body snapped to attention. "Your dog stopped eating? Entirely?"

"Oh, well, no," Eudora said. "Not entirely. She just stopped eating her dog food. She'll eat hamburger and the scrapings off our plates."

"When did this start?"

"Last month," Harry said, shoveling the last of his food into his mouth.

"We weren't worried about it at first," Eudora said. "We just assumed she liked her other dog food so much better that she was holding out for that."

"You mean, you'd purchased another brand of food that your dog liked better?"

"Yes, precisely. But the salesman disappeared on us, and there's none of his product in the pet stores yet, though we keep looking and hoping."

Harry growled at his wife, "Told you now that Hannah was dead, we'd never find that brand in a store, but you wouldn't listen."

"What did Hannah have to do with the dog food?" I asked him.

"Clean-up time," Naomi Smith called. All of the students dutifully got up—not counting me. "Who's on broom duty?" Naomi asked.

Since nobody leapt to the forefront, I decided that

"broom duty" was the very least I should do for auditing a class and eating their food. I raised my hand.

Harry took the opportunity of my having my hand in the air to whisk my plate off the table, though I wasn't done. Everyone cleaned remarkably fast, and by the time I'd swept the floor, only the Finches and I remained. Harry was standing in the doorway by then, urging us to hurry.

"How did you meet this salesman, Eudora?" I asked as Harry turned out the light just before we could reach the door.

"Right here. In class. Oh, he seemed like such a nice young man. And it was all natural, fresh ingredients. High on protein, and yet meat-free. He called it Dog TOFUd. Get it? He spelled it 'tofu,' in capital letters, then with a small *d*."

Eudora and I walked slowly down the hall, side by side, while Harry strode in front of us, occasionally glancing back with his face set in a scowl, shaking his head. We soon passed the exit where my car was parked and continued down the long corridor.

"He was all set to have his Dog TOFUd company backed by Hannah Jones," she went on. "It's a vegetarian dog food that's so good, he said our dog would choose it over her regular brand in a taste test. 'Course, we're no fools. We checked it out with Hannah, and she said she was feeding it to her own dog. She owned an adorable collie named Sage. She was going to invest millions for him to produce it, and Harry and I were to buy a lifetime supply, plus get stock options on the ground floor for a mere ten thousand dollars. Guaranteed to triple their worth in two years."

"What was his name?"

"Misty. Only she's a female."

I looked at her in confusion, then realized she thought I

was asking for her dog's name. "No, I mean what was the salesman's name?"

She let out a puff of air. "Heavens. I can't remember. I'm not even sure he ever told us." She cleared her throat, then called to her husband, already half the length of the hallway ahead of us, "Harry? What was the salesman's name?"

He turned, hitched his brown pants higher on his waist to reveal more of his white socks, and said, "Damned if I know." He turned the corner. "You two coming?"

Eudora gave him a wave to indicate that, yes, we were coming—had he been able to see the gesture, that is. We turned the corner of the sprawling, one-story senior center. "I was pretty skeptical at first. Then he demonstrated it right in our own apartment, and sure enough, Misty chose Dog TOFUd over her own brand."

And, I thought sourly, I'll bet the salesman managed to make their own dog food repugnant during the process of this taste test.

"We gave him a check, made out to his company name, and he gave us a four-week supply. Then he suddenly stopped coming to class, and we still can't find him."

"Did you report this to the police?"

She sighed. "No. Not yet. We were . . . starting to think he scammed us, and we didn't want to admit to being the typical, foolish old folks. Kept thinking he'd come back. Will you help us train Misty to eat regular dog food again?"

"Yes." And my treatment program was going to be pro bono to make up, in a small measure, for the con man. We were dealing with a scam artist here, preying on the elderly dog owners of the community. He had some routine going where he surreptitiously poured a repellent on the owner's dog food and brought in his own vegetarian brand.

If he'd mistaken Hannah Jones as being gullible or feeble-minded enough to fall for this ruse and she'd later caught on, perhaps this explained both the tainted dog food and her violent death. Hannah could have been on to his ploy. Perhaps the concept of his having done something so harmful as ruining her beloved dog's food made her so irate she grabbed her gun to threaten him, and things escalated from there.

Furthermore, perhaps Beth, as a former member of the vegetarian cooking class, happened to spot him while she was walking her dog. When Sage started barking at him, she put two and two together, and he killed her to keep her from revealing his identity.

We rounded a second corner and started down yet another long hallway. I'd realized from having seen the outside that this building was large, but this was beginning to feel as though we were traversing the Pentagon. Up ahead of us, Harry now fumbled with the lock to an apartment. A black toy poodle zipped out the door before it was fully opened and slid across the newly waxed floor, paws spread wide, but came to a skittering stop in front of Eudora.

"How is my little girl?" she cooed as she ran her fingers through the tight curls on the dog's head. She turned to me and said, "Misty, this is . . . oh, dear, I've forgotten your name."

"Babcock," her husband called out from inside the apartment. "Allida Babcock."

"Yes, and this is Misty." Eudora held the little dog, who started sniffing, up to me.

"Don't just stand there blocking the door," came Harry's voice. "Let her inside before the flies escape."

I raised my eyebrows at this last phrase, but Eudora clicked her tongue and gave her husband a dismissive gesture. She murmured to me, "That's Harry's idea of a joke. We don't have flies."

"No, but we *will* have if you stand there with the door open all the time."

Eudora marched inside to bicker with her husband, to wit, that he was "an impatient old grouch" and she was "a glue-footed slowpoke." I observed Misty in the meantime. She didn't look undernourished, though she would be eventually if all she ate were the Finches' leftovers. The air inside their small apartment had a certain unpleasant scent to it that I didn't want to mentally analyze, but otherwise the atmosphere was quite pleasant. The furnishings were sturdy and yet nice, augmented with personal bric-a-brac and pictures.

Eudora showed me to Misty's food dish, full of kibble. I scratched the kibble with a nail and then tasted. My mouth was filled with a bitter taste. I explained about the dog repellent to the Finches, then asked if they could please describe the salesman.

They exchanged glances. "Well, let's see," Eudora began. "He was tall, thin, and had a heavy beard. Brown. He had brown hair."

He had a beard a month ago? Joel Meyer! "And how old would you say he was?"

"Oh, twenties. Thirties."

I glanced at Harry, who was shaking his head. "I'd call him chunky. Almost fat. No way was he thin. Really wasn't that tall, either. And he wasn't a day younger than forty. Plus, he was clean-shaven. But she was right about the hair."

My heart sank at the discrepancies. Harry had seemed to have the better memory of the two. If the man was clean-shaven, Joel had to be crossed off my list. "Was his hair curly, straight, wavy?"

"Hard to say. He always wore a fedora, even when he

was inside. Rude, I'd call it. Least it wasn't a backward baseball cap."

This touched off quite an argument about the way the man actually looked. I was now deeply regretting that I'd agreed to come to the apartment before asking the other members and teachers of the cooking class for a description.

"Did he say what type of dog he owned?" I asked.

"A poodle," they answered in unison.

"He said his poodle looked a lot like Misty, but not quite of such obvious show quality," Eudora added.

I nodded appreciatively at Misty, who had that intelligent look in her eyes that I so appreciate in poodles. However, Misty also had large white markings on her chest and stomach that would disqualify her on sight from any professional dog show. The mention of Misty being of "show quality" was such a line, I had a feeling that the slick salesman owned a fictitious dog, which would morph into a slightly inferior version of whatever breed his prospective customers happened to own.

"Did he say what his dog's name was?"

"Goldie," Harry said.

An interesting name for a black poodle—though a common one for a golden retriever. Could this be the pet name the salesman always gave, so as not to trip on the name and spoil his sales pitch? If so, it might be a clue into the breed that the salesman actually did own. Yet the only golden in my client base was George Haggerty's Rex, and George didn't meet either of the Finches' physical description of the man.

Unable to elicit a name or a more thorough description, I decided to wait till tomorrow and give Naomi Smith a call. She should be able to give me both a name and a description of this one-time student.

I described the same procedure to deprogram Misty from her food-aversion training that I'd used successfully on Sage. Eudora assured me they would rather wait till morning to get new brands of dog food, as they were "ready to turn in." Which touched off yet another argument, as Harry insisted this was nowhere near bedtime and he was hoping for a swim. Misty was in no immediate risk, so I jotted down their number and said I'd check on Misty in the morning, then left for home.

I struggled to fall asleep later that night, questions tumbling mercilessly around in my brain. Could I at least be on the right track with the murderer? Was he in fact this dog-food salesman-cum-scam artist?

To my mild surprise the next morning, I'd apparently beaten Russell to work, as his parking space was empty. The moment I reached the bottom step and peered through my glass door, my heart skipped a beat. My office had been trashed. Both filing cabinets were knocked over, papers were strewn all across the floor, and it appeared as though a full carafe of coffee had been poured and splattered all across the room.

This had to be the work of Bill Wayne. He'd heard about my input on the financial finaglings between him and Kaitlyn, and he was seeking an outlet for his rage.

I righted a tipped-over file cabinet. At the noise, Russell rushed out of his office. I was completely surprised he was here.

"I was just trying to reach you at your mother's house," Russell said, holding his hand over his left eye. "She said you'd already left."

"Oh, my God, Russell!" I ran up to him and pulled his hand away from his eye. It was red and starting to swell. It looked painful and I winced in empathy, a gnawing feeling in my stomach. "What happened to you?"

"Someone's car was parked in my space this morning, so I had to park around the block, and by the time I got here, the guy was leaving. I tried to stop him, but he punched me in the eye and took off."

"Who did this? It must have been Bill Wayne. Was he thin and dark-haired, sunken eyes, and—"

Russell shook his head, gingerly covering his injured eye again. "It was that big guy I argued with Saturday morning."

He had to mean Beth Gleason's boyfriend. "Chet Adler?"

"If that was his name. You got any steak? That's supposed to help."

I had some T-bone dog biscuits, but I doubted that would do the trick. "Oh, Russell. That looks so painful." I pulled out my desk chair for him. "Here. Sit down. I'll get you a compress." He sat down while I rushed into the bathroom. We didn't have a washcloth, but I pulled off several sheets of paper towels, folded them, and ran cold water on them. Russell was leaning back in my chair, acting stoic, but the flesh surrounding his left eye was swelling fast. I gently placed the makeshift compress on his eye and found myself sorely tempted to caress his smooth-shaved cheek in the process. I was so disconcerted by this impulse that I jerked away rather abruptly and asked, "Have you called the police?"

"I didn't get the chance. You really only just missed him yourself by a minute or two."

On the desk behind Russell, my computer and printer were on. "I'll bet he printed out my client file."

"He had a couple sheets of paper that might have come from your printer."

"Dammit! Now he's got the phone numbers and addresses of my clients! He thinks one of them killed his girlfriend and that he needs to avenge her. I should have used some system security." When I'd set up my software, I couldn't imagine why anyone other than me would want to look at files about dog owners.

I called the police station and reached the soft-spoken detective. "Chet Adler broke into my office, stole my client listing, and punched my officemate in the face."

After a slight pause, the detective asked, "Adler is Beth Gleason's boyfriend, right?"

"Yes, and he told me he wanted to speak to my clients because he's sure one of them killed Beth."

"Did he say what gave him that idea?"

"No, not really. I guess it's just the connection between me and Sage, Hannah Jones and then Beth Gleason's dog."

There was another pause. "I don't follow. Why would Mr. Adler think the dog was significant?"

I grimaced but resisted the urge to stomp my foot. I'd been through all of this with the police before. Weren't they talking to one another? "Ever since I did that radio show, which talked about the possibility that Sage could identify Hannah Jones's killer, I've gotten some new clients who may or may not be after the dog through me. Now Chet's a loose cannon who's going to harass all my clients. He already trashed my office and punched Russell, and I want you to arrest him before he hurts someone else!"

"Calm down, miss."

"I *was* perfectly calm till you implied this break-in was just some isolated incident!"

"Let me assure you, we've got a lot of first-rate officers working on this case. I'll send someone out to take a formal report, then we can put out an arrest warrant for Mr. Adler."

He hung up before I could respond. My fear was that Chet Adler was the least of my concerns. I'd felt threatened into moving out of Kaitlyn's house. Someone had attempted to poison my dogs, and who knows what might have happened had Mom let the "organic dog food" salesman into the house. How much longer could this go on?

I dialed Naomi Smith's number. Her recorder kicked on after four rings. I left a message to call me, then went back to ministering to Russell, who was now milking his injury for all it was worth. But then, I really did feel indebted to him for trying to help me.

Half an hour later, Russell and I talked to a uniformed female officer, then I left for my scheduled morning appointment with Rex and George Haggerty. I was still wondering about the connection to him—his being my one bald client and having a name so similar to that of the door-to-door salesman wearing the toupee.

George greeted me with the statement, "Great news, Miss Babcock! I took your advice and faked Rex into thinking I'd left, and I caught Rex in the act of chewing on the furniture three times!"

"That *is* good news," I told him sincerely, though I knew how odd it was to be pleased that the dog was still gnawing away at the furniture.

"Yes, and this morning, I tried the same thing twice, for fifteen minutes the first time and over half an hour the second, and he was good the whole time. So, I hate to tell you this, Ms. Babcock, but after today, Rex no longer requires your services."

"Oh?" This was one downside of this job—there are few other professions in which one can be fired by a dog. "Isn't that just a tad optimistic on your part? I agree that Rex has responded to his reconditioning very nicely, but he still hasn't made it through an entire workday alone, has he?"

"No, but he has stopped jumping on me and now lets me lead on leash. And my wife agreed with your suggestion to build a pen for him. We've hired a contractor and everything. In fact, we're getting all new furniture. I already tried to get Goodwill to take the stuff Rex chewed on, but they said it was in too lousy shape. Makes me feel like quite the schlep when my own living room furniture isn't even good enough to give away to a charity."

The thought of a whole new living-room set under Rex's domain made me nervous, and I tried to warn George that trying to adjust a two-year-old dog who'd always stayed inside to life in a pen could be a challenge. George was a true optimist, however, so we worked on more of the basics of asserting oneself as the dog's master. At the end of the hour, I tested him by asking, "A salesman came to my door the other day who reminded me of you."

George showed no trace of nerves, but rather smiled and asked, "Really? What was he selling?"

"Organic dog food."

He chuckled. "I wonder what that means—organic dog food."

"That it's made from various organs, I guess." I studied him at length, trying to imagine him with a black Presley-like wig on, and concluded that my mother simply could not have mistaken him for a muscular man in his thirties. The talk of "organic" dog food reminded me of something. John O'Farrell had said he owned a health-food store. That could be how he got to know Hannah Jones. Could he sell "organic" dog food at this store?

"If you have any questions or concerns about Rex, don't hesitate to call."

George smiled. "Oh, we won't. You're number eight on our speed dialer on our phone."

"I'm honored." As long as numbers one through seven weren't dog psychologists, too.

When I came out, Chet Adler was seated on the hood of my car. I hesitated, considering doubling back and having George call the police, but reasoned that Chet was unlikely to do anything violent, or he would have hidden from my view.

I marched up to Chet, who was regarding me coolly. "I take it you got this address off my computer, right?"

"Maybe I just happened to be in the neighborhood. Already checked him out, though. That wimp couldn't possibly have gotten Beth's knife away from her. She was too strong and too tall for him." He spat, then dragged his sleeve across his mouth. "None of your other clients were home this morning."

"You broke the law, Chet. Both by breaking into my office and trashing it, and by assaulting Russell. What do you think you're accomplishing? Are you trying to get yourself thrown in jail, along with Beth's killer?"

He stared at the ground. "Don't have to worry about that. They're never going to get the guy who did this. Shit. I just want to look the guy in the eye, one time. I want him to tell me why he did it."

My heart was pounding. I found Chet utterly intimidating, with his large frame and violent undertones, and he was still seated on my car. "Then what? You're going to beat him to a pulp, aren't you?"

Chet rose and pointed at me. "The bastard'll deserve every instant of it! He's not worth one-tenth of what Beth's worth! She was the only one who ever treated me like a human being!"

"And then you'll get arrested and convicted. Even if you try to run, you won't be able to avoid arrest for long. To avenge the death of the one person who said you were worthwhile, you'll make your own life worthless. Do you really want to betray Beth's faith in you this way?"

He shouted in my face, "You don't get it, do you? My life already is worthless. Whoever killed Beth Gleason saw to that." He shoved past me, got into his own car parked farther down the road, and drove off.

My hands were shaking as I started my engine. What was taking the police so long to arrest Chet? I'd given them a printout of my clients' addresses and numbers. Yet here he'd been, biding his time at my very first appointment. I drove back to the office, largely to check on Russell. My heart leapt to my throat at the sight of a silver Mercedes convertible parked in my space. Bill Wayne had come to call.

"What now?" I asked myself aloud. Sadly, I was getting used to the thought that all visits from my fellow humans were going to wind up as confrontations. I parked nearby, rushed into my office, and found Kaitlyn's husband pacing the floor.

At the sound of the door opening, he pivoted to face me. "You think you're smart, don't you?" His normally haggard features were even more so now. He had a naturally heavy beard, which had two days' growth, and the dark circles around his sunken eyes were more noticeable than ever.

"Pardon?"

"Kaitlyn called that real estate agent I'd been working with and said that she wasn't going to owe me a penny for the house. That we have less equity in the house than my car is worth! I bought that car with my own money after I left her! That car is mine!"

"Yes, and I'm sure you feel the same ownership over your car that she feels regarding her house. She's been paying that mortgage by herself since you left."

"You bitch! You'd better watch your backside, 'cause I'll get you for this! That's a promise!"

With what must have been tremendous reluctance, Russell Greene, black eye and all, emerged from his office and asked, "Is there a problem here?"

"Yeah, man!" Bill shouted, pointing at me. "She's the problem! But she won't be for long!" Bill stormed out the door and up the cement steps.

Moments later, we could hear him revving his engine and trying to peel out of my parking space. Then there was an almost instantaneous honk, the squeal of brakes, and a crash. We both raced through the door and up the steps, just in time to see Bill emerging from his beloved vehicle, which had smashed into a tree. Another driver in a minivan called out his window to Bill, "I'll call the police on my cell phone."

"Did you see that?" Russell asked in awe.

"Just goes to show. There is a God. And He's got a sense of humor."

My phone was ringing as I returned to my office. The instant I answered, a sexy male voice said, "Allida, this is Dennis Corning. I need to talk to you. I'm on my car phone and can be there in ten. That all right by you?"

"Sure, why not?" I hung up. Come on down. Yell at me. Threaten me. Everyone else does. I was beginning to feel resigned to my own fate, which bothered me immensely, but I wasn't sure I could do much to change my mood.

"Another customer?" Russell asked hopefully as he returned to his office.

"Another hostile man who happens to own a dog."

Russell stopped and glanced nervously at our entrance. This was so demeaning. All Russell ever saw of me was men coming into my office to shout at me. Russell said, "I have a meeting with some prospective customers to attend. Want me to postpone it so I can stick around and help you circle the wagons?"

"Nah. I'll be fine. If nothing else, the police will be outside soon to help with the accident."

He offered again to stay, but let me convince him I'd be fine alone. I had a feeling he was going to have a hard enough time winning this job despite his black eye without having to reschedule at the last minute. It finally struck me that he'd returned my office to its former neatness while I'd been at George's—and I hadn't even thanked him.

A few minutes later, Dennis arrived, looking dapper as ever in an impeccable Italian suit. He waggled his thumb over his shoulder as he entered my office. "Did you know there's a grown man, sitting on the curb and crying, just outside your door?"

"He just crashed his Mercedes."

"Poor devil," he said, his voice rife with empathy.

"If you came here to berate me over my giving Sage to someone—"

"No, no. That's not at all why I'm here. Quite the opposite, in fact. I had a lengthy talk with my wife. Seems I owe you an apology. My wife thinks you're brilliant. We're going to refer our friends to you. In the meantime, I wondered if we could also hire you to help us select the right collie puppy for our family."

"Yes, I'd be happy to." His mention of his wife brought to the forefront a niggling thought I'd almost forgotten—Susan Corning's almost desperate need to explain how Beth Gleason had known to call *them* about adopting Sage. Beth had possessed one of those long-limbed bodies that men seem to find attractive, she'd come from a wealthy family, and she'd had terrible taste in men.

He nodded. "Well, I left my engine running and I'd better get out of there. I don't want anyone to swipe my Beamer." He pivoted and reached for the door handle.

"Were you and Beth Gleason lovers?" I asked, in a rare show of bluntness that froze him where he stood.

He turned toward me. His face gave me my answer. It bore the look of a dog, caught in a major act of disobedience. "What makes you ask that?"

"Just some things Beth said to me before she died."

He jammed his hands in his pockets and rocked on his heels for a long moment. Finally, he shrugged and said,

"It was just an innocent fling. A one-night stand. Don't tell my wife, okay? That'd break her heart."

"I won't say a word, provided you can convince me you didn't kill Beth."

"I *didn't* kill her! What possible motive would I have had? Jeez, if I killed every woman I slept with, I'd be right up there with Son of Sam."

My phone rang, and I picked up the handset instead of responding to Dennis. Before I could get as much as a hello out, my mother shouted at me, "Allida! Sage is gone! He got out of the yard somehow. Maybe he jumped the fence. I just don't know. I'm locking Doppler inside the house and heading out now with Pavlov to try to track him down. Come home right away!"

Chapter 19

This was my personal version of hell: driving a long distance through slow traffic to be able to join the useless search for my missing dog. I tried to tell myself that Sage had simply leapt the fence. If so, we would find him. A collie was an unusual and unmistakable sight. We would be able to talk to neighbors and trace his route. To keep my maniacal driving to a minimum, I mollified myself over and over again with the image of Sage leaping the six-foot wire-mesh fence surrounding our yard. It was possible. Just extremely unlikely.

I reached the Boulder-Longmont Diagonal, where traffic normally averaged ten miles above the speed limit but now seemed slow. If the killer had Sage, what would his next move be? The answer to that question was painfully obvious. My eyes filled with tears. I swiped them away impatiently and shouted at myself, "Think! Use your brain!"

How long would he keep Sage alive? He'd killed Hannah Jones with her own gun, but since that was ruled a suicide, he couldn't have possession of the gun now. He'd stabbed Beth Gleason, and as far as I knew, he'd used her weapon—her switchblade. This weapon he'd kept.

The cars ahead of me were braking for the red light at the intersection in front of the IBM plant. I smacked the heel of my hand against the steering wheel in frustration, but stopped the car, my heart pounding.

"He probably doesn't have a gun," I told myself aloud. Grisly as the thought was, it would be difficult to kill a collie with a knife. He'd tried to poison Sage yesterday, but Pavlov had foiled him. He might try that again now. If so, we might have some time. Sage would be too distressed to eat for quite a while.

"Oh, God," I murmured. Here I was, clinging to the hope that Sage was suitably upset not to eat—which would make him bark and call more attention to himself and possibly force the killer's hand.

I was driving way too fast now. Damn! The one time when I'd welcome getting pulled over so that I could try and enlist the police's help, and there were no patrol cars to be seen.

Traffic on the streets surrounding Longmont was bumper-to-bumper, and once again I lost precious minutes. My mom was as much of an expert in retrieving lost dogs as anyone could be. She would be out canvassing the neighborhood—talking to the postman, neighbors, people in parks. Pavlov was a good tracker, but I'd only trained her for the basics. She wouldn't be able to follow Sage's scent if the killer put Sage in that damned white car and drove off with him.

What about that car? Chet Adler, Dennis Corning, Keith/ Alex, Bill Wayne, Joel Meyer, George Haggerty, John O'Farrell. None of them drove a white sedan. Yet I could not believe that there was somebody behind all of this who'd never come into contact with me. Ever since my spot on Tracy's radio show, the evil acts had seemed to be choreographed around me. The killer had been keeping a careful watch, to learn what I knew or didn't know.

The white sedan must be a rental. The police could probably trace all of the white rental cars currently on loan throughout the area, which could take several hours, if not days. There had to be a faster way.

At last, I reached the perimeter of Berthoud and slowed down. If Sage were—pray to God—left to his own devices, he would head toward Boulder, probably toward Hannah Jones's house. Each time I spotted pedestrians, I pulled over and asked if they'd seen a collie within the last hour. No luck.

I reached the house. I pulled up in front, shut off the engine, snatched the keys out of the ignition, and raced up the brick walkway. I unlocked the door and threw it open, yelling, "Mom? Pavlov?" No answer. Doppler rushed up to greet me, his tail wagging madly, but I dashed to the kitchen, slid open the back door and again called, "Mom?"

The yard was empty. Doppler followed my every step, and as I locked the back door again, he lay down on his back, desperate for a show of affection. I knelt and patted him. "Good dog, Doppler. I'll get Sage back."

Yet how? I wanted to call in the blasted cavalry.

I headed through the front door to try to find Mom and Pavlov. Apparently having spotted my car, they were coming up the walkway as I locked the door behind me. Pavlov's ears were pricked up and she moved with noticeable tense energy.

"This is all my fault," Mom said without preamble. I hadn't seen her this crestfallen since her beloved golden retriever had died. "Pavlov and Doppler wanted to be inside and Sage wanted to stay out back. I didn't have Pavlov out there with him."

I shook my head and met her at the porch steps. "We can assess blame later. But how did this happen, Mom? You had the two dogs inside with you, right? But Sage never barked? And next thing you knew, he was gone?"

"Yes. I heard the sound of the pump going like a faucet had been turned on, full blast. I discovered it was the tap in front of the house. I went to shut it off and saw that someone had run a hose into the basement window well.

I assumed it was some kids playing a prank, and I ran down into the basement to check for flooding. Pavlov and Doppler followed me. I got preoccupied cleaning up the water, and I forgot about Sage, alone in the backyard."

"Jeez," I murmured. The kidnapping had been carefully orchestrated. There went the slim hope that Sage had merely leapt the fence. I felt I had to say something encouraging. "Maybe Sage managed to run away from the guy."

Just then, the neighbors across the street gave a little wave as they started to pull into their driveway. We gestured at them to wait and, Pavlov in tow, jogged over to them. They both rolled down their windows. I was too upset to remember their names.

"Have you seen our collie?" Mom asked, leaning to look in the window on the driver's side. In the meantime, I rounded the car to the passenger side where Mrs. Neighbor sat.

"That man took him," their daughter piped up from the backseat. She was in kindergarten, I knew, so she must have been about five.

Her parents turned around and looked at her. "What do you mean?"

"I was playing. I saw him. He was a big man. He had the Lassie's mouth in a cage."

"You mean the dog was in a muzzle?" I asked her.

"Uh-huh." She nodded at me. "The Lassie didn't want to go, but the man was dragging him. Then he picked him up and pushed him in the backseat."

"Did this man see you, Melanie?" her mother asked.

"No. I was playing. With stick boats. In the ditch."

"Oh, Melanie! How many times do I have to tell you—"

"What did this man look like?" I asked, cutting off the woman and her ill-timed lecture.

"He was big. He had brown hair."

"What color was his car?"

"It was white."

I straightened. Mom thanked the neighbors while they chattered away with apologies about not having known anything about this till just now. Mom said that, yes, it would be helpful if they contacted Sheriff Millay on our behalf. Then they pulled into their garage, leaving Mom and me standing there in disbelief.

"What have I done?" Mom said in a frightened whisper. She whirled on a heel and headed back toward the house. She still had a grip on Pavlov's leash, and the dog obediently trotted off after her. Mom sank down to sit on the top step of the front porch. I caught up to her, wishing I had something encouraging to offer.

"How could I have been so stupid?" she asked, shaking her head in shock. "I never put two and two together. Why didn't I stop to realize that there was a reason somebody chose now to pull a prank and flood the basement?"

"Maybe he won't . . ." I couldn't bring myself to say the word kill. ". . . hurt Sage. Maybe he'll drive him a long way away and let him go, assuming he'll never get back."

"But why? Why take the dog?"

"Sage was the link to the crime. To both murders. The guy felt like he couldn't take the risk of running into the dog sometime in the future and getting cornered." I started pacing. The hell with the cavalry! I wanted every person in Boulder to help me look for Sage!

A thought hit me. It was a long shot and probably wouldn't work. At least it was something I could do toward getting Sage back unharmed.

I snatched Pavlov's leash from Mom's loose grip. "Mom, I'm taking Pavlov back to Boulder with me while I talk to somebody who might be able to help us. Stay here and see if Sheriff Millay can do anything on this end. I'll be back as soon as I can."

With Pavlov in the backseat, I drove, mulling my plan. If I could get radio stations to put out a broadcast for listeners to be on the lookout for a muzzled collie transported in a white sedan, I might at least make things harder on the killer. Halfway to Boulder, I realized that my idea had at least one serious flaw: I needed to enlist Tracy Truett's help, and I didn't even know where she lived. I pulled off at a gas station just outside of Boulder and asked to use their phone book. There were no listings under the name "Truett."

I headed straight to Joel Meyer's house, hoping he'd be home and could get me in touch with Tracy. To my surprise, her little sports car was in the driveway. I sent up a quick prayer as I rang the doorbell. No one answered at first, so I rang a second time. Joel opened the door, wearing nothing but jeans. Though it was late afternoon, his hair was mussed as if he'd just gotten out of bed. He looked surprised to see me.

"Joel, is Tracy here?" I asked before he could even say hello.

He looked over his shoulder, and Tracy emerged from behind him, wearing nothing but a man's shirt. Her spiked hair was flat in telltale places, and her makeup was smeared. "Holy crow, is this embarrassing."

"Never mind that," I said, letting myself in and closing the door behind me. "You've got to help me. Do you have any friends in Boulder radio stations? Deejays who'll broadcast a lost dog ad?"

"Oh, honey, have you ever come to the right place. I know everybody, and they'd do that for me in a heart-beat. What's the matter? Lost your cocker?"

"No. Sage. The collie. He's been stolen. I'm afraid that's just the beginning." I looked up at Joel and wished I could discuss this out of his presence. I still hadn't ruled him off my list of suspects. Unless he had an alibi. "Um, Tracy? Have you been here all afternoon?"

She chuckled slowly and clung on Joel's bare arm. "Yep. All afternoon." She cast moon-eyes Joel's way, who also gave me a meaningful grin. As if I cared about his sexual prowess! All I cared about was the fact that this meant he couldn't have grabbed Sage two hours ago!

"Your former radio station. KBXD. Is there any chance we could air one last show? Tonight?"

"You want to get the entire station up and running after it's been closed down for half a week? To broadcast a show to get your dog back?"

I nodded.

She put her hands on her ample hips and eyed me at length. "Holy crow, kid. When you ask for favors, you don't mess around, do you?"

"I'm afraid I'll never see Sage alive again unless we can force his kidnapper to give him back. If returning Sage is the only way he can prevent having his crime and a description of his car broadcast all across the Denver-metro area, including to the police, he might give in."

Tracy shook her head. "No can do, kiddo. Sorry. The FCC would have a hissy fit. I'd lose my license. We have no way to—"

Joel interrupted, "All you'd need would be me to switch on the generators and get the broadcast antenna operational again, Greg to work the control boards, and you to do the interview. I've still got a set of keys to the place."

Tracy's jaw dropped, and she stared at him. "But the station owners will have us arrested for trespassing! I'll never be allowed to broadcast again!"

"You said you wished you could have gone out with a big splash," Joel said. "Now's your chance."

She sighed but nodded. "Let me see what I can do. If I

pull every string I can and call in every card, I might be able to get something going by sometime tonight." She sat down Indian style and pulled the phone over to her. "I'm assuming, if we can get a broadcast going, you want me to get other stations to advertise to be on the lookout for him, right?"

"That and to listen to the show tonight."

"Wait. You expect me to get a deejay to do a spiel for you advertising someone else's radio station?"

"Yes, but it'd just be this one, emergency broadcast."

"And from this, you hope to gain what? Hasn't it occurred to you that he might come to the station to stop you?"

"Of course. That's why I'll be alerting the police first, so they can catch the guy."

Tracy stared at me for a long moment, her large jaw agape. Then she picked up the phone. Glancing over her shoulder at Joel, she said, "I'm calling Greg and having him head over to the station. I think he's still on KBXD's payroll through the end of the week. He'll get in the least amount of trouble for unlocking the building." She punched the numbers, and in a moment, was barking into the phone, "Greg, Tracy. Get down to the station now. We're airing the show one last time." She cut off Greg's response with "Trust me. We'll see you there as soon as I get everything arranged. And don't say a word about this to anyone. Got that?"

Greg's protests, audible even to me from halfway across the room, were cut off as Tracy hung up on him.

"Think of the drama," Tracy said wistfully. " 'Allida Babcock to reveal the killer's identity. Tonight at nine P.M. KBXD. The *Tracy Truett Show*.' " She grinned and shivered slightly. "God. I like the sound of that."

I might like it too, if only I knew who the killer was.

But pointing this out to Tracy would only dim her enthusiasm, which I desperately needed.

She turned her gaze toward me. "The catch will be, though, we can't notify the police too far in advance, or they'll stop us. Let's not forget that we are going to be trespassing at the station. That means the other broadcasts can't advertise this too far ahead, either." She snapped her fingers. "I'll bet they'd be willing to pick up our feed! We might be able to get on every radio show in the city! Maybe even in the country!"

Joel had left the room and came back a minute later fully dressed. "I'd better head down to the station early and start refamiliarizing myself." He bent over and kissed Tracy passionately. "See you later."

We managed to pull the whole thing together for a broadcast at eight P.M. A somewhat irritable Greg—wearing the same Boyz II Men T-shirt he'd worn last Friday—let Tracy, Pavlov, and me in at seven-thirty. Tracy, too, had changed into the same light blue pants suit she'd worn the first time we met. "Joel here?" she asked, needing to shout to be heard over music that was blaring from the loud speakers.

Greg nodded. His forehead was damp with perspiration, and he stared through the lobby window as if expecting us to be followed by storm troopers. "He got here almost the same time I did. Trace, this has got to be the stupidest—"

Tracy held up her palms and brushed past him. "Never mind all that. You owe me a favor."

"I sure as hell do not! If anything, you owe me one!"

"If that's true, after tonight, I'll owe you two. 'Sides, it's not as though life's fair, my dear." She beckoned to me to follow as she marched into the hallway.

I paused long enough to thank Greg and apologize for

railroading him. To my annoyance, Tracy and Joel were embracing in the sound booth by the time I arrived. This was hardly the appropriate time. Neither of them could be expected to harbor my same gut-wrenching concern for Sage—but still!

Pavlov was jumpy and didn't want to follow me into the room, but obeyed my commands with obvious reluctance. I had brought her with me as a last line of defense for Tracy and me in the broadcast booth, itself. To my surprise, she growled and barked at Tracy and Joel.

Joel took a step back, watching Pavlov warily. She was clearly picking up on my tension. "Break a leg, girls," he said, then left the room. Tracy grinned as she watched him leave. I picked up the phone to dial 911. The line was dead.

"The phone doesn't work!" I cried to Tracy.

"That's 'cause it's completely controlled by the producer." She gestured at the interior window where Greg had just entered the control room, but his back was turned. Tracy grabbed her earphones and said into the microphone, "Greg? Allida needs to call out." He turned and nodded, then flipped a switch.

I dialed 911. My mouth went dry and I felt nauseated. I'd never done anything this risky—not to mention illegal— before. I said to the male dispatcher, "My name is Allida Babcock. I'm at KBXD. In twenty minutes, we're putting on a live broadcast during which I'm going to threaten to air the name of Beth Gleason's and Hannah Jones's killer. Unless the killer calls in and agrees to release my collie."

"Uh, ma'am, I'm not sure I understand what—"

"I need you to notify the police and surround the station, so that we'll be protected, in case the killer tries to physically stop the broadcast."

"Just hold on, ma'am. Give me the name of this person you're going to broadcast and let the police handle this."

"I don't know the name, or I'd have done that hours ago!"

"But—"

"Just get the SWAT team out here! Please!" I hung up.

Tracy watched me, her square chin resting on her hand. She rolled her eyes. "This is, like, so nutty I can't even believe it. The police are just going to storm in here and arrest us. You do realize that, don't you?"

"Maybe so, but if we don't at least try, Sage is dead." If he isn't already, I thought in despair. My hope was that the killer didn't have a gun and wasn't going to be able to easily kill a frightened, fighting collie with a knife.

Joel leaned in the door of the booth with five minutes to airtime. "Listen, babe," he said to Tracy, "a police car just pulled up outside. I'm going to talk to him and see if I can buy you some time. Good luck."

Pavlov whined and tried to shove past him. I scolded her, but reasoned that she was only picking up on the incredible tension in the room. I wanted to bolt out of here myself, so how could I blame my dog for wanting to leave?

In the meantime, Tracy flashed a huge smile Joel's way. "Love ya," she said just as he closed the door. She winked at me. "Show time! I figure I owe you this, for your having lousy taste in men and not falling for Joel yourself."

I had a major case of cotton mouth, but there was no backing out now. Moments later, Tracy was introducing me, and the next thing I knew, I was blathering about how I needed anyone who'd seen a muzzled collie in a white sedan to call the station, and that I knew the killer's identity and would broadcast his name at precisely nine P.M. to the police and everybody else if he didn't have Sage safe and sound at the station by that time.

Before I'd finished speaking, Tracy said, "We've got our first caller. Russell? You're on the air."

"Allida? Why are you doing this?" It was Russell Greene.

"I'm trying to save a beautiful collie's life. I want Sage back here safe and sound by nine P.M., or I'm broadcasting the killer's identity."

There was a pause, then Russell said, "If the person who took the dog is out there, just call my cell phone, and I'll come get him myself." Worried for Russell's safety, I shook my head wildly at Tracy as he continued, "Let me take the risks. My number is—"

Tracy flipped a switch and said, "Sorry, Russell, but we need to keep the lines open for anyone with information about Sage's current whereabouts. If we need you to act as middleman, my producer will call you."

I breathed a sigh of relief.

Tracy gave me a reassuring wink as she said into the microphone, "Once again, this is Tracy Truett, and I'm with Allida Babcock, dog psychologist here in Boulder who has just had her collie stolen. The collie can identify the killer of . . . who did you say, Allida?"

"Beth Gleason. Also Hannah Jones. Her death was made to appear like a suicide but was actually a homicide."

"Right. Yes. This is where it's happening on the airwaves tonight, I'll tell you. So whoever's got Sage, you'd better call in before it's too late, or my petite friend here's going to spread your name like margarine."

I furrowed my eyebrows, and she shrugged in an unspoken apology for her lame analogy. Greg must have made some remark to her over the earphones as well, for she made an obscene gesture to him through the window of the control booth.

"My fine-feathered producer here has just notified me that we have another caller." She pressed a button. "Hello,

Mr. Caller-person. I understand you didn't want to give your name to my producer. Is there a reason for that?"

In an ominous, low whisper, a male's voice said, "Just wanted to ask Allida there if she's checked her basement lately."

My heart leapt to my throat. "What do you mean?"

"You know how easily these basements around Colorado can flood. Especially when you leave a tap outside running."

"Bring Sage back! Now!"

He hung up.

Tracy's face had gone completely white. She signaled to Greg. "Let's go to commercial break. Be right back with more on this breaking story." Greg must have said something in her earphones, for she said, "Of course I know we don't have any sponsors! I don't care if you put on elevator music! I need a minute!"

"Oh my God," Tracy said, her face immediately damp with perspiration. "That was the guy, wasn't it?"

I nodded.

"Tell me everything you know about him," Tracy said, not meeting my eyes.

"He met both Beth and Hannah through a vegetarian cooking class. He was trying to market a totally vegetarian dog food, and was . . . ."

I let my voice fade. Tracy had risen and was shaking her head.

"We gotta get out of here!" she said.

She'd once said she never forgot a voice. "You know who it is, don't you?" I asked.

She flipped a switch and pushed the earphone tighter against her head. She waved at Greg, who was rapt with something else and ignored her. Rolling her eyes in frustration she said into the mike, "Hey, there, Boulder. If mister Greg-head would help me out for a moment here,

I was just about to suggest we put on a little appropriate music, such as, 'Help Me Make It Through the Night,' or 'How Much Is That Doggy in the Window?' " Again she flipped a couple of switches, and said, "Greg?" into the mike.

Greg was apparently speaking to somebody on the phone and couldn't hear a word Tracy was saying. Suddenly, his jaw dropped. He tore off his headphones and left the control booth.

I glanced at Tracy. "Christ," she muttered, starting to cry. "Greg can't hear us. He's got the whole thing rigged. We're toast!"

My heart started to pound. There was only one person, other than Greg, who could have "rigged" anything at the station.

Dear God! Joel must be planning to kill us all and frame Greg! I headed toward the door and asked over my shoulder, "Why did you lie to me about his alibi?" I tried to push the solid door open. It didn't budge. I whirled around and tried the nearby door to the control room. Locked. "We're locked in here!"

"What do you mean it's locked? The door to the hall-way can't be locked!"

"It's bolted from the outside!"

The lights went out. Tracy let out an ear-piercing scream. Pavlov barked wildly. A moment later a male voice cried in a singsong voice over the room's loudspeakers, "And Bingo was his name-oh!"

Chapter 20

The blackness was all but absolute. The sound booth, hallway, and control room were all inner rooms, with no exterior windows. I stumbled back toward my chair. Across the table from me, Tracy Truett was making terrified whimpers. In the vicinity of the locked doors behind me, Pavlov was still barking.

"Pavlov, cease!"

She instantly stopped, but let out a low growl.

"Why did you bring that big German shepherd with you, Allida?" the voice asked. "Do you think I'm going to let a little thing like a dog stop me from killing you?"

He laughed. The disembodied and amplified voice in the blackness was terrifying. Pavlov was likely all that was preventing Joel's immediate attack. Did Joel know how much better dogs can find their way through the dark than humans can? Maybe there was a way to use that to my advantage.

I felt around the butcher-block table for the phone. I grabbed the handset. There was no dial tone. I dropped it in disgust and said under my breath to Tracy, "You told me Joel was with you all afternoon. I believed you!"

"I thought he was," Tracy sobbed. "But I nodded out for a couple of hours. He claimed he did, too, but he must have drugged me."

At least this meant there was a slim chance Sage was

still alive. Joel had had very little time to snatch Sage, ditch the white rental car, and get back to his house with no blood on his clothing in time for Tracy to be his alibi. Plus, Greg had said that Joel arrived almost the same time he did . . . and again, no blood on Joel's clothing.

Tracy's whimpers turned to halting sobs. "I can't stand the dark! You know that! Don't do this to me!"

"Turn the lights on, Joel," I shouted to no avail. Tracy made sputtering, raspy noises. She was losing it. That there were two of us in addition to Pavlov was our only real advantage. I had to help Tracy keep her wits.

I fumbled my way around the table to stand beside her. I grabbed her arm and said into her ear, "He must be in the control room. Can you control the lighting to this room from there?"

No answer, just quiet sobbing.

"Tracy!" I cried in as loud a whisper as I dared. "You have to hold yourself together!"

She took a noisy breath. "That room's the brains for the entire building."

I had to get in there, somehow. I had to turn the broadcast back on and notify the police that the killer had us trapped. "Can Joel hear us?" I whispered.

"If he wants to. He can hear us through the mikes. His control panel for the microphones works the same as mine."

"Sorry I had to cut your broadcast short," Joel said. "I'm broadcasting a nice little tape I spliced together this afternoon, and I just needed to air enough of the live broadcast to con the police. I've got Greg's fingerprints on the tape and everything. It'll take the police a good half hour to figure out what's going on. By that time, it'll look as though I killed Greg in self-defense after he killed the two of you."

My eyes adjusted to what minuscule incidental lighting there was. I could make out Tracy's and Pavlov's silhouettes. Pavlov was pacing in front of the doors to the hallway and the control room where Joel Meyer had enthroned himself. "We need to disconnect all but one microphone."

"I can hea-r-r you," Joel taunted. "Don't think you can outsmart me, ladies. Let's not forget, I'm the one with the switchblade that's going to slit your throats! Allida, if you want to save your shepherd's life, tie her up! Now!"

Tracy still took rasping breaths as if she were suffocating, but rapidly pulled microphone jacks out from the control panel in front of her. In the meantime, I blindly disconnected two microphones and pushed them and their heavy stands to one side of the table. We now had a couple of makeshift weapons to defend ourselves. Also, we could now control what Joel could or could not hear us say.

I grabbed this last live mike, covered it with my hand, and whispered into Tracy's ear, "Take this mike. Keep him talking. When I say 'Now,' turn the volume all the way up and scream into the mike as loud as you can."

"Plotting something, girls? I wouldn't bother. Your only exits are bolted shut. I control every piece of electronic equipment from in here. So let me tell you my demands. If you do what I say, I'll turn the lights back on, okay, Trace?"

"You tell him no deal or we'll never get out of here alive," I whispered.

"I want the lights on!" she whispered back angrily.

"The darkness is our only advantage, " I retorted.

"Well? I'm waiting," he taunted.

"What do I need to do?" Tracy asked him.

"Use one of the cables to the microphones you just disconnected, and tie up that dog. As soon as it's done, I'll turn on the lights."

"No way," I answered for her. "Pavlov, come." She trotted over, and I unbuckled her collar. Now Joel wouldn't have an easy means to grab hold of her and control her.

He chuckled. "Al, you haven't seen how Tracy gets when she's caught in the dark, have you? Let me put it this way. If I were you, I'd be more afraid of being trapped in a small, dark room with her than I would be of what I'm going to do to you. At least that part will be quick and painless."

"Give us a minute. We need to discuss this," I said into the mike, then covered it with my hand. I remembered from before that the tiled ceiling was unusually low-hanging. "Can I get out and into the hall by crawling above the tiles in the ceiling?"

"No, there is a really small crawl space up there, but it's only between this room and the control booth. It's there so they can run wires."

"Time's up, campers! What's it gonna be?"

"I can't do this, Allida," Tracy whined.

"Yes, you can," I whispered back harshly to her. "No deal," I said into the microphone. "Pavlov is the only protection we've got, and we're not tying her up!"

"You need to reconsider that decision," Joel said, his voice taking on an angry edge. "Remember, I've got a big, sharp knife in here, and your precious dog will be my first victim. If you tie her, I won't harm her."

As he was talking, I whispered to Tracy to cover the mike, then I climbed onto the thick, heavy table and fumbled blindly till I sensed that I'd lifted one of the acoustic ceiling tiles. The ceiling tiles couldn't support my weight, but I reached around until I felt a joist, then swung myself up. At long last those gymnastic classes my P.E. teachers were always trying to force me to take instead of basketball had paid off.

The air was stagnant—hot and musty. I fought like hell

not to cough, which would let Joel know my location. There was just enough room for me to move on hands and knees, and yet the crawl space had been built with a long-limbed person in mind. Two four-inch ledges were wide enough for my hands and knees, but straddled a two-foot wide strip of ceiling tiles that ran down the center of the sound booth and control room. It was all I could do to keep my knees on the inner edges of the wood. This would make for slow going, but it was our only chance.

"What do you want from us, Joel?" Tracy asked. "Did you kill those women?"

"I had no choice, Trace. If Hannah would've just backed me financially and helped me with the recipe, I'd have been set for life. Only she catches on to how I'd spoiled her dog's food. She starts waving this gun at me. The damn thing went off as I was trying to wrench it away. Then I bumped into Beth Gleason accidentally. I was just on my way to meet Allida for the first time and see what the deal was with the damned collie, and I run into Beth walking him. She recognized me from class . . . and Sage starts barking at me. She would have gone straight to the police. It was crazy. She yells at the dog to run, and she pulls this switchblade out. What was I supposed to do? It was self-defense."

It was hard to orient myself. As best I could tell from the sound of Joel's voice, I was roughly halfway there. But what was the point? Joel was twice my size and muscular. I couldn't out-battle him for the controls.

To kill either of us, he would have to leave the control room and go into the sound booth. I could drop down, lock the door behind him, and get at the controls to broadcast a plea for help. That left just Pavlov to protect Tracy from Joel, but I saw no better alternative.

"Where's Greg?" Tracy asked. "Did you kill him, too?"

"Not yet. He's tied up in the back office. I'm giving

you gals sixty more seconds to tie up that dog, then I'm coming in, either way. It's up to you, Allida. You tie up your dog, she lives. You keep her loose, she's the first victim."

"Okay, okay," Tracy said. "You win. Allida's tying her up right now."

Something was running down my face—tears or sweat. Probably both. Sixty seconds! I had to move faster! Tracy was making noises that sounded as if a cable were being dragged across the table. She was trying to fake out Joel; she was too smart to tie up Pavlov.

"Want to know something funny?" Joel asked with an anguished chuckle. "This was where I stashed Sage so I could get back home before you woke up. That's what caused this whole bloody mess! Figured nobody was going to be in here, and it was the last place anyone would connect me to or think to look for the dog. Then you, Miss Bossy Bitch Truett, sent Greg out here! I couldn't get the dog out of the building without Greg seeing. Now he's going to have to take the fall for all of this. You just cost three human lives to try and save one stupid collie!"

"Let us go, Joel. It's too late. You'll never get away with this."

"Allida? Why are you so quiet?"

Damn! I had taken too long!

"She passed out," Tracy lied. "Wake up!" She made a slapping noise followed by a low groan.

It didn't work. I could see little slits of yellow below me. He'd turned on the lights in both the sound booth and his own control room.

"Where is she?"

Tracy stayed mute.

He paused. "You little bitch! What is it you think you're going to accomplish!"

His voice was directly below. The knife blade jabbed

through the ceiling tile a foot ahead of my face. I gasped, then inched forward. Dear God! I had no choice now but to try to drop down on top of him. If I mistimed it, I'd impale myself on his knife!

Again, he punched his knife through a tile centered right under my stomach. He pulled the knife back down.

"Now!" I hollered. Tracy's scream was all but ear-shattering, and I had the acoustic ceiling to muffle it. I kicked down the two-foot-by-four-foot ceiling tile, which cracked over Joel's head. He was still standing. As I'd hoped, he had dropped the knife in an attempt to scramble to the volume controls. Before he could react, I let myself drop the four feet or so to his head.

My chin knocked into the top of his head, and I saw stars, but managed to grab hold of his neck. We fell to the floor.

The amplified noise from the sound booth in this tiny room was deafening. Tracy was screaming at Joel. Pavlov was barking savagely.

Joel pushed me away and lunged for something near my leg. I kicked blindly, and soon realized I'd sent the knife skittering across the linoleum floor into the far corner.

"I'll kill you!" Joel's face and hair were covered in dust and white plaster-like fragments from the shattered ceiling. His eyes were crazed black holes. I lashed out, landing a punch to his trachea. He grunted. I scooted out from under him.

Pavlov was trying to claw through the glass window that separated us. If only Tracy were strong enough to lift her into the crawl space!

Tracy screamed again at the sight of me. Blood was everywhere, and I realized that the flesh under my chin had split.

I lunged toward the door of the sound booth. Joel rose,

grabbed me, and threw me away from the door with so much force that the back of my head smacked against the opposite wall. He got his hands around my neck.

"Chair on table!" I hollered with what could be my last breath.

Joel loosened his grip on me and turned to look into the sound booth. I gasped for air and got a partial view into the sound booth past Joel's body.

Tracy was lifting a chair onto the table.

Joel released me, swung around, and banged his fists on the glass. "No! Don't, Tracy!"

Pavlov bounded up onto the table, the chair, and disappeared into the crawl space. I threw open the door to the hallway. If I could just get to the lobby, the police would see me.

Joel tackled me.

"Pavlov, attack!" She was not yet in sight, and I'd taught her no such command. But Joel didn't know that.

Joel scrambled to his feet. I grabbed hold of his legs. Just then, Pavlov leapt down, landing on all fours. Joel fought to shut the door while I tried to wedge myself in the doorway to keep it open.

Pavlov growled deep in her chest, her teeth huge. Joel got an arm around my neck and pulled me against his chest to use me as a shield.

I grabbed his arm and curled into a ball. Pavlov lunged. Joel screamed in pain and released me. His fists pummeled Pavlov's back. Pavlov's teeth were buried in Joel's thigh.

I scrambled to my feet, raced to the sound booth, and threw the bolt. Tracy burst out, sweating and panting. She stood awestruck at the sight of Joel trying to fight off Pavlov.

Joel let out another scream of pain but broke free. Joel staggered Pavlov with a cruel blow to the muzzle. The knife was back in the control room. My head was throbbing. I felt dizzy, disoriented. I didn't have the strength to help Pavlov!

A high whine rose from the end of the hall. Sage!

"Call nine-one-one!" I hollered. Blood was gushing from my chin, but I ignored it and staggered in the direction of the sound. I needed to get Sage out of his muzzle to help Pavlov with Joel.

I threw open the last door to the hallway. Greg was lying on the floor, bound and gagged, Sage's leash tied to a desk leg beside him. I unbuckled Sage's muzzle, freed him from his leash, and Sage bounded out of the room. Tracy had followed me and snatched up the phone.

This was a waste of time, I now realized. The police should be right outside the lobby. My head was throbbing and I was starting to lose consciousness. We had to get past Joel and the dogs to get to the lobby.

I staggered back into the hallway. Joel Meyer was curled in the fetal position, Pavlov's teeth sunk into his upper arm, Sage snarling and barking.

"Police!" a man's voice called just then. Two officers burst into the hallway, just past Joel and the dogs.

"Pavlov! Cease!" I cried. My vision swam, then everything went black.

The next thing I knew, I was outside, staring up at a starless sky. I was on a gurney with a hard, plastic collar around my neck, some sort of padding pressed tightly against my wounded chin.

Russell was there, black eye and all, jogging alongside the gurney, watching me with a shocked, worried expression on his heavily shadowed features.

"Where'd you come from?" I managed to mumble.

"I was listening to the broadcast. I recognized part of it

from the other day. I called the police to tell them. I wasn't sure they believed me."

"Miss?" one of the paramedics pushing the gurney interrupted. "We need to put you in the ambulance now."

"Wait!" I looked again at Russell. "Pavlov and Sage. Are they . . ."

"They're fine. I hear Pavlov saved your life. You're lucky you have her. I called your mom, and she's meeting you at the hospital." He started to turn away, as forlorn as I'd ever seen him.

The paramedics started to lift me into the ambulance. "Just a moment," I cried to them, and they hesitated. "Russell? Remember that date at Flagstaff House you asked me about for last Saturday? Could I take a rain check, next week or so?"

I couldn't tell if my words were intelligible, till the smile on Russell's wonderful face seemed to light up the dark night.

A CONVERSATION WITH
LESLIE O'KANE

Q. You began your career as a novelist with mysteries about cartoonist/sleuth Molly Masters. What (or who) was your inspiration for Molly?

A. After my first attempt at a mystery (about a psychiatrist) was clearly not working, the leader of my critique group suggested I think about creating a character who was closer to myself. I played a game of "What if?" and asked myself what would have happened had I stuck to my original major in college—art. I realized that, as the perennial class-clown type, I would have become a cartoonist.

Q. What made you decide to create a second series with a new heroine, Allie Babcock?

A. I had listened to an interview with a pet psychologist who sometimes treats dogs that are depressed from such events as a death of someone close to them. As a murder-mystery writer, that immediately caught my interest. Everyone I ran the concept past—of a dog psychologist whose furry clients lead her into murder investigations—loved the idea.

Q. How is Allie different from Molly Masters?

A. Unlike Molly, who is happily married with two children, Allie is happily single, though she is not opposed to a romantic involvement. She is much less likely than Molly to make wisecracks and has a greater sense of dignity. Also, they differ in their upbringing—Allie lost her father when she was very young, and she tends to be more of a loner, sometimes more comfortable with dogs than with people.

Q. What inspired you to pursue a writing career? Why mysteries? Did any authors particularly influence you?

A. My mother is an avid reader, and when I was growing up, we made trips to the library every other week without fail, giving me a lifelong appreciation of books. My first-grade teacher taught us how to write the words "it" and "is" the first week of school, and I rushed home and wrote a five-page tome, entitled "It Is," that went: Is it? It is. Is it? Is it? It is. It is . . . (My plots improved once I learned more words.)

Even as a kid, I loved mystery novels. At one point I had just begun reading Agatha Christie's *The ABC Murders* and told my parents that I knew who did it—and stated the obvious clue that led me to think so. My father said, "If you were writing a mystery, would you start your book with a clue that revealed the murderer's identity?" I realized then that, no, I wouldn't, and I became forever fascinated by the art of mystery writing.

Q. Dogs often play major roles in your books. Do you have pets at home that are models for your fictional animals?

A. I have an adorable cocker spaniel and often dog-sit for a golden retriever and two more cocker spaniels. As a child, I had a collie—and he was the inspiration for Sage in *Play Dead*.

Q. Is it true that you were once taken hostage in a robbery? Please tell us about that experience.

A. That took place during a particularly rocky time in my life, when I was working in Boston as a cocktail waitress at night to put myself through college by day. I was head waitress, and just before two in the morning, I had to inform my coworkers that I'd just learned we were scheduled for a "clean-up party"—a euphemism for slave labor because the waitresses and bartenders had to clean the bar from top to bottom for three hours, in exchange for which they got pizza and beer at five A.M. This enormous customer—he looked like a former linebacker—overheard me and said that he was the superintendent of the apartment building in which our bar was located; consequently (so he reasoned) he was an employee, too, and could stay and drink. I said no, that didn't make him an employee and, furthermore, the bar was closed and he'd have to leave.

Some fifteen minutes later, after we'd locked up and begun cleaning, the French doors of the bar came flying open, and there stood Enormous Customer with a rifle under one arm and a double-barrel shotgun under the other. All I could think of at that moment was, "This guy is taking missing last call wa-a-y too seriously!" And I started to laugh. He smacked me with the shotgun and told me to quit laughing, but all humor had already gone out of the situation.

The SWAT team arrived at last, and around seven A.M. we got out of there. Unfortunately, Enormous Customer was out of there too. He escaped when the police ignored my observation that they'd only sealed the building, not the entire block—and that all the roofs were attached. The guy was big but not very bright; he was finally captured the next night following a brawl at another bar, in which he cut off a man's ear and then collapsed from exhaustion. Hence my conclusion that writing about crimes is more enjoyable than taking part in them.